NEW CANADIAN NOIR

THE *EXILE BOOK OF* NEW

CANADIAN NOIR

Edited by

Claude Lalumière and David Nickle

The *Exile Book of* Anthology Series

Number Ten

Library and Archives Canada Cataloguing in Publication

The Exile book of new Canadian noir / edited by
Claude Lalumière and David Nickle.

(The Exile book of anthology series ; number ten)
Issued in print and electronic formats.
ISBN 978-1-55096-460-8 (pbk.).--ISBN 978-1-55096-463-9 (pdf).--
ISBN 978-1-55096-461-5 (epub).--ISBN 978-1-55096-462-2 (mobi)

1. Noir fiction, Canadian (English). 2. Canadian fiction (English)--21st century. I. Nickle, David, 1964-, editor II. Lalumière, Claude, editor III. Title: New Canadian noir. IV. Series: Exile book of anthology series ; no. 10

PS8323.N64E95 2015 C813'.087208 C2014-908418-8
C2014-908419-6

Design and Composition by Mishi Uroboros / Cover Photograph by MC Fischer
Typeset in Fairfield, U73 and Akzidenz Grotesk fonts at Moons of Jupiter Studios

Published by Exile Editions Ltd ~ www.ExileEditions.com
144483 Southgate Road 14 – GD, Holstein, Ontario, N0G 2A0
Printed and Bound in Canada in 2015, by Imprimerie Gauvin

We gratefully acknowledge the Canada Council for the Arts,
the Government of Canada through the Canada Book Fund (CBF),
the Ontario Arts Council, and the Ontario Media Development Corporation
for their support toward our publishing activities.

Conseil des Arts du Canada Canada Council for the Arts

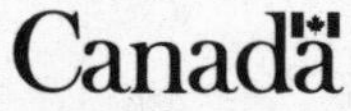

Canadian Sales: The Canadian Manda Group, 664 Annette Street,
Toronto ON M6S 2C8 www.mandagroup.com 416 516 0911

North American and international distribution, and U.S. sales:
Independent Publishers Group, 814 North Franklin Street,
Chicago IL 60610 www.ipgbook.com toll free: 1 800 888 4741

CONTENTS

INTRODUCTION
ALL NEW, ALL CANADIAN, ALL NOIR

New Canadian Noir is not an anthology of crime fiction. Not quite. Call it crime-ish.

One of the most exciting things about fiction these days is that, after going through several generations of relatively rigorous boundaries, genres are bleeding into each other with casual abandon, and that seems to be especially vivid in Canada, where the old, tired clichés of CanLit are being retired in favour of a more diverse, less easily defined, less confining literary repertoire.

Noir, to my mind, has never been a genre so much as a tone, an overlay, a mood. It just happens to have been applied more explicitly to crime fiction than to other genres.

When we conceived of this book, we resisted the temptation to define what we meant by *noir*. We were much more interested in what it meant to Canadian writers. But we did want to make sure that writers knew that we weren't merely looking for the familiar formula of the hard-luck grifter or hard-boiled detective being undone by the twin perils of nihilistic self-destructiveness and merciless violence (but, hey, we'd take a look at that stuff, too). We wanted to see it all – every possible iteration of what noir could mean to daring writers unafraid to explore the dark and weird interzones of their imaginations. Our call for submissions reflected that desire; we announced that we wanted "dark fiction that spans across genres to capture the whole spectrum of the noir esthetic: its traditional form within crime fiction; its imaginative forays into horror, fantasy, and surrealism; its dystopian consequences within speculative fiction; its disquieting mood in erotica; its grim journeys into frontier fiction; its stark expression in literary realism." The stories we received surpassed our yearning for diversity.

Although we did not ask our all-Canadian roster of writers to limit the settings to Canada, we were very happy to see noir portraits of major Canadian cities – Montreal, Toronto, Vancouver, Halifax, Calgary; to explore far-flung regions such as Nunavut and the Okanagan Valley; to have one story narrated with a pronounced Newfoundland inflection.

What this anthology is, is a snapshot of the Canadian noir imagination as it is being expressed now, across both genres and geography. It is noir. It is pan-Canadian. And it's all new.

Claude Lalumière

SUN MOON STARS RAIN

Silvia Moreno-Garcia

James.

Beautiful, beautiful James. Not the same boy I'd first met all those years ago. A few strands of grey in his blond hair, a few too many sleepless nights leaving a mark on his face, but still a strikingly handsome man beneath the ratty jacket and grime.

Folks call him JD or Jimmy, but he's still James to me.

"What do you want? It's late," I say.

"Xochi, can I come in?" he asks.

"Didn't you hear me? It's late. I've got work tomorrow."

"Xochi, please. Come on. Let me in for a few minutes."

"Can't do."

"Xochi, I really need your help."

I first met James when we were both nineteen at a party in Chinatown which he'd crashed. I was in love with him within an hour. It made me physically sick, his absence creating a gnawing void in my stomach, his presence sending me into bouts of hyperactivity. Agonies of longing and tremulous desires that subsided once it became evident James would prefer to shack up with a post-apocalyptic mutant squid-ape rather than me if the occasion presented itself.

As a result, fifteen years later, I was over my childish infatuation but never quite immune to the charm of James. He'd imprinted on me, I suppose.

I let him in and James begins looking for a place to sit down. For a studio apartment in Vancouver my place is actually quite large. They've subdivided apartments so much that people can literally be living in a closet, but this is an older building and there's more footage than you'd expect. I even have a little den attached to the side, which I don't like very much because the previous tenant painted suns and stars and a great moon over the ceiling, all in these girly purples and pinks and golds, but I've always been too lazy to paint over it. The super won't do it. So there it stays.

Ten years from now I suppose it'll be swallowed by the sea, what with the global warming and all. But that doesn't concern me. There's always the Yukon, which is looking quite pleasant, as the world gets hotter with all the El Niños pounding at the coasts.

At some point in the distant past James and I had talked about trying to see how things were in the far north, final frontier and all, à la *White Fang*. But he'd gone and become a junkie and an alcoholic – which, I guess, at least is true to the spirit of Jack London – and I'd never really done any of the things we'd yakked about. Then again, I guess most things don't work out the way we plan them. Not for people like us, anyway.

"What is it – women, drugs, or money?" I ask as I walk to the kitchen and pour myself some gin. I don't offer James a glass. It's the expensive variety and I'm not into sharing my spoils. He drinks too much already, anyway.

James moves the boxes with books I have on the couch, takes off his jacket, and sits down. I can see the jacket has holes all over the place. Much good it must do him on a rainy day, which is every day in this part of the country.

"You really read all of these?" he asks.

"Don't say some stupid shit you know the answer to just to deflect my question," I tell him, 'cause yeah, I read, and not the e-reader thingy. Books are supposed to be artifacts, not just text on a screen, ya know."

He doesn't reply.

"So it's all three," I say. "Look, I'm not lending you money."

"I didn't talk about lending me anything," he says.

"Well, there's only one damn reason why you'd crawl over here."

"Xochi, I need a gun."

"I want a pony. Preferably in a curry sauce."

"I need it."

"Yeah, like I can get one."

"You're a security guard."

"Working in Canada, man. They barely allow us to carry a fucking flashlight and just to have handcuffs I had to pass an AST course. And I had to buy my own handcuffs, damn assholes wouldn't provide them. Did you have an aneurysm and forget about that?"

Truth is, I do have a gun. More than one gun: there's the one I keep behind the picture of the Virgin of Guadalupe (she looks like a nice lady) and another one on the shelf, in a hollowed-out book (arts and crafts count for something). But I don't trust James with that shit. First thing he'd do with a weapon is sell it or accidentally blow off a foot. Moron.

"I really do need it. Look, it is women and it is money. But not the way you think."

"Fuck if it isn't. You've got no money to pay for some new prostitute that's caught your fancy and—"

"It's Christine."

Christine Chao? That was a surprise. Christine was ancient history. James had had a dozen relationships and more than a dozen years to mope after her. "What about her?"

"She contacted me two weeks ago. Said she needed to talk. So I said yes. Turns out she's dating this guy, some important bastard who ain't so nice. Lots of dough. She wants to leave him but she can't. He won't let her. So she's trying to figure some way out of town. Wants to try her luck overseas, cut all ties. She wants to start again, new name. She's wondering if I can help her."

"Forging papers?"

"No, catching salmon. Of course forging papers," James mutters.

"So you do it."

"No. I *try* to do it. Before I can finish the job and give her the passport there's something on the net that Christine Chao's gone missing and next thing I know two big fuckers are looking for me at The Yellow Door."

"Can you be more specific?"

"Can I be more specific? Two dudes with knives, how about that. Look, my roommate's not answering the phone, and Christine's vanished. I need to lay low for a couple days, get that gun, and get my ass over to Mexico."

Good old Mexico. Down to Cancun, no doubt, like every other loser with a lack of imagination who'd run afoul of someone on the West Coast and thought the streets in the south were paved with tanned babes and cash.

I finish my drink and set the glass down on the kitchen table. "You can't stay here," I say, grabbing his jacket and throwing it at him. "I have no guns and it's past my bedtime. Get your ass out."

"Look, Christine gave me this. As a down payment, you know," he says, pulling out a gold necklace and showing it to me. "You can have it."

"No, she didn't give it to you as payment. You would have hawked it if she had. Did she steal it? Are people looking for this piece of shit?"

"I don't know. All I know is I've been having some rotten luck and I'm ready to pay whatever it takes to get rid of it, okay?"

That's the thing about me, you know. I can always get rid of James's problems. I remember when he dated Christine and the looks she gave me, like she was wondering why some hot smooth-talker like James would be hanging out with a bitch as ugly as me, with the fucked-up teeth and the fucked-up skin. And it was, it has always been, because I could save him from himself. Maybe there was a time I liked being his own personal superhero, but that shit got old real fast.

"Hey, look, all I'm saying is let me hang out for a bit, let me figure this out."

"You've gone from wanting a damn gun to a hotel room. Nice bargain you strike."

"Alright, just…just a roof for the night. I'll sleep on the floor, not even the couch. What's that gonna cost you? We've known each other for what, fifteen years?"

"Fifteen long fucking years, James," I mutter.

"Well, yeah. You can't throw fifteen years down the drain. All the stuff I did for you..."

That amounts to barely nothing, of course.

"...come on, Xochi."

"I'll say the same thing I said the last three times you got yourself into something stupid: fuck off."

A knock on the door makes us both turn our heads. Before I can say anything there comes a loud voice I recognize.

"Xo Doza, it's Wick."

I motion to James to head into the den, and he does. I don't grab my gun. It would look too suspicious. But I have my knife tucked safely at the wrist.

I open the door, and there's Wick with two dudes I haven't met before. But if they're with Wick then they're also bounty hunters sniffing some trail. Bail bondsmen and bounty hunters are illegal here, but Wick and her friends don't exactly do stuff by the book.

"What's up, Wick?" I ask.

"I got a line out for your buddy JD is what's up."

"He's been playing cards again? Don't bother. He always manages to get the cash."

"You think they'd get me to collect some measly tab? Who the hell do you think I am?"

"Well, I have no fucking idea what you're doing lately, and I don't care. Fuck off. I've got a gig in a couple of hours and I need my beauty sleep."

Wick takes out her phone and shows it to me. Big round number, she shows me. Lotta zeroes. I tilt my head and frown.

"That much?"

"That much, baby."

"Who's looking for him?"

"Doesn't matter. Have you seen him?"

"He owes me money."

"That's not an answer."

"No, Wick. Haven't seen him. Now let me get my power nap," I say and move to close the door.

Wick steps forward. She's tall; she's a damn six-foot-two of Amazonian muscle and I'm much shorter, much lighter. I'm knives and punches and I work the occasional special event. Lately I've been doing night work at an abandoned factory. Lots of foot patrols and chasing bums away. Bums. Not the same line of work as Wick.

"Look, Xo Doza, girl, I like you. You're smart. You're quiet. You're a nice person. But this is a lot of money. Tell you what. I give you a 10 percenter if you let me walk quietly into your apartment. If you don't let me, I walk in, break your skull, and smash your boy's face into a pulp anyway. So you get a smashed skull and no money. I'll give you three minutes to gather your thoughts."

My first thought is: no way. This is James we are talking about.

My second thought is: exactly.

If our positions were reversed I know James would gracefully bow out of the way and let three fuckers beat me up, no problem, ma'am.

My third is whatever shit James has gotten himself into is too thick for me to wade into. It's probably time for the Yukon, anyway.

James was bound to have a bad ending. I just expected him to go in a slightly different fashion, killed by too much booze and drugs, not Christine Chao.

I have a knife but it's three of them. James is no good for fighting, couldn't fight his way out of a paper bag. That's me and three, then.

Sure, once upon a time I was crazy-crazy for James but that was when I was nineteen and James was this pristine daydream.

If I could grab my gun and put a couple of good ones in Wick, maybe. But what about the other two?

James.

Beautiful, beautiful James.

I stand by the doorway thinking very, very hard and to tell you the truth, I don't know, man.

What's that gonna cost you?

I don't know anymore. I just don't know.

MOOT

Corey Redekop

"You're moot."

◂ ▸

She was worth a stare, and knew it. Late twenties. A face of superbly crafted beauty. Five feet nine inches of unblemished curvature sheathed within a dress formulated to be gawked at.

Not what I was used to seeing at nine in the morning. Or any time. My clientele tended toward the shabby.

She'd walked in as I was polishing my eye. Dumb luck I hadn't bothered to turn the lights on. The dim from the morning sun barely cut the smog, let alone the window that hadn't known clean since the Allies won. I popped it in before she could notice.

"Miss Carmen Lopez. *Miss* Lopez, if you'd be so kind, *Mr.* Pasko." Her lips smiled. The rest of her didn't bother. No one ever truly smiled in my office.

"I might be so kind." I propped my feet up, showing off socks that had been new when Roosevelt took office. The first time. "I aim to please, Miss Lopez. Says so on my business card. But if you're here for personality, I have a different office for that. And I'm disinclined to put on airs without a look at your bankbook." I leaned back, slid a cigarette into my mouth, and flicked a matchstick with my thumbnail. If I'd been wearing my fedora I'd have tilted it over my eyes.

Ever since Bogart's *Maltese* shtick, people expected a show for their buck, and I was happy to play the part if it meant a client. But where I once followed up dry witticisms with professionalism, I now intentionally prodded. Helped maintain a distance. If you were at my door, you'd likely as not be put off by a little brusqueness anyway.

Her fingers whitened around her handbag. She wasn't used to lip. "Mr. Pasko—"

"Dudley, please." I took a long drag, imagining the rush that once upon a time calmed my nerves.

"—I am looking for someone, and you come…recommended."

"By whom?"

"Does that matter?"

"I suppose not." I puffed out a few half-hearted rings. "But I offer a discount for referrals."

"Money is no object, Mr. Pasko."

"Never is, until it is."

She withdrew an envelope from her purse and laid it on my desk. I ignored it. "Why don't you tell me why you're here? I hate letting money get in the way of friendship."

I motioned to the chair nearer my desk. She looked at me, uncertain.

"Please sit. I rent it by the hour."

She cleared her throat. "I think I'd rather stand over here. If it's all the same."

The door must have looked inviting, she kept inching toward it.

"Something on your mind, Carmen?"

She took a breath and said, "You're moot, Mr. Pasko."

I sighed, camouflage blown. "Well done, most don't notice. What was the tell?"

"You haven't blinked since I came in."

"That'd do it." I slipped my sunglasses on. "Better?"

"By degrees. Also, your eyes are different colours."

I sat up at that, rattled. "What?"

"Your left eye is brown. The other is green. Were they like that before?"

I clawed a mirror from my desk drawer and peered in, not seeing what she saw. I'd lived in tones of grey for months. Forgetting myself, I scooped the right out, scowling.

"Are you sure?" I asked.

"Quite."

"I'll kill him." I shoved the marble back in. "He swore they were twins."

"It's hardly noticeable."

"Not the point. In my line, appearance is important." I spat the cigarette to the floor and ground it beneath my toes, forgetting that my shoes were in the closet. I heard the flesh crisp as embers singed through the wool of my left argyle, not feeling a thing.

"Now that my mootness has been uncovered, sit and spill, will you? It only looks like I have all day."

I gave her a moment. She gnawed at a fingernail, caught herself, and sat, crossing her legs. In another life that would've been it for me.

"I do apologize, Mr. Pasko. I wasn't expecting..."

I waved her quiet. "No one ever gets used to it. Moots, I mean."

"You look..." She struggled for the word. "...real. Alive, I mean."

"My pay mostly goes to upkeep these days."

"Why do you...?" Miss Lopez blushed, ashamed of her curiosity. "Please forgive me. I shouldn't pry."

I finished her thought. "Why play lifer? Tell the truth, would you have come to my door otherwise?"

"Perhaps not," she admitted. "It's not that I'm deathist, you understand. My maid is moot. But she's not...what's the word? She's not smart?"

"I prefer the term 'sentient reanimate.'"

"Yes. Cora's beginning to..." She looked around, hesitant to utter such unpleasantries. "...spoil. There was a burglary. She was struck with a crowbar. Here." Miss Lopez drew a line across her forehead with her finger. "It's unpleasant, of course. She makes almost as much mess as she cleans. We took her to Greytown once. I thought she'd prefer it there, among her own, but she wandered back the next day. Not that I mind. Cora's family."

Family. I swallowed my irritation at her necrophobia. Family, just not *capital F* family. Family, but not family enough to set Cora up in a resurrection community.

"Start again," I said, taking out a pad and pencil. "Begin with why."

She composed herself. "It's my sister. Isabel's always been unpredictable. Went to *all* the best schools, because none could handle her for more than a month. Can't sit still, won't take anything seriously. A hellraiser, as my father says. She's only sixteen, and already she has been involved with men. And drugs. My family has spent a great deal to keep her out of the papers."

"And she's taken off for parts unknown." Kid nobody understands runs away, takes up with a bad scene. Not the oldest in the book, but a classic for a reason. "Have you called the police? They're helpful with missing persons, especially well-off missing persons."

"We'd prefer this be handled quietly. My father feels Isabel has embarrassed us enough."

"Your dime. Luckily, you've caught me with a gap in my schedule. I get thirty per plus expenses, which you'll receive itemized once I've found her or the trail runs cold."

It was more than I usually charged, but she could afford it. Plus, my doc wasn't the cheapest in town, and I was only going to get worse. Especially if I killed him for the peeper switcheroo.

"There's more." Her eyes began to mist. "Isabel was never interested in religion. We couldn't even get her through Sunday school. But when Cora returned last year, Isabel started going to church."

"Not surprising. I hear attendance in the pews has quadrupled since this all started."

"Suicides, too," she said.

I nodded, fiddling at my shirt cuffs.

"It hit Isabel particularly hard. Cora is the closest thing to a mother Isabel knows. She was the one who discovered the body. Cora returned in Isabel's arms."

"Unsettling."

"After that, Isabel started taking things more seriously. After the inconstancy of death became clear."

Inconstancy. I liked that. Nicer than random chance or fickle finger of fate. Or worse, God's Will Be Done.

"So Isabel found God. Not usual for a runaway."

"It's my fault. We are good Christians, Mr. Pasko. But Isabel never does anything halfway. She prays loudly all hours of the day, she preaches chapter and verse to anyone and everyone. When she's not at church, she has her head buried in the family Bible. I'm ashamed to say this, but her belief has become frightening."

"There's religious, and there's *religious*."

"You understand, then."

"Too well." I glanced at the corner of my desk. She followed my gaze and frowned, curious at the picture frame lying there, face-down.

"And then Isabel left," I said, louder than I meant to.

"Yes, Monday. We had been arguing again. This obsession, especially with death, it's unhealthy for her. Then Isabel didn't show up for breakfast. Cora was agitated, but I didn't think much of it. I thought perhaps Isabel had gone to an early Mass. Later on, I noticed the safe in my father's office was open."

"She took money?"

"A few thousand dollars. We haven't heard from her since."

"How about your church? Anything going on there? Hate to say, it wouldn't be the first time a trusting young woman was taken advantage of."

I scratched at my wrist absently while Miss Lopez assured me at length of Reverend Carlson's impeccable reputation. We both remembered the Bishop O'Shea case. For an entire year it had consumed the city's attention. A clergyman taking advantage of young girls has a way of firing up the populace.

"What about the maid?"

"Oh, Cora's practically doornail." If she thought the term would bother me, she didn't show it. "Honestly, I'm thinking of putting her down."

There's only so much oblivious mootism I can take. "I'm sure that's for the best. Cora's not really family. Will you have it stuffed?"

She blanched. "Oh, that's not what I—"

"Get the bones resined? Use it as a hat rack?"

"That isn't fair," she protested.

"None of this is. But your moot's the one that recommended me."

Her mouth gaped at that. "How did you know?"

"Who else could you have asked? It's probably not quite the doornail you think."

I'd have to talk to the moot, that much was plain. After a few more questions, I saw Miss Lopez out with the promise to expect me at her house that afternoon for a moot-to-moot chat.

After all, even a rusty doornail has its uses.

◂ ▸

I wrote myself a note to eviscerate my physician – or at least get a refund – and opened the envelope. Inside, a sheaf of centuries promised another year of function, maybe two if I could barter Doc down on a few procedures.

As a rule, moots invest any savings they accumulated in life in priests and charlatans and quacks – anyone promising something beyond their shambling non-existence. There are *many* ways – grisly ways, blood-soaked ways – to escape the clutches of unlife, but most moots, sentient and doornail alike, continue to crave spiritual assurances on the state of their immortal souls.

I'd never gone in for the godbotherer bit. In my opinion, whatever deity was in charge had either died, left work early, or simply stopped caring.

Myself, I kept to the routine. I had little else to do. My family was gone, my unplanned early retirement refused.

Rather than try again, I stuck around and took my punishment.

Beneath the cash lay a photo of Isabel in all her sixteen-years-of-life exuberance. Youthfully curvy, face pleasingly baby-fatted. Polka-dot dress fit for both church suppers and driving young men wild. A wide-brimmed hat shadowed a mischievous gap-toothed grin that would keep any boy she deigned to favour with a smile occupied with dirty thoughts and dirtier socks.

Regretting it but helpless to do otherwise, I lifted the picture frame and held it next to the photo. They could have been sisters. So and Jo gazed out at me, arms around each other's shoulders, their toothy grins infectious enough to bring one to my lips even as a lump formed in my throat.

Three years dead, and still my body refused to forget.

I put the picture back, face up. I pocketed the photo and deposited the bulk of the cash in my floor safe beneath the desk, grabbing a Michigan bankroll I kept there for emergencies. After a second of thought, I loaded and holstered my gun, a Colt Detective Special I named after my wife.

Like the pistol, Marion promised safety.

And delivered death.

◀ ▶

I typically neatened up for house calls. Laundered pinstriped suit, shined patent leathers, tie fully Windsored, chin shorn of shadow. The prospect of interrogating a moot dissuaded me from looking my best.

At the sight of my rumpled apathy, the Lopez butler promptly broke the first rule of butlering and allowed his blank features the momentary gift of undisguised loathing. I followed his stiff-backed majesty through the manor, marching past the requisite displays of animals cut down mid-snarl and traversing a kitchen fit to feed an entire restaurant filled with the highest of high society.

Miss Lopez waited for us in a sparsely furnished bedroom at the back of the house. The room was likely a humble affair, by her standards. I could fit my entire office within its walls with enough room left over for a round of miniature golf.

After shooing the butler off, Miss Lopez moved to the bed, sitting next to a grotesque uniformed in maid's cap and dress. I shook Cora's offered hand, scarcely hiding my disgust as I felt the dried joints crackle.

"She just came back from shopping," Miss Lopez said. "She can still read a grocery list, although sometimes she forgets to pay."

I pulled up a chair and looked in its eyes, snapping my fingers. The right eye focused lazily on the motion. The left wandered. I removed its cap and examined the canyon gouged into its skull. Beyond the blackened edges of bone, the brain glistened.

"It's wet," I said.

"We spritz her every day. Dr. Feingold told us the moisture would help keep her mind sharp."

"He's lying. Or incompetent. Overpaid either way." I fit the cap back snugly over Cora's patchy scalp. "Makes no matter if the brain's protected—" I knocked my head with my knuckles. "—or on a shelf. You'd have as much success if you filled the crater with tar. Brains just eventually stop on their own. When they've had enough, I guess."

Cora's lips peeled up, showing gums long absent of pearly whites. I smiled back. "No tongue?"

"She lost it early on. But she can still write." Its head bobbed in agreement. Miss Lopez handed me a notebook, pages black with scrawl. The first few pages were barely legible. The last, hieroglyphic.

"Not much time left, Cora," I said. Its eye looked to the floor dejectedly. From what I saw on the page, the moot had a few months at best before complete body shutdown. What happened after that is anyone's guess.

I scanned ahead to the last page, to a chicken scratch of a word.

P A S C O

"This why I'm here?"

"I thought it was nonsense at first," Miss Lopez said, "but she was so adamant." Cora poked a finger at the scribble, then at me, asking a question. I dipped my head, and its smile returned. Still some higher functions in there. Maybe a year.

"Isabel used to talk to her at night. I could hear murmurs, but I didn't feel it was my place to pry. I thought Isabel was simply keeping her company." She put a hand on the moot's shoulder. "Cora always was the family sounding board, weren't you?" It nuzzled her hand with its cheek and groaned.

"And after Isabel disappeared," I said, "you asked it where she might have gone."

"Yes, Cora wrote this down. I had a devil of a time figuring out what she meant. Until we actually met I wasn't sure I was right, that it was a name." She frowned. "I don't know how Cora would have known of you."

"Maybe it heard my name somewhere. Cora, do you ever meet other moots? Maybe while shopping?"

Cora's eye remained glassy, as whatever remained that was still human parsed my question. After a lull, it shrugged.

I felt like I was questioning a particularly dense gorilla.

I took Cora's hands and looked into the good eye, willing it to remember. "Cora, do you remember Isabel? Nod for yes."

It cautiously lowered its chin and raised it again. *Yes.*

"Did Isabel talk to you?" *Yes.* "Do you remember what she talked about?" *Yes.* "Did Isabel ever talk about running away?"

The seconds ticked by; then, *yes*. A single tear escaped and trickled down the cracks of its dead flesh. Miss Lopez gasped. I waved her silent, hiding my own disquiet. It might have been coincidence, but moots don't normally retain enough moisture to cry. I took it as a last sign of intelligence, dying within a withering prison.

"Could you write where you think she'd go?" I put the notebook in its lap and worked a pencil into its grasping fingers. It hurriedly began squiggling streaks of lead across, up, and down the page, still moving after Miss Lopez gently pried the pencil away.

I rubbed at my temples in frustration. "Would anyone else know where Isabel went?"

Its face went blank; then, *yes*. Cora started slowly flipping through the journal, scanning the nonsense. We waited as it cautiously studied each page's gibberish until it grunted excitedly, stabbing a finger to the paper.

In a space of lines thick with ink, a tiny oasis of clarity.

N E X

"Nex," I said. "Does that mean anything to you, Miss Lopez?"

"No. Cora, is this a person?" *Yes.*

"And this Nex knows where Isabel is?" *Yes yes yes yes yes.*

"So what now?" asked Miss Lopez.

I took the journal from the moot's grip and ripped the page out, shoving it in my pocket. "Now I hit the streets." I stood to leave. "There's a few snitches I know. I'll let you know if anything pans. Hopefully this isn't just your moot sending me on a snipe hunt."

◂ ▸

"Did you have to keep calling her that?" Her voice quivered as she walked me down the main hall to the drabness of the world beyond luxury.

I ignored the question.

"*It*. *Your moot*. Cora is not an *it*, Mr. Pasko."

I stopped at the door and faced her. "Miss Lopez, I appreciate your courtesy on behalf of the help, but Cora isn't a *who* anymore. She and I, we're *its*. And I was under the impression I had been hired for my detective skills, not my manners."

I walked down the path, turning back when I reached my car. She stood in the archway, in every way perfect, and not for the first time I bemoaned my mootness. "You're not doing it any favours by keeping it around," I yelled. "Take my advice, book a crematorium. Cora will be much happier as a pile of ash."

She yelled something back as I lurched into the driver's seat. I turned the ignition, letting the engine complain, pretending not to understand what I heard so clearly.

I drove away, idly fingering the scars on my wrists, mulling over her question.

Why haven't you, then?

Excellent question.

◀ ▶

Over the next while I hit up my usual sources, trotting out Isabel's smile in places a young woman should never frequent, to faces a young woman should never meet. Getting nothing but deadpan stares and obscene single entendres, I sprinkled the name Nex about, along with a few fins. All I earned was a lighter wallet.

I started hitting airports, train and bus stations, taxi stands. Zip. Ditto hospitals and morgues. If Isabel had left town, it wasn't via public transport or pine box. Reaching out to my last few friends on the police force was similarly dispiriting. I started visiting churches, synagogues, arbitrary places of worship. Isabel's face brought me downturned mouths and *Isn't that a shame*s, but no results.

My reports to Miss Lopez were perfunctory. She told me Cora had slid further downhill. I think it was keeping itself going by sheer will, hoping that someone would bring Isabel back.

I sat in my office and bit my lip until it should have bled, walking though options. Isabel's pic was propped up next to the girls'. So, Jo, Isabel. My eye flickered over the trio.

Three expressions of utter guilelessness. Faces alit with heady expectancy. They could go anywhere, do anything. They were hope. They were life.

But they sat here, on my desk, captured in moments of wonder. Frozen in possibility.

These children did not belong in my office. Their being here was a violation. They should never have put their faith in me.

I knew where I had to go. I had always known – and had wasted days.

I put my head down, hands over face, resigned, loathing myself.

I hate moots.

◂ ▸

Every city has a Greytown. Ours is a northside slum once intended to quarter miscellaneous population detritus: junkies, immigrants, juicer hoboes between train hops.

Soon after Moot Point – that day when death became debatable and funeral homes lost business – a decision was made from on high to reorganize the social hierarchy. Ghetto denizens found themselves shifted to more suitable surroundings, and the new Greytown was abandoned to moots. While no laws actively *forbade* a conscious corpse from lingering in Lifeville, moots were politely *encouraged* to consider Greytown their new home.

A handful of jazz clubs operated on its borders. Joints with names like The Belly Up, The Dirt Nap, The Worm Bait – dismal haunts where lifers got their giggles slumming with the dead. The music wasn't anywhere near good, moot combos being reliant on fate to supply them with musicians still gifted with lips to blow and fingers to tickle ivories. Any moot of real talent inevitably found itself onstage at a lifer's club, eking whatever pleasure it could from its extended sojourn aboveground. I'd caught Charlie Parker at the Carleton while on a case. If anything, death had only improved its playing, adding an indefinable touch of despair that resonated long after the tunes had ended.

My best bet was The Death Knell, the closest a Greytown club would ever come to respectability. After tipping the lifer doorman with a growl and a flash of Marion's ample assets, I took a seat at a booth and motioned for the waitress. A group of businessmen was laughing uproariously as the moot behind the bar painstakingly assembled a fleet of complicated cocktails with its one good arm. The joke was on them, I knew. Not only was the hooch watered down, it was a safe bet the bartender was leaking juice from one of its open orifices into every glass.

The waitress walked up – another moot, all appendages intact and body deloused should a discerning customer wish to order an Open Coffin, a nice-nellyism for corpse coitus. I slipped her a fin and asked for the manager. While I waited, I took in the onstage trio. The saxophonist managed to blurt out a passable "Harlem Nocturne," even with the hindrance of an open torso. A dwarf in clown makeup added a touch of macabre theatricality to the set by squeezing the sax player's lungs like bagpipes, to the delight of the audience.

"You know, Terry wasn't reborn like that." A moot with skin dark as java, one whitened eye, and a body that was an altar to infidelity slid in next to me.

"Good to see you, Jimmy."

"Tut, tut. Madame Destiny of the Nine Spheres, when I'm at work."

"Apologies. I like the eye."

"Flatterer. Rubes love it. They think it bestows some kind of extra perception into," it shifted its voice down and took on a robust Jamaican patois, *"the vast all-ah-knowing cloud-uh of the great beyond!*" The moot tapped its head against the back wall of the booth and its left eye, the blue one, popped out and bounced into my waiting palm. "They were both white once, but clients were beginning to think I was blind, not psychic. So out went leftie."

Business was obviously doing well, well enough that few would suspect Jymma Olfonse was one of the oldest moots in town. In life she had been a card sharp with a gift for prophetic fabrication. I'd crossed her palms a few times and she'd never steered me wrong, but since my death I'd kept away.

After its murder and resurrection at the hands of a disgruntled client, Jimmy took up with some resourceful miscreants who could craft opportunity out of atrocity, renovated an abandoned dive, and became a success. All its profits must have gone into body upkeep, which, I could see, was worth every penny. Even up close there wasn't a trace of moot. Except for the eye, and the bruises around its neck, which Jimmy kept visible as a badge of some sort of honour.

I tossed the marble back. Jimmy slipped it in and blinked it into place.

"There was nothing wrong with Terry's body, he just isn't a very good musician. He needed a gimmick, so he cut his chest open and gets the shortie to man the bellows. How could I ever turn that down?"

"You're all heart."

"Ain't that the truth. Plus, I'd swear he's a better player now." It laughed at that, a laugh in sound only. "Brass tacks, Duds."

"Is the reunion over?"

"You died years ago, yet I only see you now? You've hurt my feelings."

"Something tells me you'll get over it." I handed Jimmy the photo. "I'm looking for this girl." I ignored its smutty *tsk tsk*. "I've caught a missing kid case. Can't find her among the living. Maybe she's found her way down here."

Jimmy considered Isabel's face. "Cute. Too cute for a place like this. Sorry, don't recognize her."

"I figured." I slid the crumpled journal page over and tapped it with my fingertip. "This mean anything to you?"

Jimmy let the paper lie, reading the scribble from above. Even with one eye false and the other cloudy, I could see them frost over. "Nothing to me," it said. "Looks like gibberish."

"I'd never play poker with you, Jimmy. Doesn't mean I can't read a lie."

Jimmy looked at me, something blazing behind its one good eye. "How's the family?" it leered. "Keeping well?"

I stiffened. "Stick to the subject."

"Those girls still run you ragged?" Jimmy leaned forward, painted lips carved into a smile that wouldn't fool a blind man. Its voice was empty as my wife's marriage vows. "Why, they must be adults by now. Any grandkids on the horizon?"

I fought the urge to drive my fist through that smirk. "You're still a sick twist, Jimmy," I managed.

"And you're still dull. Death hasn't changed that." Jimmy feigned a yawn. "Show yourself out, Pasko. I'm not interested in what you're selling."

The moot made to leave. I grabbed its forearms, pushing my mug up close. "Let's not mince. I don't like being here, so let's bypass the dance. I've got a girl who went all churchy, stole some cash, and vamoosed. A doornail writes a note, that's all I have to go on. You know something. Who's this Nex?"

"What should you care, some spoiled breather brat wants to dance on her grave?" It spat in my face. "Look at yourself. Detective Pasko, always worried about the lifers."

"What do you know about it?"

"Everyone knows. You're shuffling blind in the light. You've lost touch with who you are. There isn't a Greytowner around who doesn't know this word. And none of them will tell you a thing."

"Talk," I said, squeezing tight. "Or I'll cause you so much hurt you'll go bankrupt trying to put yourself back together again."

"You're a traitor to your race, Pasko. You know what we call you? The self-hating moot. The lifer lover. The great dead dick, pretending a pulse."

"*Talk.*" I snapped its left arm like a matchstick. Letting go, I whipped out Marion and pointed her at the approaching doorman. The room went quiet, the band ceasing its desecration of Cole Porter, all eyes now on the Dudley Pasko floorshow.

I looked back at Jimmy, arm bones splintered through skin, its face mild, as if I had just suggested we go grab a bite.

"How's Marion, Dud? You allowed conjugal rights? Keeping the bed warm for when she gets out?"

I pressed the gun against Jimmy's neck. "I'll puncture your brainstem, babe."

"Did the razor hurt, Duds? Such a clichéd exit. I'd figured you to eat your gun."

"You'll be a brain in a jar. Really limit your career choices."

"Boring," it said. "I never liked you in life, Dud. I like you less now. The ol' S&M."

"What?"

"That's where you'll find your girl. That's where they all go."

I let go, warily watching the doorman as I stood to leave. "And what happens at St. Mike's?"

Jimmy looked at me, almost sadly, rubbing the open bone. "Maybe you'll wake up."

◀ ▶

St. Michael's of the Celestial Anima Cathedral had been an oozing blotch of pessimism since its erection. Nestled among some of the shoddiest buildings in the ghetto, it should have been a beacon of hope by default. Instead, its grand archways and eloquent gothic spires somehow expressed a sardonic outlook on the futility of existence, as if its low-balling architects had foreseen mootkind and infused the stonework with apathy. It made a perverted sort of sense that Bishop O'Shea found a home there.

After his conviction following one too many kicks at the underage can for the Holy See to ignore, the ol' S&M had been unceremoniously forsaken. Even moots didn't bother with it, preferring to attend services in one of the other Greytown churches.

The roads grew steadily worse the farther you trekked toward Greytown's heart, and it was full night by the time I made my way to St. Mike's. I'd had to walk the final dozen blocks, the streets barely walkways through a wilderness of concrete and steel, lit only by the occasional working streetlamp.

I approached the façade cautiously. A few candles flickered behind its windows, beams of sickly light fighting vainly against the murk. From within, a lone voice warbled in the theatrical cadence of what could only be a sermon. After a pause, a chorus of "Amen." A wheezy pump organ began to gasp a barely recognizable rendition of "Gladly the Cross-Eyed Bear."

I tried the doors. Locked. I took a few steps back, looking for another way in.

"Help you?"

I swallowed a yelp. A hatchway in the door had slid silently open and a bored-looking lifer looked out, his tumble-down face lit from beneath by a candle.

"Sorry, you frightened me." I made a show of regaining my composure. "Is this St. Michael's? I'm not sure if I have the right place…"

"You here for the sermon?"

"Yes, the sermon. I apologize for being so late." I could make out a collar and cassock, but if this mook was a man of the cloth, I was the pope. Most clergymen I've come across have fewer facial scars. And more teeth. "The roads, you see…"

The man smirked. "Helps keep out unwanted guests." He squinted at me. "I don't think I know you, Mr…?"

"Smith." I took my hat off and held it to my chest in both hands, taking a step back into the shadows. From behind the fake priest I heard the music mercifully end. A shout of "Hallelujah!" reverberated through the passageways. "Dudley Smith."

"This is a private meeting, Mr. Smith. And I don't know you." The trapdoor began to shut.

I reached out and blocked the opening. "There must be some mistake," I stammered while I pulled at the panel. "Madame Destiny said I would be welcome. She said Nex was the one I needed to see. Please, I've brought the money."

He paused. "Show it."

I hurriedly fumbled at my pockets and finally held up my billfold, letting it drop through my grasp. "Dammit." I bent down, hugged myself to the door below the opening. "Sorry, it's dark out here," I called out. "Could I get a light?"

The man pushed his head through the opening for a better look. I reached up, linked my fingers behind his head, and yanked, crushing his throat against the wood and holding fast. He shook briefly while his lungs wondered where all the air went.

I let go and he slid back, thudding to the floor. Reaching in, I fiddled around blindly for the latch until the door swung open with a creak that couldn't sound more ominous. I picked up my wallet and stepped inside, kicking the false priest as I passed. Half to make sure he was out cold. Half to make sure he knew I had been there.

The voice became clearer as I crept forward in the murk, holding Marion out in front. I heard "death," and "God," and "absolution." A lot of "Amen!"s. And finally, as I neared the inner entrance to the main chapel, "communion."

I pulled the door open a crack and peeked in. Candles lined the walls, directing balletic shadows about the room. At the opposite end, an enormous wooden crucifix loomed over an apse, the eyes of its tortured inhabitant wide and judgmental. Beneath its gaze, between the pews, a group of about thirty worshippers lined themselves up. I couldn't make out their faces, not in the gloom, not with my eye. I opened the door as wide as I dared and slipped inside.

The organist launched into an abysmal interpretation of "Amazing Grace." The queue calmly shuffled forward. I sidled up the left aisle, keeping to the dark. A figure in religious vestments stood atop the dais, placing a communion wafer in each obediently open mouth and offering liquid from a garish chalice. The music droned on, the organist a suspiciously mature altar boy.

I edged closer, crouching behind a pew. I could see faces now. The parishioners were all lifers – old and young, men and women, several races. The only thing they seemed to have in common was their attendance. Those finished with communion had retaken their seats. A few had their heads lowered in prayer. Or slumber.

I scanned the parishioners, not seeing her.

I felt a slight prickling in my upper back. Then, my chest. I tried to stand but remained fixed to the pew. The knife pinned me to the wood like a butterfly on display.

"Still moving, Mr. Smith?" The voice breathed in my ear, each word a croak, as if their speaker recently had his windpipe violently pulped. "What a clever little moot you are." The most definitely not a priest pried Marion from my hand while I futilely pushed against the bench. "I don't like clever little moots, not at all."

The barrel of my gun pressed up behind my ear.

"Careful with that, she's a present from Mom."

He cocked the hammer, a disrespectful click that ripped through the quiet. The priest paused and looked over, sizing up the situation. I could make out a wispy Van Dyke staining a weak chin, lips equally at home in a smile as a scowl. Its eyes glinted, lenses opaque with scratches. A tendril of fear tickled my gut as the former Bishop O'Shea took me in, frowned, then resumed its theological ministrations.

"You work for a moot?" A few of the faithful had noticed me. None looked particularly compelled to intervene.

"Quiet," the henchpriest hissed.

I scanned the faces. A few candles had snuffed themselves out, making identification difficult. Near the procession's end I thought I could see a ponytail, maybe a dress.

"Seems odd, you working for a moot," I went on. "What with your noticeable antipathies."

"I don't like moots. I do like getting paid." He motioned the gun at the lineup. "These people? Five large each."

An elderly Chinese couple stepped forward in unison and accepted the Eucharist. I watched them potter back to their seats, the man staggering near the end, the woman weakly pulling him along. I looked back and saw Isabel Lopez joyfully open her mouth to accept a wafer placed serenely on her tongue by the good bishop. She took a few tastes from the vessel, crossed herself, and peacefully retook her seat, the last supplicant of the evening.

"What now?" I said. "We all go in peace? Something like that?"

"Now, Detective," O'Shea intoned, "we begin the crossing." It spread its arms outward to the congregation and began reciting the Lord's Prayer. Smiles lit their faces – those with eyes still open. Isabel's face beamed with sleepy contentedness. Her eyelids drooped closed, then opened again. All around her, members of the congregation began to drop their heads.

"You have done so well, children," said the moot, its prayer complete. "Very soon now, you take the next step toward eternity."

"Sounds like quite the deal," I called out. "Anyone get in on this who *doesn't* have five grand?"

The henchman pistol-whipped the back of my head. I put my hands up, performing the actions of the wounded. My legs tensed beneath me.

"Ignore this heathen," the moot continued, unfazed. "He is unworthy of the gift God has bestowed upon him. Embrace the darkness when it comes, it shall last merely a moment. And then..." The smile of a kindly Samaritan creased its face as it gestured to the wooden messiah "...you shall know the rapture of his righteous love."

"Rapture?" I shouted. "That's the grift?"

"I said!"

Another blow to my head.

"Be!"

Another wallop.

"Quiet!"

I pushed up with my legs. The knife resisted, its blade carving into me, sliding off a rib. I yanked myself left and fell free, dodging the next blow.

Off-balance, the henchman lurched forward into the pews. I grabbed the knife, now loosened in its berth, prying it free. Before the henchpriest could regain his footing I blundered toward him, knife out, an ample flap of me dangling loose beneath my arm. The blade met his chest as Marion's barrel met mine.

He pulled the trigger twice as I plunged the knife in. I felt one of my lungs deflate. He fired once while he fell, once more while he bled out. I pried Marion from his grip as he died.

The organist was scrabbling for something beneath his robes. I quickly put a bullet in his neck before he could draw. O'Shea managed two steps before I shot out its kneecap.

I climbed over the worshippers. Isabel's head was chin to chest. I slapped her face. Her eyes fluttered.

"You're too late," O'Shea said. It'd propped itself up against the organist and was examining its lack of knee. "It's over. It's all over now."

I pried her eyelids open with my fingertips. She pushed at my hands, moaning.

"Isabel, stay with me," I said. My voice was thin, harsh. My one lung pushed harder. "Carmen wants you back. I'm here to take you home. Stay awake."

"She's already dead."

I shook her shoulders. "Cora's waiting for you, Isabel." Saliva dribbled from her mouth. Her breathing shallowed.

I stood, reloading Marion as I strode to O'Shea. "Antidote?"

It shook its head. I plugged the bishop's other kneecap. It took the violence quietly.

"Why?"

It sighed, picking at the new wound. "Because they *want* this existence. They *crave* it. They come here *begging* to be moot. Who am I to deny someone their fondest wish?"

"How many?"

"Hundreds. Thousands." I shot it twice more in the chest.

"How many have come back?"

It dismissed the question with a weak wave of its hand. "Not that many. After they die, we leave. When we come back, any rebirths are gone, we clean up the leftovers and divide the cash. I give my share to the few bastards I've left around. I can at least do that."

"Seeking absolution?"

"Absolution no longer exists. I could tell them this, but it would make no difference. They simply cannot accept the truth of it."

"Truth?"

"That there is nothing beyond this world. No Heaven, no afterlife. No God." It snorted a laugh. "After all I've done, all the people I hurt, I couldn't even suffer the torments of a hell."

I knew it was right. I had experienced the nothing, and returned. I spent years outrunning the dark that awaited me.

I looked to Isabel. Her breathing had stilled.

"They're so jealous," O'Shea continued. "They think we're God's children. Every moot a messiah. It offends them. They can't bear to be *ignored*. Not when they're so *deserving*. So they seek me out, they make a payment for past sins, and I remove their pain."

I sank into a pew and cradled my head in my hands.

"You fool them," I said at last, furious. At Isabel. At O'Shea. At me. "No one would willingly do this to themselves." I fought to get the words out, refusing to believe the fundamental untruth of them.

O'Shea looked at me, philosophical. "I'm only an instrument. They're just afraid to do it themselves. I give them a show and help them cross the river."

The congregation died as I watched. One by one.

"Faith doesn't move mountains, Detective. It just obscures the view."

I checked my gun. Three bullets left. Thought things over.

"I hadn't heard you'd died," I said.

"I was shivved in the yard. Nasty business. After I returned, I played doornail. The prison didn't want me, so the church dropped me off in Greytown. As I suspected they would. It didn't take long to find gentlemen willing to fund my new church. Even less time to find clients."

"And Nex?"

"Short for necrophilia. My own little joke."

I stared at Isabel. Looked at her life. Wondered what she could have become.

Thought about Marion. About So and Jo.

"What now, Detective?"

I counted my bullets again.

"You won't let me go unpunished, will you?"

I looked to the bishop. Its eyes were pleading.

"I deserve punishment."

I looked back to Isabel.

"You want to do it."

I caressed my scars.

"End me."

One for So.

"*End me!*"

One for Jo.

"I'm going to wait," I decided. "Until something happens."

I waited a long time.

◀ ▶

I called Miss Lopez, told her I quit, Isabel's trail had gone cold. I hung up when she asked for specifics.

I pass the days now shuffling through Greytown's streets, gun by my side. Most moots avoid eye contact, lurch to the other side of the street. They've heard the stories; even if they haven't, self-preservation demands the response.

I ignore them. If they are cognizant enough to avoid me, they're plainly capable of making up their own deteriorating minds.

Once in a great while, one will get it in its head to take me on. It'll lumber up to the sidewalk beneath my Greytown apartment window and groan a threat, sometimes heave a brick ineffectually into the air.

It's usually the new arrivals. They haven't figured out yet what it means to be dead. They think me a vigilante. A sheriff no one elected in a town no one wants to live in. I give them a chance to leave me alone. Then I let Marion speak for me.

Sometimes, they're older moots, looking for a way out, knowing I'll provide one. All they'd have to do is ask. But they believe it better to go in a blaze of glory than a mewling plea to end it all.

To moots, I am the avenging angel now. Or the nightmare of nightmares.

Same result either way.

Other days I can't bring myself to face the grey. I stay in my apartment, waiting out existence, O'Shea's brain set companionably beside me in its bowl. I fancy I can hear the man within shrieking into the void.

Neither of us deserves to escape our hells.

I stare at the wall. Feeling myself slowly rot away. Wishing it were quicker. Glad that it isn't.

On the wall in front of me, two photos make up my world.

Sophia and Josephine: the two I couldn't save.

Isabel: the one I did.

DONNER PARTIES

Keith Cadieux

Lewis Keseberg is the name he uses to rent the basement of the rundown rooming house. He leaves an envelope of cash in the mailbox every month, has seen the landlord only once, and either there are no other tenants or they never leave their units.

To call it an apartment is too generous: two rooms with poured concrete for walls and floor. Squat, splintered windows sit at eye level inside, ground level outside. The sound of tires going past intermingle with other noises: a rattling refrigerator, a steady sewer-filling drip. The floor is slick with water, which runs into a small metal drain.

He wears a sleeveless white undershirt, worn khaki trousers, and plain white socks. Water squelches out of the fabric and between his toes with each step but he prefers this to the feel of cement on his bare feet. He sports a full beard, a spade, that reaches to his chest. The long whiskers drip down onto the front of his wet clothes.

His fingertips are pruned and slippery with wet. Loosely, by the handle, he grips a gallon jug filled with water. He paces and stops at the edge of the drain, plants his feet, takes a few deep breaths, and brings the jug to his lips. He tilts his head back and drinks, making loud pulsing sounds as he forces down the liquid. His palate notes hints of copper. His esophagus stings with cold before going numb. His stomach shrieks and distends as it's forced into holding so much fluid. He tilts too far, and water spills out the sides of his mouth. He loses his focus, coughs, splutters, and has to pull the jug away. There are still a few cups' worth left in the jug.

He rests his hands on his sore belly, tries to catch his breath but belches instead. The square, stone room reverberates briefly, then the sound of the burp is overtaken by a rush of water as he vomits fluid onto the floor. He bends forward at the waist, pushes hard on his middle, like squeezing juice from a lemon.

He dumps out the bit left in the jug. The sound of dripping quickens. He straightens up and moves over to the side of the room where there is a sink with no counter. He refills the jug at the tap, to the very top.

He needs fewer breaths this time and brings the container back up to his mouth to drink. And drink. This time he drains the gallon without a hiccup. He doesn't think he's spilled any, but he's too soaked to be sure. He straddles the drain, presses hard and low on his belly, and forces everything out again. He makes a fist around his beard, wrings out the excess.

This is part of his training. Gorging on water stretches the stomach.

Set up against the wall opposite the sink is a folding dinette table. The legs wobble on the sloping floor. The tabletop is covered with medical and anatomical textbooks, all thick, heavy hardcovers. Some are piled neatly, others opened to specific pages and laid atop each other. He is always careful not to get them wet, but the pages are wavy and moist. The glossy finish of the coloured paper is dulled in straight lines where he has run a damp fingertip along the words, memorizing all the terms and structures and layouts of the stomach, its surrounding muscles, the placement of nearby organs, the distribution of nerve endings, where fat tends to roll over, how deep the stomach lining, the careful coilings of the intestines. He knows this information by heart but reading the words over again is part of the training as well. Part of the ritual.

There is one book that doesn't fit with the others. A thin paperback, popular history rather than a textbook. He reads and rereads familiar words, savouring a favourite texture: *When they asked him why he had not eaten the ox legs, he replied, "They have not as good a flavour."* He closes this book first and sets it at one end of the table. He closes the others one by one and sets them in a neat stack on the floor in the corner. The table now cleared, he steps over to the noisy fridge, the bone-metal rattle louder with the door open, and takes out a glass punch bowl filled with fresh stewing beef. He sets the bowl on the dinette table and pulls over a kitchen chair from against the far wall. He peels back the plastic wrap and eats the small cubes of cold meat. Eating is part of the training, too. The pieces are slippery and slide easily down the throat, thanks to a recipe of his own – sugar, corn starch, a touch of water – that makes the liquid viscous and slick, though admittedly it doesn't do much for the flavour. With pinched fingers he lifts out and eats each morsel one at a time without chewing. Chewing slows everything down and the whole point is to consume as much as quickly as possible. He won't eat again until tomorrow night.

He stands, rinses the bowl, and leaves it in the sink. He wipes his mouth and face with a handful of tap water. At the other end of the basement is the empty bedroom. A separate outfit hangs neatly from wooden hangers over the doorknob, expensive shoes set atop an empty cardboard box, so as to be off the ground. He undresses, tosses the wet clothes in the corner, and puts on the good, clean clothes. He turns out the lights, the raspy breath of the fridge still louder than the elegant clack of his footsteps. He locks the door behind him, the sound of the key against the tumblers like cracking soup bones.

◀ ▶

The next night is dry and cold, but he enjoys the walk. The smells are crisp, his steps slow. Sunrise is still a few hours away. In one hand he swings a metal lunchbox, the kind he imagines construction workers eat from, up high on the girders. He smells the sauced, salty smoke of food vendors. His stomach growls.

He walks deep into downtown, crosses through an outdoor parking lot. He kicks a walnut-sized rock ahead of him for a few strides. The skip of the stone and his footsteps are the only sounds. His hands are cold; he puts them in his pockets, walks with his head high against the chilled breeze.

He stops in front of a long and low-roofed brick building. There is a FOR SALE sign in the window. No phone number is written on it. The power lines overhead buzz, as though coursing with honeybees. It is darker here than the rest of the block. He steps to a nearby lamppost, glass crunching under his shoes, and looks up as he sits on the curb. He lets his gaze rise slowly like steam to the top of the pole where the bulb is broken. He breathes deep, enjoying the scent of the air, the taste of anticipation. His stomach rumbles again.

He hears shambling feet, soles never lifted off the ground, and rusty shopping-cart wheels. A shuffle and squeak. A greasy man makes his way up the road. Keseberg stays sitting, enjoying his quiet moment, but the man walks straight to him, hand outstretched. He has glassy eyes, like washed and polished apples.

"Spare change?" the man says.

Keseberg admires the man's beard a moment, almost as long as his except grimy and riddled with grey. He gets up to take a five-dollar bill from his pocket and hands it over. "Nice beard," he says. "How do you keep your food out of it?"

There is no answer. The man continues up the block as though never interrupted. Keseberg stands in the same spot and turns to watch him go. The man reaches the end of the street, wheels around, and wanders back the way he has just come. The money now tucked away, hand outstretched again, eyes empty of recognition.

"Any change, sir?" the man says. It's Keseberg who doesn't respond this time. The man is unperturbed and moves to the far end of the block and turns onto the next street. Once he's out of sight, Keseberg slips into the old building.

Inside is a dark and unswept staircase leading down, though the lights in the room at the bottom are on. He takes the steps slowly and has to lean his head to one side to avoid hitting the angled ceiling. The lower level sprawls into a broad, open space. More than a hundred people, by rough estimate, mill and murmur about. They stand in small groups, huddle around support beams. Everyone whispers, a few chuckle nervously – a mixture of contained excitement and morbid curiosity simmering all around, bubbling at the edges.

As Keseberg steps deeper into the room, the crowd moves aside and fills in promptly behind him as he passes, like sauce parting thickly around a spoon. He meets the stares of those who turn to him, looking in their eyes for signs that they recognize him. He wonders how many have seen him eat before, how many know him by name.

"That's Lewis Keseberg," he hears crest over the thrum. He nudges people aside, looking for the source. He sees a youngish-looking woman, her tattooed face close to the ear of a tall male companion who seems a little younger. She points.

He approaches the pair swiftly, a smile liberally spread across his face. "I don't believe I've had the pleasure," he says, leaning forward. The woman looks sheepish and takes a step back and to the side, just enough to put her companion between herself and Keseberg. "Are you fans?" he presses. "Surely not first-timers?" The tall man deepens his furrowed brow and takes his own step back. Both ease their way backward, regaining their anonymity in the crowd. "No need for rudeness," Keseberg says, and shrugs.

He makes it to the front of the crowd, beyond which is a serving counter and past that a long-defunct kitchen with dusty and dulled stainless steel surfaces, entirely devoid now of any appliances. As he takes in the full scope of the room – the layout of the open space with the kitchen behind, the neighbourhood around the building – he realizes what this space was normally used for: it's a soup kitchen. This makes him smile. Tables and chairs have been cleared away to allow more standing room, which is much needed.

In front of the counter are three wheeled tables, each covered with a clean and pressed sheet. Under the covering, the familiar rising and falling shape signals that everything is in place and ready. The contest will start soon. The fluorescent bulbs overhead have been changed and there are tall halogen work lights at either end of the row.

Two of the tables are already claimed, their eaters nearby. Keseberg steps behind the one remaining, sets his lunchbox on a nearby tray, and leans back against the counter, hands in pockets. The metal tabletop in front of him is shaped like a deep, oversized cookie sheet with a steep lip all around. Something straight out of a morgue. There is a digital console on the side with a weight readout: 176 lbs.

He nods to the eater next to him who nods back and takes a similar position at the counter. They share a moment of familiarity. "Hello, Armin," Keseberg says. Armin doesn't answer but this doesn't faze either of them. There is a woman hovering at the farthest station but she takes no notice of them.

There are no nameplates or announcers, only the whispers that linger after the tables and places have been cleared. The phantom rumours of those few witnesses, trying to convince those who haven't seen and don't believe such underground events really happen.

A woman in a tie and round frameless glasses approaches the row of slabs. She snaps on latex gloves and drapes a stethoscope across the back of her neck. She wants the eaters' attention. Keseberg takes his hands from his pockets and crosses his arms. He leans to one side and says, "You know, the first time I competed, the event doctor actually wore scrubs and a mask." Armin shows a hint of a smile. "Glad to see it didn't become a trend," Keseberg says.

The event doctor nods to each eater in turn and pulls away the sheets. The whispering crowd catches its breath and holds it. A nude and lightly drugged man lies on each slab. The doctor steps over to the one in front of Keseberg and presses two fingers under the corner of the jaw, below the ear. She pushes her glasses higher up on her nose and watches the man's chest rise and fall once before moving to the next.

Keseberg eyes the woman at the far end. "Any word on her?"

Armin, in the middle, turns to him. "The Red Widow, apparently."

Keseberg squints against the light, still looking at the far station. "I'm not sure I like that," he says.

A man holding a clipboard and pen steps beside the doctor, who raises one arm, holds her watch at eye level, and exchanges a long glance with him. The whole room watches her. The silence grows frenzied, roiling. She drops her arm, the signal to begin.

Keseberg opens his lunchbox and takes out two knives. He has refined his tool set to just these. He takes a long moment to look everything over, assess, even though the other two have already rushed to take their first few bites. He will not be pressed into making careless blunders. The sleeper before him is young, dishevelled, but clean. His lips are cracked, one or two sores in the crook of the elbow.

He chooses his filet knife first, long and slender, and makes a very shallow cut across the stomach, left to right, through the navel. The sleeper's eyes flutter but don't open. That done, he changes to his slicing knife, with the granton edge, and starts in earnest at the shoulder. He carves a generous mouthful, a cube of stew meat, but doesn't lift it out right away. He gives the heart rate a chance to elevate, lets the juices swap around a little. Once it's coated over, he picks it up in his fingers, pops it in his mouth, and swallows without chewing. Warm and pleasing.

He feels prickles of sweat at his temples, in the small of his back. The lights are hot but give an excellent view around the whole room. He sees the crowd surge and bulge, though it never comes too close to the tables. The doctor paces from station to station, keeping her distance as well, so as not to interfere. He moves slowly, takes in the moment, the sights and sounds. The smells and flavours. There is some commotion over at Armin's table, where the sleeper is awake and fighting.

They are never tied down, the sleepers. That would be cruel. Restraint and control are part of good technique and up to the eaters. The commotion works into the crowd, which roars with excitement and encouragement, but for whom is unclear. Keseberg looks down to see his own sleeper's eyes open and looking confusedly at the cut in the stomach. He begins to sit up; Keseberg helps roll him onto his side into a fetal position. The sleeper clutches at his belly, tries to press the cut closed.

"That's good thinking," Keseberg says, leaning over him close. He breaks good manners and speaks with his mouth full. "Don't let anything slip out." Though the cut isn't deep enough for that, just a distraction that helps maintain control.

Armin, on the other hand, has lost that. He is no longer eating at all, only struggling to hold the sleeper down. With every move, the crowd's reaction grows. After a moment, Armin has no choice but to grab a heavy cleaver and bring it down with a roar.

"Back!" the event doctor says as she steps to the table. She places her fingers on the sleeper's neck and, when she doesn't feel anything, nods to the record keeper who takes down the time on his clipboard. The doctor moves around to read the scale and the recorder notes the difference from the starting weight, which is just over two pounds. It's a poor showing. Armin swears under his breath and passes behind Keseberg on his way around the counter.

The far station is suspiciously quiet, by contrast. That sleeper hasn't woken up at all. It happens from time to time, a miscalculation in the anaesthetic. The doctor checks the pulse. "He's dead," she says, and waves the Red Widow away. The recorder comes around to check the scale. Her showing is well over six pounds.

This leaves Keseberg the clear winner but he keeps eating. The doctor steps closer to his table, watching over the rim of her glasses. The sleeper is so preoccupied with the cut across his stomach that he doesn't seem to notice what Keseberg is up to. The recorder keeps his pen and clipboard poised and ready. Keseberg eats. He doesn't stop because he's full, or even because he's already won. Just puts his training to use.

The room is hushed, everyone curious to see how long it could possibly go on. A few at the front, if they strain their ears, can hear lips smacking. They start to whisper; Keseberg strains to hear them. He hears his name, hushed, as though his existence were a secret that they can't wait to share.

He almost feels the need to offer whispers of his own, to draw from his favourite words, read and reread for their savoury texture. Those words that inspired his adopted identity, that explain where the name comes from. Those words that describe the fourth team of rescuers expecting to find the last four survivors of the Donner party trapped in the Sierra Nevada mountains and finding instead three dead – partially eaten – a wealth of ignored provisions including three ox legs, and only one man alive: Lewis Keseberg.

Sometimes, he passes strangers on the street, hears them mention with a hush, "They're called Donner Parties. My cousin said he's been to one. It's true, I swear."

The doctor has her fingers on the sleeper's neck but she keeps quiet. There is still a faint pulse, but it's fading. Keseberg slows but continues to eat. The crowd looks on, the rush ebbing away. The lights flicker. And Keseberg eats. And eats. The real shame is that eventually it will end. He will have to stop. But for now, at least, he sees no reason to.

UNREDEEMABLE

Michael S. Chong

I collect cans and bottles to make money. It is honest, hard work. I am getting older and cannot make money any way else. I do not get government money because I worked with my husband at our laundry, never paying into the system. With my late husband's gambling and no pension, I needed some way to survive and I would never ask my son for money. I lost much of my savings investing in one of his business ideas that failed.

Going through the trash of others and collecting cans and bottles is hard work, but I have always worked. I get by with my limited English and have a roof over my head. I know people who do what I do who live on the streets and they are crazy, sick on drugs and alcohol. I have done every job no one else would want to do. I've washed dishes in a seafood restaurant, pressed clothes in a laundry and spent a few years picking worms. No one ever took care of me, even when my husband was still alive or even before in China when I was living with my family. I have always had to take care of myself.

My father left us when I was young to go to America, following his father, who left much earlier. Money was easier to earn in America, the gold mountain. You could work hard enough to make enough money to support an entire extended family back home. I was the last to leave. I was left with my grandmother in China and then Hong Kong during the war. All my uncles and brothers had already left for California. When the Japanese came we hid, otherwise they would have done terrible things to us. We hid in cellars and saw them go through. Some bad things happened to some people but that was in the past.

While escaping the war, my grandmother and I took refuge in a bombed-out shell of a building until dawn. At night, there were bandits who knew those leaving carried valuables so my grandmother dressed us poor and we walked during daylight hours. While looking for a corner to rest, we came across a badly wounded Japanese soldier, his uniform red from his blood: legs, in the dark, looked like ruined shards of flesh. Barely in his teens, the Japanese soldier started to yell, thinking we were there to hurt him. My grandmother told me to turn around but I watched her take off her scarf, cover the soldier's mouth and nose, muffling his screams, then take his life. He might have called others to find us and kill us. It was work that needed to be done, she told me later.

We made it to Hong Kong while the Nationalists and the Communists battled among themselves in our hometown and the surrounding Big Circle region. I met my husband while we were there. He had been school friends with my older brother and was returning from Canada to look for a girl who had disappeared during the war. He looked me up, and since I had had a crush on him as a child, when he asked me to marry him, I did.

It's funny, I remember the past better than I remember things that happened yesterday. My memory is not what it used to be, but the distant past seems clear. I worry I am losing my wits.

A Chinese friend of mine, Shu Chen, a few years younger, also collecting bottles, seems to be remembering events different than I do. I mean, she mentions mahjong games or dim sum meals and remembers it totally different than I do. Maybe I'm wrong. Maybe we're both wrong. Getting old is not for the weak.

I first met Shu Chen early dawn, just when it was getting light out, around the time I first needed to start gathering cans and bottles. We met while I was in the northern part of my route, collecting on one side of the street, and she was on the other, working her way toward me.

When we met in the middle, I spoke to her in my dialect and she understood, being originally from a neighbouring county in China. She looked like she would be. We agreed right away to share the street or let the first person that arrived have the takings. We have a system called *guanxi* that is a personal connection between people where if one does a favour for another they are indebted to them, the opposite of the Western way. We became fast friends, since at our ages most of our friends from earlier in our lives have disappeared or passed away.

It is good to have friends out there while working since some of the other collectors are not so nice. They yell at you, telling you that the street you're on is theirs even if you have never seen them before. How can someone own a street? There are enough cans and bottles in the city for everyone, so I never complain. I just walked on.

For all the bad people you meet, there are many good people. On my regular route, there are homeowners who make sure to leave their bottles out for me so I do not have to go through their trash and get dirty from the garbage. They smile and wave as I walk onto their property to get the bottles.

Why these people did not walk the few blocks to return their bottles, I could understand. The ten cents for wine bottles and five cents for beer cans and bottles is not enough of an incentive for them to leave the comfort of their homes.

For me, I make almost fifty dollars on a good day. That is enough to support me for a whole week. My expenses are low. When money is tight, I survive on canned fish, rice and discount vegetables, the ones that are sold for much less because they are wilted. Just like me.

I know people look down on me or feel sorry for me when they see me out there in the mornings going from garbage can to recycling bin, opening bags and pouring out leftover fluids. I am supporting myself, as one should in this life. If I didn't collect cans and bottles, I don't know what I would do.

Some of the neighbourhoods I work in are rich. I mean the houses are big, the lots are large, and the cars in the driveways look expensive. Their trash seems fancy and pricey too. I mean their food is all processed and high-end. I guess to afford lifestyles and homes like they have, they both have to work and that does not allow time to make food from scratch. They all seem to eat a lot of pizza, both frozen and delivered.

The only food treat I give myself is an occasional dim sum meal with Shu Chen, and even then we go to a cheap restaurant in Chinatown that sells dumplings at a discount if you arrive before 11 a.m. and even cheaper if you are a senior. The tea is free and both of us rarely get more than three dishes each, but stay a couple of hours and enjoy the atmosphere and the company.

Shu Chen has no family in the city. Her late husband died quite young of a heart attack and her only child, a daughter, lives on the West Coast and never visits. I guess I am her only family. One time in the winter, she did not show up for a day and did not answer her phone. I heard where she was from Bobby, a young bottle collector, who smelled bad, dressed like a bum, and I think was a drunk, but he was always nice to Shu Chen and me, always being respectful of territories. Bobby had found her fallen down with a sprained ankle, called an ambulance, then found me. Rushing to the hospital, I found her sitting up reading a week-old Chinese newspaper. She smiled when she saw me and told me someone was probably getting all of our bottles.

Recuperating and lucky she hadn't broken her hip, Shu Chen was off her feet for the next couple of weeks. I took care of her when not collecting. We would play cards and talk about the past, old friends, and all the hearts we broke. She did the same for me when I was out with the flu one spring. We are lucky we found each other.

Without collecting bottles, I would still be alone most of the time. Even if I did have enough savings for retirement, where I could sit around watching kung-fu soap operas all day and eating sweets, I would still probably collect bottles. It gets me out of my room; I get outside, breathe fresh air, and see the world. Where others see trash, I see money, freedom, and independence. Sometimes, kind people offer me money like I was a beggar but I refuse it. I work for money, and the city is my workplace.

What makes this job a little hazardous are the creeps who do it for the drug and alcohol money. They have no respect for people. I have had bums physically threaten me when I was collecting. Addicted tourists. They usually slurred their words and seemed crazy and I was not about to lose my life for a few dollars. Shu Chen was different. She took on a few of these bad types, telling me they were weak from their addictions and, if they were willing to beat up an old woman for some change, life would get them in the end. Like a lapsed Buddhist-Taoist, which most Chinese in the West were, Shu Chen thought karma would get the bad ones in the end. Me, I wasn't so sure.

Shu Chen told me she had to hit a bum over the head once with her searching stick after he tried taking her cart. Shu Chen and I both used metal fold-up shopping carts. That, good rubber gloves, some garbage bags, and an old broomstick to stir up the recycling bins to uncover the redeemable bottles and cans, were all the equipment we needed. The ones worth money always seemed to be at the bottom.

Bobby was badly beaten up once. They never caught the punk who did it and I don't think the police even cared too much. Shu Chen and I made sure Bobby, who lived in a small closet-sized basement apartment, had enough to eat while he got better. Bobby was a little slow, but always smiling, and seemed to look out for Shu Chen and me. He would always tell us when there was some new location that had too many cans and bottles for him to collect and he would always share the day-old baked goods that were given to him by a kindly baker on his route. The Danishes and croissants he gave us were dry but went down well with hot tea, which we carried in thermoses during our working times.

I don't think he had any family, any that he kept in touch with; at least he never mentioned any. Sometimes he acted a little off, talking to himself so quietly you could not hear what he said, but you could sense he had a rough life. His face and hands were always a little dirty but his clothes seemed neat, if not a little smelly.

Bobby was the one who told me he saw some strange man redeeming cans and bottles from Shu Chen's cart at the local beer store we went to. He waited for the man to get his money and then followed him back to a rooming house in the bad part of the neighbourhood. Bobby described the man, saying he wore black clothes and had a beard, shaved head, and looked middle-aged.

I left my cart with Bobby and walked Shu Chen's area, then went to her room in a building not far from the park. I could not find her so I checked the hospitals and even went to the local police station. There was no sign of Shu Chen anywhere.

Bobby found me sitting in the park near Shu Chen's apartment. He was pushing my cart and looked as if he had been crying. I had been a little, too.

"Have you found her?" Bobby asked.

"No, nothing."

"Maybe she's with family and the guy just found her cart."

"I don't think so."

"Maybe the police can help."

"They don't care."

"Yeah."

"Show me where this man lives."

"What are you going to do?"

"I just want to talk to him."

"I don't think that's a good idea. We should let the cops know."

"No, they don't care about people like us."

"That's not true."

"That time you were beat up, did the police do anything?"

"No."

"They don't care about us."

Bobby stood there with his head down for a while, like he was confused, then said, "Okay, but I'm coming with you."

"It is better if I go alone."

"No, it's not safe."

"I'm just going to ask him if he has seen Shu. He might not talk if there are two of us."

Bobby looked down, lost in thought. "Okay, but I'll watch from just out of sight. I'll be in yelling distance."

"You're a good man, Bobby," I said.

He shook his head and said, "I just want to help."

We walked in silence the ten blocks or so south toward the lake. Bobby insisted on pushing my cart for me. When we got to the house the man lived in, it was late in the afternoon. People were starting to come home from their jobs.

The houses and the state of them showed a neighbourhood that had seen better days. The house the stranger lived in was a semi-detached. One side was stuccoed, with a well-kept lawn with bleeding heart flowers and irises trimming it, while the other had an empty patch of dirt strewn with weeds.

Bobby waited around the corner while I walked up with my cart. I did my regular routine: leaving my cart on the sidewalk, and taking my searching stick, I walked up the side of the house where they kept their recycling bin. Bobby wasn't sure where the strange man's apartment was but saw him walk down the alley to the back of the house. I did the same, looking into the small basement windows, covered with what looked like aluminum foil. Opening, then looking into the recycling bin and swirling the contents with my stick, I was surprised to see a half-dozen tall beer cans.

Around the back, beside a small wooden patio and a closed glass door, there was a short entryway down to a door that had a crack haloing the doorknob, as if someone had tried to kick it in or out. Through the small window I could see shadows. I knocked and there was no response. Using my stick, I banged on the door. There were some muffled voices, then the door opened to a crack held taut by the chain. A face matching the one described by Bobby peered out, but it seemed thinner than I thought it would be. His pupils were pinpricks.

"What do you want?" he said with the rough voice of a heavy smoker.

"Have you seen an old Chinese woman like me around?"

"What?" He looked at me with confusion. "You want upstairs. Try the front door." He slammed shut the door and relocked the three deadbolts.

I kept knocking until he came to the door again. It took a long time.

He unlocked the three deadbolts, and unchained, and opened the door this time. The man was skinny with broad shoulders and an indented chest like he used to work out with weights but stopped.

"Lady, I told you to go check upstairs."

"Have you seen my friend, an old Chinese woman like me, about my height, grey hair, she collects bottles in the neighbourhood?"

"No offence, but all you Chinese look alike to me. Ask upstairs. They're Chinese or something." With that, he slammed the door, then I heard loud music. He would not come back to the door again.

I went to the front door and rang the bell but there was no answer, even after I waited for a while. Looking in the partially curtained windows, it looked like a regular home with a couch and TV, empty, with the owners still at their work.

Taking my cart, I went to find Bobby, who was just down the street grabbing some beer cans from a recycling bin, and told him what happened.

"Was he acting strange?" he asked.

"I think he was on drugs but I don't know."

"How about I get in there when he's not home and look around?"

"Too dangerous."

"It's a basement apartment, they're easy to get into and small. It won't take me long."

"I don't know, maybe we find her."

"I hope so," Bobby said.

With that, we walked our separate ways home. That night, I called Shu Chen's phone number so many times I lost count. By the end, her old answering machine was full with my pleas for her to call me when she got the message.

I had trouble sleeping that night. I dreamed of Shu Chen and me swimming like I did as a girl back in China. Shu Chen was ahead of me, just swimming out of my reach, and I could not really see her other than the kicking of her feet, but knew it was her and kept trying to catch up. There was no shore to be seen, like we were in the middle of the ocean. I woke up before dawn, drenched in sweat.

After having a steamed bun I microwaved in my little kitchen alcove, I walked to Shu Chen's room above a storefront that sold used furniture. She had given me her keys that one time when she was recuperating and had never asked for them back. Her small room was dark when I let myself in. Checking her stand-up dresser, all her clothes were there and her one piece of luggage was still sitting nestled in the back, the handle tattered from age, but she had wrapped twine and elastic bands around it to hold it together. I knew her so well, I knew the outfit she was wearing when she disappeared, a white brimmed hat stained to pale yellow, dark green pants and her pink quilted top with little blue flowers like daisies, the pattern so small they looked like houndstooth if you didn't look close enough. The place, like mine, smelled of mothballs. On a wall she had a photo of her and me at a mahjong game, smiling like we both won. I started to cry.

I knew that when I passed maybe my son and his family would mourn but no one else. Shu Chen's daughter probably wouldn't even come, but I knew I should contact her if too much time passed before we found out what happened to Shu Chen. From what Shu Chen told me about her daughter, I doubt she would even care, which made me cry harder, with deep moans for my lost friend. The world was so cruel to good people like Shu Chen, who never hurt anybody. Our lives were so hard and to end like this made everything seem worse than I could endure any longer.

While walking home, just wanting to lie down, sleep, and make it all go away, I saw Bobby running my way. He was holding something in his hand and talking so quickly I could not understand him, and then I saw the yellowed hat of Shu Chen. She wore that hat so much it was probably her late husband's.

"I found it in his place," Bobby said. "Jimmy, his name's Jimmy, I found some letter from the government. He's an ex-con or something."

I took the hat from his hands and stared at it. "How did you get in?"

"After I left you, I turned around and started watching his place from across the street on the porch of an abandoned house. After it got dark, I saw him stumbling down the street, mumbling like he was wasted. I knew I had some time to get in so I pried open a window and slipped through. His place was crazy messy. I doubt he'd notice anything missing except his drugs. He had all kinds of pills in there. None of the bottles had Jimmy's name on them."

Still holding the hat and staring at it, I felt the material, rubbing it with my fingertips and said, "This is hers."

"Yeah, I know. There was nothing else though."

"This is proof."

"Yeah, I'm thinking he had something to do with it."

"It's proof. Enough for me."

Bobby just smiled. "Maybe I can follow him and see where he goes next time."

"Yes, next time," I said. "Bye, Bobby." I walked away, still clutching Shu Chen's hat.

A week went by in which I only slept a few hours and I still had heard nothing from Shu Chen, so I tried calling her daughter, but never spoke to her, only leaving her a message. She never got back to me.

I had stopped working and spent my days walking by Jimmy's, dropping in on Shu Chen's and just tracing her regular route. I guess I was looking for clues or a sign or something, I was not really sure, feeling confused from lack of sleep and not eating properly.

After some time doing this, I decided I had to get into Jimmy's place and look around myself. Slow Bobby could have missed something my eyes would catch, so I formulated a plan.

I went to the local liquor store and bought a large bottle of Polish vodka that was 76 percent alcohol, which cost me about three days of work, then put it into a gift bag I got at the dollar store, writing "To Jimmy" on its little tag. I walked over to Jimmy's and left it outside his door around dusk, then wasted time for a few hours walking Shu Chen's route once more. At the time, I don't know exactly why, but it felt right, and maybe in the back of my mind I was honouring her.

When I was sure Jimmy had had enough time with the bottle, I went back and knocked on the door. It took a while but I was patient enough. He opened the door very drunk, weaving on his feet, unable to focus his eyes. While he said some incoherent words in his drunken stupor, I brushed past him and he almost fell to the ground. His apartment was as messy as Bobby had said, with overflowing ashtrays all over the floor, the counters, and the table in the middle of the room. It smelled like stale sweat and urine. I felt him grab my shoulders, but he was so drunk that the momentum of swinging around knocked his feet out from underneath him. He lay there on his back, beside the empty bottle of vodka, huffing and wheezing with his eyes closed, this man who did something to Shu Chen.

My gloved hands found one of the garbage bags I kept in my pockets, and I shrouded it over his head, tying it in a knot around his neck while all the time he still hadn't moved. The bag started to suck and blow right where the hole of his mouth was, then he started to get sick, filling the bag with vomit, and his arms and legs started to flail about like he was having a bad nightmare, and all along I just stood there and watched, trying not to miss anything. After some time, I nudged his unmoving body with the toe of my running shoe.

Remembering why I came, I looked around in a haze, surprised to find no pills anywhere, thinking maybe Bobby had taken them. I left then, shutting the door behind me, and started walking. I was just walking, wanting to go somewhere else, to find some place where I could trade Jimmy's life for Shu Chen's and we could go play mahjong, then get some dumplings and tea, talking and laughing like we used to.

I found myself near Bobby's, so I thought I would tell him what had happened, since I felt like I had to tell someone and Bobby might know what to do next.

I came up to Bobby's apartment through the alley and saw Shu Chen's cart by the trash bins in the back. It was partially covered by some large greasy rag, but I would recognize it anywhere. Maybe Bobby had brought it back from the beer store after he saw Jimmy getting cash for its contents. Or maybe Bobby was lying the entire time and I had just killed an innocent man. Either way, I would need another bottle of liquor. Bobby and I would either celebrate, or I had more work to do.

THIS IS THE PARTY

Rich Larson

This is the Party:

Had Khuat is constellated by fire dancers all up and down its black beach, by lithe Thai bone-and-sinew slumsurfers, with their rock-star manes and anglicized nicknames, wearing fire-proof skinsuits or nothing at all as they cartwheel, cavort, carve up the dark.

More bodies twist and turn up on skyscraping platforms that rise like Ozymandias from the sand, dancers perfected by a subtle knife, sculpted by silicon and surgery and genetics. Floating cams transpose them onto frayed clouds, weaving their writhing silhouettes into the laser show's neon.

Below, on machine-sifted sand soft as flour, the Party guests drink and stumble and dance around the base of an artificial volcano belching steam. Freon-chilled champagne foams and splashes in wobbling arcs. Dopamine plugs slide into ear canals, up reddened nostrils. The guests mostly wear Gucci and Rag and lunar imports, and all of them wear masks, either mirrored or holo-retro.

In this bacchanalia, Prosper is reborn. His blood runs slick with alcohol and his head is shredded by a mild hallucinogen, but he knows he is Prosper Rexroat, he knows he is twenty-three, he knows he is from San Francisco, and he knows, dimly, that he came here on the suborbital with Holly, but if he can barely stand then Holly is prone somewhere on the sand and so he can do whatever, whoever he wants.

Parties have always been Prosper's element. Why would the Party be any different?

◀ ▶

Prosper wakes when adrenaline clouds into his IV bag, swims up his veins and strokes his brainstem. He reassembles himself from a hipbone, a sore calf, a cheek on rough fabric. His skin is numb. He opens his eyes.

The clock above the gurney tells him a lie. It says 5:27 a.m., August 18, 2127, but Prosper knows he is twenty-three years old, not forty-seven years old. There's a woman standing over him, turned away. He knows it's Holly, though her posture is subtly changed, her smell is different.

She turns. Her sea-green eyes are webbed with cracks.

"Why are you so fucking old?" he asks, voice catching on a dozen hooks.

She says nothing.

"Rip Van Winkle," Prosper says. "I pass out on a beach and wake up in the future. Because those fucking lucies were diced. I'm in a hospital sweating out the trip. Still seeing shit." He pauses. "Or is it a coma? Have I been in a coma? Am I old, too?"

He remembers falling twice: once down onto soft white sand, glass in hand, then once falling down into a column of steam, but he can't remember which fall was dream. Maybe both.

"You're a clone," Holly says at last, and her voice is pewter. "The eighth."

Up on the monitor, Prosper's heart line writhes like a snake.

◀ ▶

Holly Rexroat-Carrow, née Holly Carrow, killed her husband for the first time on a sun-drenched August afternoon, one liquor-drenched week after he left her and other earthly possessions to take the deep sleep to Ganymede with a digitattooed Ukrainian actress.

Divorce proceedings stalled by cryogenesis and a lawyer AI in need of diagnostic, Holly spent seven days in a gin-and-tonic haze. She cut lines on the smartglass kitchen counters and cut lines on her wrist in the shower, just shallowly.

In the mornings she slept as long as she could without overdosing on Dozr, so when the San Francisco FleshFac called at 11:35, Holly heard nothing. When they called at 12:35, she ignored it. When they called at 1:35, she clawed through cumulative hangover and answered, thinking, half-dreaming, that it was Prosper.

"This is a call regarding the organ policy of Prosper Rexroat-Carrow." The clinic's phoneghost had a slight Italian accent, calm and cultured.

"This is Mrs. Rexroat-Carrow." The title stung on its way out of her mouth.

"Good afternoon, Mrs. Rexroat-Carrow. This call is to inform your husband that his clones have reached transplant maturity. The San Francisco FleshFac would like to extend an invitation for IRL or remote inspection of said clones at your and your husband's leisure."

Holly picked a looped hair follicle off her pillow, twirling the dark strand between two fingers. Prosper never told her he'd taken out an organ policy, but she knew of it, vaguely, as she knew of other things he'd never told her, like the string of bleached blondes she'd convinced herself were only a physical release, a bodily function. She thought of Olga Kurylenko's tanned thighs and felt gutsick.

Prosper would want the clones put on ice and shuttled after him. Holly opened her mouth to tell the clinic as much. She stopped.

"I'm afraid my husband is offworld on business, but I'll take a look at them," she said instead, her tongue thick and clumsy with three days' silence. "If that's alright."

While directions uploaded to her Audi, Holly slouched toward the kitchen. She filled a glass with the same Luna vodka stickying her bathroom tiles. The smell made her gag and the taste made her hollow stomach heave. As she drank she shuffled through drawers of pristine utensils, knives, and electric peelers. She went to the car with her glass in one hand and a tenderizer dangling from the other.

The San Francisco FleshFac was well outside the city, out in the dust and vineyards and faux-villas still stubbornly aping Tuscany. Holly lay back on the drive, closing her eyes in the cool dark and opening them only when her car dropped its indicator and turned onto a long stretch lined by twists of AI-generated sculpture. The clinic itself was a behemoth of smoked glass and concrete and biostructure, swooping architecture more in line with a gallery than a hospital. Prosper had always had a taste for the exorbitant.

An automated greeter ushered her inside, an automated usher directed her down a sun-sliced hall, an automated door scanned her iris, and then she was alone in the red womb of the clone room. There were three of them, three perfect

Prospers prone under frosted glass. Holly walked circuits around them, trailing her fingers along the humming cool bioshells, hating the curve of his lips, full as the day she met him, the symmetry of his bones, the girth of his cock. Perfect as he'd been the summer they fell together.

She thumbed the release to a deep click and a serpentine hiss. Prosper's face was a lake with no ripples, tranquil the way his face a thousand light years away was tranquil, frozen veins flushed with saline, the woman he loved one cryopod over. Holly opened her bag with trembling hands, retrieved the tenderizer, and set to work demolishing his face. She swung with grim rhythm until she finally cracked skull; neurons in the blank brain made the clone spasm, squirting clotted grey and red over her hands, slicking her grip on the mallet and making her flinch backward.

When the clone was finally inert meat, an automated usher directed her toward the lavatories. As she washed her trembling hands, it explained soothingly about liability and replacement costs and legal actions. It asked if she had found the clones dissatisfactory in some way.

"I'll pay for any additional cleaning and disposal costs incurred," Holly said, voice smooth and tight for the first time in seven days. "The clone was beautifully grown. In fact, my husband and I would like another. To replace it."

The usher's head bobbed on its pneumatic neck. It didn't try to understand. Holly wished, fervent in the moment, that she was the same.

◀ ▶

Parties have always been Prosper's element; the Party is no different. He slides from copse to cultured copse of revellers, speaking silver-tongued in English, German, body language. He draws them and sloughs them, touching this arm, this stomach, this ass, as if he owns every body on the black beach. Wherever he takes his unbreakable smile, he hears about two things: the Host and the Lotto.

They pull up their cuffs from their blue-veined wrists to show him the digitattooed numbers; a girl rolls up the sleeve of his shirt to remind him of his own. He doesn't remember when the impermanent ink was punched into his forearm, but he doesn't remember who slapped glow-paint across his crotch or where his Versace loafers have gone, either.

The Lotto is unbelievable the first time he hears of it, macabre the second, magnetic the third. Each and every guest has a randomized sequence stitched into their skin. One of those sequences is the winner. When the Host arrives, the winner dies. Some years by drowning, some years by fire, some years by gutting, electrocution, helium-hefted gallows. But this is all secondhand, because attending the Party is only ever permitted once, and all external electronics are confiscated, all implants damper-clamped. And attending in itself costs as much as an organ policy. More.

Prosper knows Holly cannot possibly know this, could not have known this when they trawled down Thailand's coast and ferried to Koh Phangan to find the sort of partying that hadn't existed since the military coup. She would have never agreed to come. Maybe he knew and didn't tell her, but with the sand slithering like quicksilver and the night swelling and contracting around his skull it's hard to remember what he knows and what he's told.

◀ ▶

Prosper wrestles up from the IVs and body monitors and tells Holly-who-is-not-Holly that he is not a clone. "Clones don't have memories," he says. "They're vegetables." But he is groping down his leg, down under the thermal blanket, searching for his scar.

"What's the last thing you remember, then?" she asks simply.

"We're in Thailand," Prosper says. "Koh Phangan."

"Yes. We're here every year."

Prosper stops, racks his memory, reaching back past the party on Gaussian-blurred beach with the strange tattoos and some sort of game, some sort of lottery. "We rented gills to go diving," he says. "We tried to fuck in the water but it was too cold. Went back to the bungalow for Singhas. The mosquito net has a hole and you were drunk so you tried sewing it shut. But I told you, I told you the only mosquitos here are vaccinators." The scenes are unfurling in his head now and spilling out of his mouth. "We went out. They were casting ads for a muay thai fight, but we just wanted to get drowsed so we hit a club for shisha. Your hair was in your mouth."

Holly-who-is-Holly, even though she's somehow old, closes her eyes for a moment. Her lids are scrubbed of makeup and look paper-thin. Prosper feels he's getting close to something.

"You were saying how maybe you wanted to get your lips reshaped, or collagened, or something, because we're in Thailand anyways and they still have all the best cosmosurgeons, but I said no, I said your lips are perfect, and then you said what about tattoos, the bamboo kind, we could do that together."

Prosper can hear the conversation, half-shouted in an oceanside nightclub with lime-green drink specials slithering over the walls, marijuana smoke billowing back and forth between them. He looks down at his wrist, where the IV slides into his skin, and for a moment his eyes project a string of cobalt-blue numbers onto the unblemished white.

"But on our way to the tattoo shop we saw that little brain-box place, the place that sterilized all their plugs real good, and we still wanted to try it out, so we did the fantasy fuck module. They called it that, on the sign. When we finished, I was blue-balled so hard you couldn't stop laughing, remember? And before we left we got a cold copy—"

"So it would be like we were always young and in love and in Koh Phangan, circa summer of 2103." Holly's eyes were open. "Two neural imprints, two little ghosts of ourselves in code. You lost mine the morning we flew for Bangkok, because it was in the pocket of those blue shorts that you left in the laundry, but I never lost yours. I still have it."

Prosper feels the top of his head removed. He knows Holly, he knows this is too elaborate for her, too vicious a joke, and her eyes are so old. "You can't put a neural imprint into a clone's brain. It's just. It's just fucking code, alright? It's not..."

Prosper tears at the blankets, seeing for the first time that his skin is burned and bubbled in swathes, damage plastered in some sort of medi-gel, but the place on his thigh where the scar should be is milky white, untouched.

◂ ▸

For a long time, Holly didn't visit the FleshFac. She tried to not even think about the FleshFac. Then Prosper started peeling her life apart. He'd left behind at least a dozen bankbugs that began locking her out of former joint accounts, funnelling funds to places she couldn't reach or even see;

until he thawed on the other end, the lawyer AI assured her, there was no effective way to take legal action. Even when he did, the time delay would stay glacial.

It wasn't losing the money that hurt – more the meticulousness of it all. Prosper had been planning to leave her for a long time. So Holly had her hair razored to the latest fashion, her implants lifted, her lips slicked carmine like war paint, and went alone to the Marina District to find someone Prosper would have hated. She hadn't been properly IRL laid in ages.

In a dopamine parlour, she met a man whose name wasn't important to her. He had wolfish eyes, beautiful bones, and LEDs in his gunmetal teeth that scrolled slogans like *existentialism is the only way, cunts* and *nous sommes des cadavres exquis*. When their stools migrated together Holly felt dizzied in a way the Antarctican rosé could not account for. She suspected pheromones, but didn't care.

She bought him a drink; he told her he was a mortality artist. While their legs mingled under the table, he explained that death was the Platonic form of life, or something equally inane. Holly's attention only sparked when he said he was planning to kill a clone on live feed. Her stomach gave a churn on the wine, her spine stiffened.

"People aren't affected by clone snuff anymore," the man said. "They know there's nothing in the shell, and brain-dead doesn't sell. But there's this new technique, this thing with neural imprints, cold copies. I'm going to write my memories into a clone's brain, and then I'm going to murder myself."

"People pay for that?" Holly asked, removing his hand from her cooling thigh.

"They'd pay a fortune if they thought it was a real person," the man snorted. "Because they're the Philistines, aren't they?

But they'll pay enough, yes. Though I hate catering to sadists. It's a necessity. I need capital for my work."

But those wolfish eyes said otherwise, and Holly wondered if hers looked the same in the bar's half-light. She determined to find someone else, someone young and vapid and drowned by testosterone in the womb, but before she left the dopamine parlour she took the man's contact information. She thumbed it in under Business.

◀ ▶

On the beach Prosper thinks of finding Holly, but a woman with red-slicked lips is hanging on his shoulder, and then there's hubbub from the shore, because the Host is arriving, and he forgets. A scalpel of a speedboat tears toward the beach, halogens slashing at the dark. The guests howl their anticipation. Prosper howls loudest, waving his discarded shirt like he was hailing a taxi, and it catches on through the crowd.

The engine cuts, the boat sloshes to shore on its afterkick, and Prosper has his first glimpse of the Host as she disembarks: tall, regal on stilt heels, wrapped in soft whites. A floating cam darts in and suddenly her face is flashing across the sky. Her jaw is trimmed, her neck is taut from lifts, and her eyes are a thousand times deeper, hollower, older than they should be, but he could never mistake them.

Impossibility freezes him to the sand as the Host makes her way out along the thronged beach. It freezes him as the numbers inked to his wrist bloom across the dark sky. Prosper realizes he is in a dream, or has always been in one. He reaches down for a scar the edge of a rusted metal chair left on his thigh at five, but the skin is smooth under his fingers.

◀ ▶

Now Prosper is silent and Holly is talking. He can only halfway hear her through the blood rushing in his ears. He is a clone, clone, clone.

"Sometimes we twist your telomeres to age you up," she's saying. "Put a clamp in your spine, powder your hair. We have a whole team of plastic surgeons now. Sometimes we pump you with estrogen, give you tits, work on your face. Blonde damsels do better on the ratings, but for those we have to keep you lucied out of your mind."

Prosper is remembering fragments from last night, people he spoke with, things he heard. Some years by drowning, some years by fire.

"But this is you," Holly says. "You at twenty-three with no alterations."

"Did I die?" Prosper demands.

"The original Prosper Rexroat is still alive." Holly pauses. "Meaning you're a technical non-person. He's on Ganymede. He has children." The smooth plaster of her voice is stretching thin. "He launched seven years ago. Like a fortieth fucking birthday present to himself."

Years mean nothing to Prosper now, they are fog and dust. But he seizes on *alive*. "If I'm alive, why did you clone me?" he croaks. "Why am I here?"

"You're here to die," she says, and this time it's her voice that breaks. "Like you do every year."

Prosper remembers the dark beach, remembers falling into a cauldron of searing steam. Maybe he was dead, then. Maybe he was dead and in purgatory.

◀ ▶

The Party was Holly's idea, and finding guests over the nets was easier than she anticipated. Only six of them, that first year, four men and two women, all wealthy and restless with an inchoate dark in their eyes. Anonymity was paramount.

The preparations had taken months. Holly had pulled Prosper's old cold copy from its box in her dresser to take it in for testing. She was assured that the imprint had maintained its integrity over the years but was asked politely to leave when she inquired about putting it into a clone's brain. For that, she had to take the suborbital to Taiwan.

If she hadn't been so quick to find a willing biotechnician, if things hadn't fallen so smoothly together, maybe it never would have gotten off the ground. But she found Yeo, and Yeo was willing. With her dwindling funds, Holly flew Yeo and Prosper's second clone to a facility in Bangkok for the upload procedure.

She attended. It happened in a seedy concrete bunker, morgue-cold, because neural transfer was a dark shade of legal grey even in Thailand. Yeo's team worked in coordinated silence, communicating by sub-audible microphones in their bunny suits. The clatter of Holly's Louboutin pumps seemed impossibly loud in her own ears.

Prosper never woke up, not really. Holly told herself as much. He stayed in a dopamine haze all the way from Bangkok to Koh Phangan, where she'd rented an isolated stretch of beach and cliff. Holly didn't attend the Party in person, but she watched. Six figures standing apart from each other up above the gnashing waves, hair whipped by a warm wind, and then the seventh brought up with a hood over his head.

That first year, the Lotto was to decide who killed him. She'd pulled the idea of digitattoos from the offworld lotteries that sent less-monied migrants in the colony camps to Mars or Ganymede. The winner was a philanthropist who owned billions in solar sail stock, and he pushed with both hands instead of using the handgun. From the private live feed in her hotel, Holly watched Prosper plunge down toward razored rock and the diver waiting to retrieve his corpse. When his body struck stone she felt the same release she'd experienced at the FleshFac.

If the guests suspected a clone, they made no sign of it. They wanted so badly to believe, and Holly was the same.

◂ ▸

The crowd was hungry mouths, and Prosper wonders how he didn't notice that voracity before. They funnel him through, eyes hot and hard, and as he is dragged up the quickcrete stairs, up to the lip of the volcano, he cranes his head back up to the sky. As he waits on the lip, he stares into Holly's sea-green eyes, cold and tired, wreathed by scalding steam.

◂ ▸

"Seven years?" Prosper demands. "You've done this for seven fucking years? Murdered me seven fucking times?"

"Law moves slowly," Holly says. "You still can't murder a clone."

"So why am I here? Why didn't you finish the job last night at your Party?"

Holly looks away. "A thermostat glitch."

"No. No. You woke me up on purpose." Prosper thrashes upright again and starts unplugging the IVs with deliberate ferocity. "You didn't have to tell me this." The gurney wails as Prosper frees himself of the tubes with a slick wet sound, a sharp throb.

"You left me with fucking nothing, Prosper," Holly snaps, then clenches her teeth, looks pained.

Prosper gets up from the bed on his second try. "Not me."

"No." Holly's voice goes limp. "Not you. I'm sorry."

"You sending him the live feed or something?" Prosper demands. "Sending all this warped shit to Ganymede?"

Holly's eyes flash hot. "Never."

"Because you want me to think you've forgotten all about me, but you're still here playing pretend every year." Prosper tries to take a step forward and nearly falls. "Still punishing him," he gasps, snatching for the edge of the gurney. His skin is beginning to burn all over again.

"You enjoy it," Holly says, throat raw. "You're happy. You're the centre of attention. You're the gravity well."

Prosper gathers himself and staggers forward, past Holly, into an antiseptic white corridor. The trailing cords slither after him like snakes. A man in a surgical mask stands frozen as he passes.

"I just have to ask you something," Holly's voice comes from behind him.

Prosper stumbles on, his vision collapsing and expanding, dark and light. He stops to steady himself on the wall and shouts over his shoulder. "Why would you tell me all this? I can't tell you why I fucking left. I haven't yet. You hate me for something I never even knew I was going to do."

Holly shakes her head. "I don't hate him anymore. Not for years." She pauses. "But I still want to know."

Prosper sinks to a crouch. His head is hollow and spinning; pain is groping tendrils through every inch of him. The wall is not a wall. Through the fogged glass he sees a figure drifting in crucifix, tethered by feeding tubes.

"Know what?" he asks.

"If you ever did love me."

Prosper presses his face against the glass and suddenly looks into sea-green eyes, glazed by chemicals but no longer old, no longer tired. It's not him drifting there in the nutrient bath. Holly. The Holly he remembers.

"That's why I had to ask," Holly says. "Because you're the last clone. I don't hate him anymore. He won." She smiles horribly. "Now I just hate myself. It'll be me on the beach from now on. I had a new imprint made." She steps closer. "So. Did you ever, Prosper?"

They become statues in the cold corridor as the silence stretches, and stretches, and Prosper longs for the oblivion of the beach, for music and motion and frenzy, and he knows now he will never answer.

And the Party will never be over.

HEDGEHOGS

Kevin Cockle

She's downwind from me, so I don't smell her, but I hear her pretty good. Heart like a puppy's heart – strong and rapid. She's trying to be quiet but it's pointless – autumn – too many dead leaves, too much dry grass around for her to be stealthy. Anyhow, I let her make her approach.

"Hey," I say before she can speak, just to let her know I know she's there.

"Hey," she answers. Voice high, piping, and young.

I turn in my seat on an old throwaway ottoman, putting the gunmetal grey of the Bow River at my back. The water's greasy, not like I remember it at all, but I've grown used to the odour.

Tracy looks good – thin, but looks like she's had a few good meals this week. Black cable-knit sweater over black jeans; black boots two sizes too big for her – big silver buckles like ski boots. Dark brown eyes too big for her face; long brown hair in a braid.

I see her looking at me – looking right at my face. I listen close to her heart, and there's no change. No change in cadence at all.

"How do you do that?" I ask. Having just heard her voice, I'm extra-aware of my own. That artificially low, resonant, battlefield timbre they gave me. I murmur the words to keep from booming up and down the river valley.

"What?" she says, eyes bright.

"You should be scared shitless, kid."

"Yeah. You're not so bad."

I smile, pop a river-stone slick with green algae into my mouth. I grind away, shattering the stone, tasting the minerals as I break them down.

She grins, thinks it's cool when I eat rocks and shit off the ground. She looks so young when she smiles – ten, or something. I'm not so good at judging age anymore. And age doesn't mean what it used to mean, anyway.

"They want to talk to you," Tracy says, walking onto the stones of the rivershore, looking out onto the leaden water.

"Yeah?" That's new. Things must be awful desperate, they want to talk to me.

"Yeah. There's trouble."

"Not yet there's not. I show up, there'll be trouble."

"You're not so bad."

I think about Tracy's heart rate, her weird calm, her perspiration and ocular cues. I don't faze her, and in turn she doesn't set me off. It might not actually be healthy, a kid being as unflappable as she is. Not everyone's like that; when people get jumpy, it brings out the worst in me. Or best, I guess. Context is everything.

"You're a sweetheart," I say, "but most people get scared, I show up. They can't control themselves."

"Mom wanted me to give you this." Tracy roots in a pocket, pulls out a bottle of pills, tosses it to me. I recognize the little powder-blue pellets without reading the prescription: military grade adrenal suppressants. Tracy's mom works at one of the lower-tier private clinics across town. I pop one of these babies, I can handle people's fear without going into attack mode. For a while.

"Okay then," I smile, showing her my big incisors for a cheap thrill. "Tell 'em I'll be by in half an hour."

◂ ▸

The big Mex hits the wall about halfway to the ceiling, body parallel to the floor. His body cracks drywall and I hear him groan, but I also hear a hammer being cocked behind me. I turn and smile, take the nine-millimetre shell in my chest. Don't like to get shot, but the psychological effect on the bad guys when they see me doing it is usually worth the aggravation.

It is this time, that's for sure.

The shooter – a scrawny white skinhead – pulls the trigger again and again in panic. Small calibre non-explosive rounds ain't gonna get it done. I stride toward him, bat the gun out of his outstretched hand, then pick him up by the throat.

The first guy – not the guy I threw into the wall – but the guy I punched in the chest when I first crashed the joint – that guy has finally caught his breath. I throw the skinhead into him and they both go down hard – skinhead breaking a wrist en route.

Wall guy's just whimpering. Something's broken loose inside him, something's shifted out of position. He'll stay put.

I walk to the pile of thugs and kick the guy on the bottom in the mouth. I wear custom combat-boots in size 26 or so. Steel-toed.

Skinhead's whining, trying to scramble up off his buddy, so I help him up by the back of his neck and the seat of his pants.

Carrying him, I walk into the broken-down kitchen of the townhouse-condo. We're right above the garage, so basically a floor above ground level.

Out the window he goes – half of the glass was broken anyway so I doubt it'll hurt property values much. He hits once off the slope of the garage roof, then tumbles down from there to asphalt. The condo board and a bunch of the neighbours look up at me from the street. If I hadn't taken one of those little blue pills, there'd be more than enough panic out among those people to draw me to them. They're doing a good job though, outwardly. Standing and staring, hands in pockets, nobody wanting to appear provocative in any way, shape, or form.

Holes in my shirt from the bullets. I pull at my rubberized skin, ejecting the compressed lead while I walk back to the dining room. Mouth-kick guy's on his back, moaning, hands up near his mouth, but afraid to touch broken teeth.

Wall guy's trying to push up off his chest, so I walk over and crouch down, my knees popping like coals settling in a fire.

"Where's your lab?" I say. Can't smell their stash, but it's gotta be around here somewhere. That was the story anyway: meth heads operating out of a vacant unit; residents nervous about the business being done.

"Nothing…man, there's nothing…" He's having trouble breathing. Punctured lung from a broken rib, I reckon.

I'm listening close, smelling him close; don't think he's lying.

Not dealers, but definitely punks.

Things're worse than I thought.

◂ ▸

"Can we get you something to drink?" the woman asks – Tracy's mom. Tracy looks younger than she is; mom looks older than she is. Premature grey; heavy lines around the eyes. Corners of the mouth defaulting down; nervous little ticks in her lips, eyelids. I shake my head no to her offer of a drink.

She's holding it together pretty well, but I pop another pill just in case. Living room on the courtyard's kind of nice – big sliding balcony doors leading out onto a small deck. Community vegetable garden taking up most of the lawn space. I sit on the couch, figuring it's the only thing in the room that can take the weight of my reinforced skeleton. Scuffed hardwood floor's kind of warped, but well kept; a monitor in the corner, some chairs and food put out for the half-dozen condo board guys. Place is rundown – they put these things up in the 1980s – but Tracy's mom is doing the best she can with it. Beth, I think the woman's name is.

"They weren't dealers, far as I could tell," I report. "Anyway, they weren't set up yet if they were."

"Well, we appreciate what you did regardless," a small, slope-shouldered, balding gent with wire-rimmed eyeglasses says to me. I gather he's the president of the condo board, and I gather he wasn't consulted about my little intervention. He holds his gaze pretty level, staring at my snout instead of my "eyes." Can't blame him. Something erratic about his pulse, but hey – he's probably never been face to face with a Gunboat before.

"Definitely," someone else says – heavy-set black woman with a kerchief around her head. "Thank you."

Murmured agreement from the rest of the assembled. Older folks mostly, all hollow cheeks and worried eyes.

"There's lots of abandoned units," Beth says, smiling. "You don't have to live down at the river. Really, I mean...if you want to, you could take one."

"That's probably not a great idea," I say. "Thanks though."

"We're taking up a collection," the president says, sitting upright with hands on his knees. He's an adaptable guy. Having been left out of the decision-making at the start, he's taking over the process now. "We'll get you paid by the end of the day."

"Appreciate it," I say, "but you might want to think things over a bit."

"What do you mean?" he asks.

"Well, the Mexican kid told me they were paid a decent amount of money to take up residence where they did. Hassling you at the garbage bins; partying late...that was their job."

"Their job?" Tracy's mom, suddenly spooked. I can practically feel her thinking about her kid. Concern like that has a smell. "What are you saying?"

"Does the name Zitadelle Management mean anything to you?"

"Well yeah, that's our property manager," the president says, frowning. Heart pounding. He should have that checked.

"Makes sense," I say.

"How?" Tracy's mom.

"Rundown condo development from the 1980s five minutes away from downtown? Riverside property? Walking distance to the last legacy park in the city? Breakup and land value is worth more than you guys. Look at the neighbourhoods around you – all those mansions? Surprised you've lasted this long."

I look at their silent faces, their thoughtful eyes as they work through the math. Pisses me off, seeing them put it all together. That moment when you realize you're just another disposable commodity. You've been out-competed; you're out of gas, out of moves. No cops left outside of the homicide division, no municipal government to speak of, just folks with money and folks without. These ones hanging on by their fucking fingernails. Doing whatever they can to stay in the country of their birth, even though all the work for people like these is mostly overseas.

Pisses me off I fought for this. I was created to enforce this.

Have to get a hold of myself. Getting angry won't end well.

"Maybe I will take a unit," I say, playing a hunch. "For a while. It has to be one that doesn't have neighbours."

"I can show you," Tracy pipes up. Beth glances a glance that says no, but the kid obviously isn't in the habit of heeding her elders. Tracy's smiling, happy to help.

I smell the anxiety in the room, but also some relief. Nobody's super-comfortable with me, but some of them like the idea of muscle in the 'hood. Their muscle. Some way to answer; some way to push back.

Not everybody though. Most of my deep-diagnostics are shot, but I've still got hyper-sensory input and good old-fashioned instincts. I can parse the different kinds of fear the way normal folks distinguish different flavours.

I know somebody's not happy at all with my decision.

◀ ▶

I look up through the hole in the roof of my second-floor bedroom. Nighttime now; clear night, dim stars.

I lie back on a crusty foam mattress, hands behind my head. The mattress, along with other telltale signs, indicates to me that I'm not the first vagrant to occupy the joint. I don't need shelter now of course – I'm rated for minus 90 degrees centigrade, can metabolize whatever's available for food – but there is something about having a roof, even a partial roof, over your head. Feels nostalgic. Reminds me I wasn't always a Gunboat.

Somewhere up there in low Earth orbit is the "Deck" – the space station command for JSOC Inc. Once, I would've been connected directly – like a direct line to Mount Olympus, with access to all the world's data, and the processing muscle to handle it. Once, I could have called down hell itself from space, and had done, in mountains and jungles a world away from here.

Lying here in the dark, I can smell the smell of burning village again. Burning flesh. It's funny how the smell stays with you, that it's the smell you can conjure up with relentless fidelity.

"You better get in here before you break your neck," I say into the night. Tracy's head comes into view at the side of the hole. She does a little balance check, then lowers herself into the room like a cat burglar.

"Hey," Tracy says.

"What're you, my sidekick?"

"You wish."

"You can't hang around me, kid. God forbid you ever do actually surprise me."

"I think that it's good you're here."

"'Good is ideologically constructed.'"

"Huh?"

"Lemme ask you something. You ever drown cats or kill birds for fun – anything like that?"

"No."

I consider the answer. Her heart doesn't skip a beat, even with a question like that out of the blue. I have no idea if she's lying. Finally, I say: "You bring a phone?"

Tracy pulls a wafer phone out of her back pocket, unfolding it, then activating it. A bright electric blue lights up the oval of her face. She walks over, hands the phone to me, sits down cross-legged just off the mattress.

I sit up. Suddenly, I think maybe I don't want to do this. I make a call, I start figuring things out...pretty soon things get complicated.

I'm winding down. I've been decommissioned. I'm obsolete. I should just go back to the river and let things take their course. That was the plan, after all.

Most of the shit I've done, it wasn't my fault. There's no such thing as a non-combatant these days. I don't sit around blaming myself and feeling guilty for the way the world works.

Fuck it: I make the call.

Toll-free to a ground station; voice ident; relay to a substation, then signal-stitched to satellite. Mac answers from the Deck on the third ring.

"Who's 'Tracy'?" he says.

"It's me, Mac," I say. He'll know. Fifty years as my dedicated handler on Deck, he'd know my voice anywhere. Parts of me are pushing one hundred; God knows how old Mac is. We both know who Ferris Bueller is. What a VCR was. What "universal healthcare" meant.

"Jonas," he says, too nerveless to sound surprised, but I know he is, deep down. "Been a while."

"Weird talking to you on a phone, that's for sure." Once upon a time, Mac's voice just would have sounded in my head, like the voice of God.

"Weird's one way of saying it. Not-protocol would be another."

"I need a favour. A Deck favour. Can't do it myself, remember?"

"You're offline, Jonas. Retired. Supposedly staying out of trouble."

"I need you to light me up for about fifteen minutes Mac. Need to run some connections. Just Big Data diagnostics, nothing else."

"Just diagnostics," he says. "Who you planning to kill?"

"I'd say 'planning' is an overstatement in this case. Doubt it will come to that."

"How's it going down there, Jonas? Really. You all right?"

"You gonna help, or…"

There's a long pause. It's not illegal, what I'm asking Mac to do, but it'll be monitored, and recorded. Whatever I'm up to could come back on him, if it breaks wrong. Against that, I can sense Mac weighing our history together. Everything I did, he was there, in my head, helping. I've never seen his face, but I've never been closer to another human being. Not even my wife, God bless her soul.

Eventually Mac says: "Fifteen minutes."

Seconds later my heads-up display reactivates and I can hear Tracy perk up at the sight. In the dark, my bug-black eye-coverings must be giving off some eerie glow. A new thrill for her – something to go with the teeth.

I get to work, knowing Mac won't give me one second more than the fifteen minutes discussed.

It doesn't take five to prove what I kinda, sorta already knew.

◀ ▶

"Holy...shit..." the condo president sputters, sitting up in bed. I've opened the drapes of his bedroom window to the moonlight so he can be dimly aware of my bulk in the gloom. I smell the stink of fear wafting off his skin and smile at the juice it gives me. Way they figured it – the geniuses who built me – by tuning my own aggression matrix to react to the fear I invariably cause, a kind of killing-feedback loop develops. The more vicious I get, the more terrorists freak out, and so on. Once I commit, there's no turning back, no hesitation. My own nervous system won't let me back off.

Just the sound of this guy's heart slapping around in his chest makes me visualize tearing his throat out with my teeth. Really gets me going, actually. But I don't flip the switch just yet.

"You need to calm down, Don," I say, voice rumbling in the small confines of the room. Naturally, his pulse spikes. "Don Wilcox, thirty-eight. Divorced. Freelance data processor and IT huckster; Amway salesman; financial planner; all-around bottom-feeding piece of shit. Elected to the condo board of Bow Groves six months ago. Zitadelle Management has no Calgary office, but you trace it up the chain and you can see they're part of a REIT out of Houston. They've done the math, and it's time to plough this complex under. Bought you off; gave you the money to hire those thugs, and that's really just your first move, am I right? Smart, hiring them online without any face-time. Not bad."

"How...how did you get in here..."

"I know, right? Seven feet, four hundred pounds give or take, you'd think you'd hear me coming, but you know what? Stealth's a big part of the package. They thought of everything, believe me. Anyway. Up and at 'em, Don."

"What…what're you…"

"It's just after midnight. You've got till sunrise to get packed and get gone."

"Gone?"

"You're moving out. And you're never coming back. Now here's the thing, Don: some part of you is thinking about calling the property manager. You're thinking they can send some muscle up here, you can lever me out of the picture and just strong-arm the remaining families like you probably should've done in the first place. But you know me, you know what I am. The second you make that call, I'll see it. You can't hide from Gunboats, Don: that's the whole, entire point of us. We see what you're doing, then we come to get you. That's why I can afford to let you leave with your life, Don. Because you're as good as dead the moment I want you to be."

I stare at him in the moonlight, knowing all he can see is the deep black where my eyes should be. It's all a bluff, of course. A fully functional, wired-up Gunboat could do those things, but a first-gen rust-bucket who's been taken off the grid? Not a chance.

I can smell the fear on Don though, and I know the flavour. He doesn't have the balls for a double-cross. Doesn't have the brains to see that all this is way too small-time for a sanctioned Gunboat intervention. He's pissing himself with gratitude that he'll be allowed to skulk away like a thief in the night.

Good enough.

◂ ▸

It's a nice fall night – cool, but not yet frosting up. I walk back to my unit, boots echoing loud on the empty streets between townhouses. This is a huge complex – damn near a kilometre long, two blocks deep of grey, two-storey row-units of varying sizes. In the dark, it's still kind of pretty in here, with old-growth trees along the main roads leading back to the Trans-Canada and large green areas separating various sections of the development. These condos are threadbare buildings though – lots of water-damaged walls, collapsed roofs, wonky garage doors. It's only a matter of time this place goes under, resident Gunboat or no.

I know there are pockets like this all over the city. Analogue neighbourhoods, not wired up, not smart, filled with analog people who try with their smartphones and videogames to pass as digital, but nobody's fooled. Communities like surrounded armies in hedgehog formation, cut off from all hope, gradually dwindling under the relentless pressure of market forces. Yay, "freedom" – glad I fought for that. Sure sounded good when I volunteered for the Gunboat program.

I turn onto my street, noting the absence of street lighting in this part of the complex. Just as well. I figure I'll stay indoors during the day, stretch my legs at night. Anybody needs me, they can send Tracy to come fetch. Spooky kid.

My driveway, then a little cobblestone walk to my front stairs – all shrouded in shadow.

There's an open box filled with root vegetables and processed meat in plastic wrap. There's a bag of coins and notes backed by various companies, and good throughout Alberta. There's a card – a handwritten thank-you card – and that makes me chuckle. Just like these people, write a card for a guy.

I put the coins and card into the box and scoop the whole thing up.

Can't say it's home, but I will say this: it reminds me of home. Reminds me of a time when people owned stuff, expected to stick to places. Reminds me of me when I wanted those things. There's a doomed little idea of home here in the darkness.

I'll take it.

SAFETY

Michael Mirolla

She's in the apartment alone, waiting for her husband of two days to return from work, when the doorbell rings. It couldn't be him. Too early yet. So she opens the door cautiously and keeps the chain in place. The pleasant face with a thick moustache smiles and explains that he's there to repair the phone. Trouble has been traced to her landline. And he's come to fix it. That is, if she'll let him in, he says chuckling pleasantly. "One moment," she says and, making as if to release the chain, slams the door in his face.

"You can't fool me!" she yells, trembling with a combination of fright and anger. "No sir. You can't fool me. There's nothing the matter with our landline for the simple reason we don't have one. So you'd better leave right now because my husband's on his way home. And I'm going to dial 911 on my cell phone."

"Sorry to have bothered you, Miss," a muffled yet still pleasant voice says apologetically. "I guess it's the apartment next to yours that's having problems. These machines aren't too particular sometimes. Sorry again. Hope I haven't inconvenienced you."

"Not at all," she whispers, listening intently as his steps fade down the hall. And grateful that the bluff about a cellphone worked. She's ordered one but hasn't yet managed to pick it up. Perhaps she'd been too hard on the man. Perhaps it had been a genuine error on his part. She's always been of the opinion that telephone repairmen aren't too bright as a group.

For the next twenty minutes, she sits in what she figures is the exact centre of the living-room floor (their furniture on order but having not yet arrived) and contemplates the walls. She folds her legs beneath her and visualizes the finished apartment – the multicoloured matching drapes and curtains, a beautiful warm sofa, antique dressers, a King Arthur oaken table and chairs, a four-poster bed with or without canopy. She has almost decided a name for the baby when a tapping across the bedroom window shocks her out of the reverie. She lets out a yelp and bites her hand. There, framed by the first few flakes of snow and dangling upside down, is the unshaven face of a man, smiling at her through yellow gap-spaced teeth. He has a steaming rag in his hand. She backs out of his line of sight, her heart threatening to leap out of her chest and go thumping across the floor. The tapping resumes. My God, she asks herself, are the windows closed? Is he going to smash the glass and leap through, a shard in his hand? Already she can smell his breath, feel his raw calloused fingers gripping her throat. But there is no smashing of windowpanes, no sudden descent into the bedroom. Only the tapping. She walks cautiously to the kitchen and peers out. Oh Jesus, what a fool! What a complete idiot she's made of herself. The man dangling upside down is busy scrubbing the dirt-encrusted windows, the very windows she'd complained to the landlord about. "Yes, ma'am," he'd said. "We'll clean them till they sparkle." In order to do so, the man had to reach in between thick iron bars spaced four inches apart. In fact, it was she who'd insisted on such a precaution. She goes back into the bedroom and unpins the temporary curtains – bedsheets, actually – much to the pantomimed dismay of the man on the scaffolding who, at one point just before his face disappears, has one hand over his heart and the other wiping away imaginary tears. She laughs, then peeks through the curtains for one last time. He is now threatening to jump off, taking little leaps from one end and landing at the other.

She starts humming to herself, cradling the warmth she feels inside. Her stomach rumbles. She goes into the kitchen and pulls open the fridge door, remembering the horror the first time she'd looked inside and several cockroaches had come tumbling out, nearly frozen to death. But a half-can of spray and several hours scrubbing had taken care of that. Now, neat piles of cold cuts, cheeses, and vegetables are flanked by vitaminized apple juice and Double Grade A Extra-Large eggs. She pulls out the cheddar and a piece of celery and cuts both into strips. These she places fan-like in an alternating pattern on a dish from which a bluebird is forever bursting out of what seems a fig cracked in two. It had been a gift from her mother-in-law, who had late in life taken up the feminist ideology, complete with its sexual imagery.

She puts a piece of cheddar on a piece of celery and bites down. The softness followed by a solid crunch has a satisfying texture to it. She leans back on the rickety chair, a leftover from her husband's bachelor days, and sighs. The snow is coming down faster now and it's pleasant to watch as it covers the city's customary greyness. But it's nothing like the countryside she's left behind. Maybe someday, when their children are grown and they have a little bit put away, they might invest in a small farm. After all, her husband is an up-and-comer – the boss had said so himself – and money will be no problem. In fact, she might pitch in as well, go back to school, upgrade her skills, as the fancy magazines put it. She immediately visualizes herself seated behind a large desk in a huge office, a Dictaphone in one hand, a baby in the other. "Hold all calls," she says, and offers her breast to the gurgling infant. The buzzer rings. "I said hold all calls!" The buzzer rings again, followed by a knock.

She falls forward on the chair. The buzzer rings for a third time. It's the doorbell.

"Yes, who is it?" she says, leaning her ear against the closed door.

"It's your friendly mailman, madam," a stentorian voice answers. "A special delivery package for Harold or Jenny Jones."

"Slip it under the door, please." She tears a piece of dry skin from her lip and chews on it.

"Madam," the mailman says, his voice overflowing with reasonableness, "it's a parcel, not a letter. Besides, you have to sign the receipt."

"Just a minute," she says, and leans back. What to do? She has been expecting a package for several days – a Sears catalogue baby doll negligee. It's to be a surprise for her husband. Not that she really needs it. Yet. But one can never be too well armed.

"Madam, I'd like to stand out here all day but I've other parcels to deliver. If you don't want it just say so. I'll leave a card and you can pick it up at the post office."

"No! No, it's all right. I'll open the door." She turns the lock and pulls it back till the chain is taut. Another smiling face greets her (to think she'd been told that all city functionaries were dour and glum) and says he doesn't blame her for being cautious. "You can never be too careful in the city. Lots and lots of crazies out here." He eases the package through the opening. It's wrapped in plain brown paper held together by a frayed bow that has been obviously reused many times. "Sign here, madam. X marks the spot." The mailman holds out a piece of paper and a pen. Only his hairy arm and hand are visible. She reaches up to take the paper and he grips her wrist as if in a vice. "Gotcha!" he says gently, yanking her toward him like a rag doll. She screams and, without meaning to, puts all her weight against the door. His fingers catch between the door and the frame. Yelping, he lets go her wrist and withdraws his hand. She tries to shut the door completely but discovers she can't. He's jammed his foot into the opening. "Now, now, my dear," he says breathing heavily, his arm snaking in, hoping to trap her again, "why don't you just make things easy on yourself and release the chain? You know it's only a matter of time anyway." He rams his shoulder against the door. The chain holds but the impact sends her flying. For several blind seconds she lays sprawled on the floor, listening to his ever-increasing invective, to the things he would do to her once he gets in. He rams the door again. One of the screws comes loose.

She tries to scream but there's a large bone in her throat. Softly, calmly, she pulls at her hair. Several strands fall out and cascade to the floor. Where's her husband when she needs him? She goes into the bedroom and works to open a window. It won't budge, sealed shut by the new paint and the winter cold. The man on the scaffolding waves to her, then starts to tap dance. From the front door, the banging and the heavy breathing increase. "It won't be long now, sweetie. Won't be long. Look, I'm taking off my clothes so you won't have to wait once I get in." She goes from room to room turning on all the lights. In the kitchen, she finds herself staring at the table – actually two pieces of wood strung across a pair of sawhorses. On it are alternating pieces of cheese and celery and – balancing across a fork – the carving knife. Something inside her jumps. She remembers, back on the farm, the clean slit it made across the pig's neck, leaving almost no sign of its passage. Wood from the front door splinters. She reaches for the knife and, holding it with both hands to keep it from shaking, advances toward the door. Most of the screws holding the chain have fallen off. That it still holds is a miracle. "The best money can buy," the landlord had said. "Actually, don't tell anyone else, but my brother is a locksmith." She kneels at the foot of the door and waits for the pseudo-postman to ram it again. Then she drives the knife down into his foot. The first blow misses and she has to rock it back and forth to pull it out of the hardwood floor. She stabs again, this time slashing the edge of leather. "You fuckin' bitch!" he screams and pulls the foot back just as she comes down for a third time. "You goddamn fuckin' cunt! You tried to stab me! I can't believe it! You good-for-nothing whore!" He pulls at the door again but it is too late. She's already managed to lock it.

"Oh now, wait a minute," he says, suddenly speaking very softly, as if he were whispering directly in her ear. "Wait just a minute. You're asking for it. You really are. All I was going to do was show you a few tricks. And I bet you would've liked it too. I bet you would've moaned for more. But now you got me mad. I don't like people trying to stab me. That's not playing fair. So you go ahead and lock the front door. You just go ahead. Don't worry about me. I'll find another way to your heart. Why, I'll ooze in through the cracks in your plaster. Or maybe through the skylight. That's it. You just go into the bathroom, take your clothes off and make yourself comfortable. I'll be right there. See you soonest."

Shaking to the point where she can hardly stand up, she still forces herself to check every window in the apartment, making sure they all have metal bars across them. It's now dark out. The man on the scaffolding is gone, his bucket left dangling precariously. She pulls the skylight shut. For one ridiculous moment she actually has a terrible urge to take a bath. But it passes. To reduce the number of openings, she locks the kitchen, bedroom, and bathroom doors. She's left in the living room, sitting once again in the exact centre of it, beneath the bas-relief of two sexless angels from the middle of which hangs a cheap chandelier. Holding the carving knife against her chest and feeling the coolness of the blade between her breasts, she dozes off. It's the kind of sleep that provides no rest and makes her feel more fatigued as time passes. As well, it distorts her sense of reality to the extent that, when the first knocks come, she isn't certain of their origin.

"Honey, I'm back. Open the door, will you? I think I've lost my keys again."

Her husband! She leaps up and runs to the door. She's about to pull it open when she stops. Can she be so sure it's her husband? What if – ?

"Honey, what's wrong? Is the door stuck or something?"

"What's your name?" she asks suddenly.

"My name? Honey, what is this? I'm tired. It's been a long day. Let me in."

"Yes, your name. And mine. What are they?"

"Oh, for Pete's sake. Harold. And Jenny. There. Now are you going to open up?"

She unlocks it, but keeps the chain on.

"The chain, you silly goose." He laughs – and that's when she knows for sure it's him. She undoes the chain and falls into his arms with a moan.

"Honey, is something the matter?" he asks as he locks the door behind him.

She kisses his strangely cold face and blubbers out her story: how glad she is to see him after the horrors of the day; how they have to move from the apartment; no, from the city; how he is never to leave her alone again, not even for a minute; how they'd better get that cell phone. Pronto.

"Promise me you won't," she pleads, burying her head in his strong chest.

"Won't what?" he says, his voice rumbling basso profundo in her ear.

"Leave me alone. Promise."

"I promise," he says, and begins slowly to peel away the lifelike mask.

To reveal a pleasant face with a thick moustache.

To reveal an unshaven man with yellow gap-spaced teeth.

To reveal the postman's smiling features.

To reveal that of her husband of two days.

PEARLS AND SWINE

Colleen Anderson

The guy who casually enters the almost claustrophobically narrow shop seems to gather shadows and light to himself. He ignores the warm wood and wallpapered walls, the photos of cops with Gatling guns and one of Bonnie and Clyde, and the etchings of various guns, as well as the cop who is leaving as he glides to the counter. He glances at the sign, *Treat em well and they won't desert you in a pinch.* His hand goes in under his jacket and pulls out a derringer. Laying it carefully upon Diana's counter, he then pulls out and lays down its mate.

Diana never lets her guard down in her shop. She's never had trouble either. Speers' Gun Maintenance and Accessories is a neutral ground. Everyone knows that if Diana can't clean or fix your gun there's no one else in town who can. Good guys and bad guys come to her place. No one wants to be in a critical situation and have his gun fail.

This man has warm brown skin and a familiarity that would make some people drop their guard. He wears a loose black jacket, baggy pants, and a white T-shirt. On someone else his clothes would look as if they were two sizes too big – but not on him. Long and lanky, the kind of guy who looks better in clothes than out of them. Naked, he would look close to starving but not there yet. He balances that vulnerability with his reputation.

Johnny Jawbreaker. Diana pushes escaping tendrils of hair back into hairpins, and picks up the twin derringers. Johnny Jawbreaker's profession is a mystery, but that's true of most of her clients. Yet, he is known for being faster with his guns than with his fists.

He grins. "I want pearl handles for these babies. And a design; something with a heart surrounded by ivy, and an animal."

Diana's tall, but still she must look up to meet his eyes. Not-quite-tamed wisps of black hair fall on his brow. Something clacks against his teeth, and a wisp of licorice sails out on his breath – the jawbreakers he's famous for. Of course, it's possible there are other jaws he breaks as well. He smiles again, with the jawbreaker between his teeth, then sucks it into the warm cavern of his mouth.

She pushes her hands into the pockets of her worn jeans, trying to ignore the sensuality of his mouth. "What kind of animal?"

He shrugs. "I'll leave that to you. Something that fits in – and represents wildness."

Diana has seen all types before. Those who often go for the pearl handles are hollow like their guns. They are collectors who can't afford originals, or they think the designer handle will give a measure of self-worth, or respect that they can't gain otherwise. Others hope for a sliver of reputation that says, *Back off, I know how to use these*. Confidence has to be in the man, not the gun, or a man won't stay one for much longer.

Johnny is confidence born. He doesn't try for cool or control; he exudes them naturally, and Diana suddenly wants to touch him, feel the vibration of his will touch hers. She caresses the smooth metal of his weapons, loving the coolness they return, wondering if Johnny is as hard as his guns.

"Three weeks from today," she answers, and names her price.

Johnny nods, then waves in a half salute. "Thank you, ma'am."

It's the "ma'am" that makes her realize Johnny has only seen her as a labourer, someone with whom to conduct business, not as a woman at all. Somehow it is important that he does notice her; that he realizes she is as unique as the designs he wants on the gun handles.

Diana Speers needs no man. She's proved that over and over. Best shooter around, her own business by twenty-five, knows more about guns than any man within a hundred miles, and able to make it on her own. Daddy had taught her a lot, and to trust no one. She'd learned that lesson best of all when he'd abandoned her at sixteen.

Diana wants to know the inner workings of a man such as Johnny Jawbreaker. It's the same reason she likes guns: all mechanical, guts and bearings on the inside, but on the outside, like sculpture, interesting quirks and turns that make you wonder again what's hidden.

◂ ▸

A man she's never seen before drops by the shop to say something to a taller, muscular blond guy who is staring at the photos on the wall while waiting for Diana to wrap up a package. The customer, chewing a toothpick, his hands clenched in his pockets, turns and raises one eyebrow at the new guy, who responds in a voice as soft and unprepossessing as his attitude. "Johnny wants us to be on time for tonight. Big show he doesn't wanna miss."

Not a bad looker, Diana notices, but innocuous and invisible as those models who all look the same. Too all-American.

The tall guy grunts. "Where we going tonight?"

"Savoir Faire. You know Johnny and babes; he likes 'em better than jazz, and at the Faire he's got both."

Diana pushes the guns across the counter. "Here you go. Treat 'em well and they'll be good for a few thousand rounds."

The customer winks. "As always, thanks." He shoves some bills her way.

She closes up early. At home, she showers, then digs through her closet floor. Hip waders, running shoes, steel-toed boots and sandals jump out of the closet like maddened fleas. "There!" She backs out holding a pair of patent-leather candy-apple red pumps. Her wet hair slithering over her shoulders, Diana dusts the shoes off on the towel wrapped about her. "Alright, guys. You don't get out much. Time to do your stuff."

The towel slips away as she bends over to put on the shoes. In the mirror, Diana examines herself: nothing but red shoes and wet flesh flushed by the shower. She runs her hands over her milk-chocolate nipples, over her ribs, the flat plane of her belly and down along her hips. "He'll notice me. Now, which dress? Class with sexy."

A quick comb and gel through wild hair, a dash of carmine to her lips, a caress of silk the shade of fresh cream over her bare body – Diana is ready to bring light and colour to the shades of night.

◀ ▶

The restaurant is amber light and earthy wood, subdued and elegant with touches of brass. The cool air has puckered her nipples. Their slight bulge is plain through her clinging silk dress. Her ears flicker highlights of diamond, enough to draw the maître d's eyes from her dress. Almost hesitantly, he asks, "Reservation?"

She shakes her head, flashes a small, not overly friendly smile. "Table for one." Looking around, she spots the clumped shadow of Johnny's table. One or two women are at the table but none sit near him. "I'd like a table over there, near the painting."

The painting is dark; late summer trees, woods filled with winking shadows, and the sense of something hidden, waiting.

The maître d' checks his list – and her body – again. "I'll see what I can do. One moment."

Diana considers slipping him a fifty but decides to see how far she can go on will and sensuality. She pays no attention to anyone in the room while she waits. In moments she is ushered in and seated. Crossing her legs, showing shin, she pulls out her cigarette. There is no need to look around.

It doesn't take long. She scans the menu, then takes out her lighter. Johnny lightly brushes her shoulder, kneeling down to light her cigarette. Like the shadows that seem to cross him, his lighter too is dark, ebony. At least he didn't send one of his guys to come and ask her over. He dressed in a loose jacket, black pants that fit smartly with a black belt and tight T-shirt. Tonight he is all shadow until he smiles at her and rolls a jawbreaker across his teeth. "Care to join our table? Your beauty should not go to waste by being alone."

Diana slowly drags on her cigarette, then blows out the smoke. "I'm rarely alone." Then she rises; for a moment she looks down at him as he looks up. Surely that is not awe upon his face, but merely the momentary wonder of a child confronted with a Christmas morning haul.

The other women are gone and his guys look sullen, but brighten momentarily at her arrival. After she's seated, Johnny straightens up and leans forward. "You're the pistol woman."

"Diana Speers. You're Johnny Jawbreaker." She holds out her hand.

He shakes it but continues to hold on. "Johnny Morton. Jawbreaker's because of these." He sticks out his tongue with the hard candy pearl on its tip, then he sensually, slowly, sucks it back.

The waiter appears for drinks. "Gin martini, dry, with a twist of lime," she orders.

Johnny pops out his jawbreaker. "Scotch, straight up." After the waiter leaves, he turns to her on the wide plush seat. "How's the guns?"

She hopes he doesn't show his true calibre as lacking. The conversation will have to change. "I never mix business with pleasure."

"Good point," he nods. "Why are you here, for the food or the music?"

She stubs out her cigarette in the ashtray beside his jawbreaker. "The atmosphere, something sultry and slow, the way it wraps around you and then insinuates itself."

His fist props up his tilted head, and he glances about, his gaze coming back to settle on her. "I come for good food, great music, the scent of flowers mixed with the smokiness of alcohol and bass. And for the beauty; the people, the decor, it's all one great work of art."

The drinks come. Diana sips, feels the cool lava slide down her throat, heating up her stomach. The food arrives, then more talk, but Diana's tongue sticks on words. She's more used to the language of hands, from carving handles and fixing guns, than the intricately woven language of words. Not that she does not know them but the distraction of smoke and sound and flavours make her words turn to fog before they drift from her mouth. She settles for another smoke and offers one to Johnny.

He shakes his head. "No, thanks. That's how I got the name Jawbreaker; always sucking them to quit smoking. Now I'm hooked on them. One habit gone, replaced by another." He snaps his fingers. The two guys watching the band turn toward him.

"I think you guys need some air."

Reluctantly, the shorter guy agrees. "Uh, yeah I think we do. See you in a few. Come on, Mark. I want to show you something."

As they leave, Johnny leans forward, his finger tracing figure eights on Diana's bare leg. "You have smoky eyes."

"Comes from working with guns. They leave their tales in your skin, one way or another. Me, they filled my life. For my care, they tell me their secrets."

His finger scratches a trail along Diana's thigh. She wants to shiver but holds it in, for now. Johnny's other hand goes to her hair, slides down to caress her neck and shoulders.

"You make me forget my words. Secrets, your skin holds secrets too. But such a beautiful neck should not be unadorned. It needs something to call attention to its wonder."

He leans forward then, close enough that his breath warms her neck and the vibration of his voice on her ears does cause her to shiver. She closes her eyes momentarily as the tremors course down through her spine and to her belly.

"I want to give you something."

A light dew has gathered between her legs. She longs for his fingers to creep under the edge of her dress and twirl the wanton curls of her mound.

Her tongue caresses her lips, an effort to move the sensations into a more controllable realm. "I bet you say that to all the girls."

A laugh, then he leans back with a tight squeeze to her thigh. "I do, but I give each of them something different." He pauses, then says, "Come, I'd like to take you for a drive."

He grabs her hand and the heat makes her electric.

A time-jagged ride through streets in a long, sleek and airy car, Johnny at the wheel, Diana tries to hold herself back. His men follow behind. Then she's climbing behind him up tiled stairs as he tells her the history of the adobe-style building with brick- and sand-coloured terra cotta. He opens the door, pulls her in and has her wrapped tightly in his arms, his mouth seeking hers. His hands are up under her dress, on her thighs and hips, digging in, turning her into the dessert they skipped. Diana wonders briefly about Johnny, but then gives in, begins to knead his buttocks, and pull him against her. Their hips touch and a delicious rubberiness spreads through her limbs. There's a rap on the door.

Johnny sighs and looks into her eyes. "Wait just a minute."

He steps outside. Diana has long enough to notice the penchant for black and chrome. A stainless-steel look, too much like the cold rooms in a meat warehouse. Chilled, she turns back as the door opens.

His dark hazelnut eyes look at her. "I've got to go – some business I have to take care of." He pulls her head in for a long kiss. Then, "I want to see you tomorrow, but..." he breathes in her ears, which sets her vibrating, "I want you to suck me now."

Diana freezes. The safety's released, the hammer pulled back. "Why, Johnny," she drawls, "you don't need me for that. Any five-bit whore would do it with the same lack of intimacy. If I'm not different enough, you don't need me." Inside, worming its way into her thoughts, the realization that nothing is perfect, or as she wishes. *Fool.*

His hands clench at his sides, his jaw muscles ripple under his flesh. A softly cursed, "Damn..." then: "That's not how I meant it. Look, I'm sorry." He lays a hand alongside her cheek. "I would like to see you tomorrow. Come by the docks, to the Costanza Imports Warehouse. I'll meet you there, then take you out on my yacht. Quiet dinner and talk only, if you wish. And I still want to give you something."

Her mind fires thoughts like a Gatling gun. *Should I even bother? But I want him. I knew better than to hope for more than physical. Go on, take him for a ride.* "Perhaps I will, but remember, Johnny Jawbreaker, the only business I get involved in is my own. Don't involve me in yours."

He shrugs and gives a quirky little smile. "Come by at 8:30. All business will be concluded by then. It will only be pleasure. I'll see that one of the boys gives you a ride home."

She waves her hand. "Just call me a taxi. I wouldn't want to take their time from you." Nor have them know where she lives.

◀ ▶

Detective Galbraith is picking up his guns and two others for his partner. He brings them in regular as clockwork for cleaning. He leans on the counter pressing fingers to fingers, watching Diana as she finishes wiping the oil from the last one. He smiles and leans forward some more. His broad jaw and light, icy blue eyes make his teeth look larger than they are.

"What do you say, Diana? I could take you away from all this."

He's been trying a long time. "Sure, Dan. From frying pan to fire, from guns out of action to guns in action. No one points guns at me here." She wraps the last gunmetal weapon in black cloth and hands them all to Galbraith. "And what makes you think I want to be taken from this?"

He straightens and tucks the guns away in a satchel. "Surely you don't like cleaning those smelly, greasy instruments of death?"

She lets out a smile. "Now that's only conjecture that they cause death. After all, none of my own have. And have you ever known me to do something I don't like?"

"Ah, touché." He gives her the point and reluctantly leaves.

She closes up and is at the warehouse exactly at 8:30. This time of night it's mostly deserted and even more so with the fog that's settled in, breathing sleepy vapours over the wet dock, white tendrils fingering their way up the metal sides of buildings.

Everything looks like ink and mercury, the colour seemingly leeched out by the long-gone sun and the hungry tongues of fog. Even Diana has dressed in black and silver – and red lips, a taste of being alive in this still-life night. It's possible she's become nothing but a game to Johnny, most likely just another night's distraction but, she has to remember, that's all she really wants too. Detective Dan would be steady and reliable, but Diana has always liked working with guns for the danger they hint at; like Johnny. She's attracted to his mystery. And he has a sense of style, even if his place was utilitarian and cold.

Her shoes tap a deep staccato beat as she moves slowly toward the warehouse. Her black skirt grabs the dampness and licks about her legs. If she has to run, she'll toss the shoes, but there's no danger to Johnny. She has worn neither underwear nor bra under her leather vest.

At the grey Costanza building, she stands outside gigantic double doors. As if sensing her, a small door to the side opens up and Johnny's gangly guard beckons her in. It's dark inside but the doors at the opposite end are open. Through the silvery white light she can see the distant specks of the transport ships waiting in dock. They look like ghost barges, waiting to ferry souls to some unfathomable destination.

Some fog swirls in after her, reluctantly relinquishing its hold, knowing that it has the entrances blocked. There is one glowering bare bulb keeping the shadows at bay where crates and boxes shyly hunker. Johnny leans against a desk, intently leafing through a ledger. A slight crease has formed between his brows, and a shock of raven hair falls over his eyes. Diana wonders if she could smooth out that frown.

Johnny, dressed all in black again, his evening uniform, looks up as she draws near and puts down the ledger.

"It looks like you're still working. Perhaps I should leave."

He motions his men to leave the building as he pulls her close. "The work just ended."

The sound of the big doors being drawn shut rumbles through her, or is it his growl? His scent is tangy, metallic, with the slight sea air and a deeper earthy musk. One hand presses into the small of her back, the other on her neck. He nuzzles her shoulder and ear, then his lips find hers.

She wants to remain cool, distant, but the heat in her is burning away her clarity. Voluntarily pulled into the kiss, Diana lets her body soften.

Johnny pulls back slightly. His fingers search out the zipper of her vest and pull it down, then trace whorls over her breasts. His other hand dips into his pocket and pulls out a strand of nearly two dozen loosely strung pearls, ranging from ten to thirty carats. They look oily in the light; grey, whitish-silver, black. The pearls seem at odds with themselves, like oil and water, formed of confrontation. Johnny presses their cool spheres against Diana's cheek, then slides them down her neck and between her breasts. His lips follow the cool trail, heating it like cometary fire.

She can't help but hold on to him, her nails digging in as the sensation increases. Diana tries to hang on, not yet give in.

He kisses her, his tongue slithering into the cave of her mouth, filling her, heating her. The pearls, following like hungry children after his fingers, crawl up her thigh, burrowing under her skirt and toward the moist downy juncture of her legs. Diana sags into Johnny, suddenly powerless to do anything but let his fingers complete their task. Then his fingers search out and slide along the wet folds of her flesh, seeking her own pink pearl. So slowly that she almost dissipates into fog herself, his fingers slither into her vagina.

Diana attacks his neck, nipping at ears and throat. One point of contact is not enough. She wants to burrow into him too, to swirl into one large man-woman pearl. Her hands skim over his body, coming to rest on his fly. She releases his erection and strokes the warm skin.

Johnny's fingers have stopped seeking mysteries and have begun to push each lustrous pearl into the tide pool of her molten vagina. As each pearl is pushed deeper into her, Diana cannot help gasping, filled with the tantalizing knowledge of his audacity, and the seductive indiscretion in wanting all those pearls to make her one great fleshy oyster. As the last pearl is slipped in, Johnny stops, and then pulls out one.

It is like a bottle being uncorked and Diana sags against his warm flesh, her hands pulling him closer. Tremors ripple through her. She wants to be pried open, to feel his penile blade move into her and nose among her cache of pearls. There is wetness in her; and sliding down her breast, a tincture of sweat and lust and fog.

Johnny still leans on the desk. Diana is about to push him back and climb on top when there is a sharp retort on the metal doors. His brown eyes open wide, like the car-seeking deer's, then they slit as he barks out, "What is it?"

"Trouble, boss. Blues. Gotta go now."

Johnny sighs and gently pushes Diana back. Her skirt slithers down her thighs to hang demurely once again. She sways, uncertain if she can stand on her own. Turning back into muddy shadows, Johnny presses his erection back into his pants and cages it once again. He straightens his shirt and jacket, and then passes a hand through his hair. A jawbreaker, a sugar pearl, appears in his hand and is thrown into his mouth.

"Sorry about this. I'll have to leave the dinner and yacht for another night." He reaches briefly between her legs and gives a tug on the one dangling pearl. "This isn't what I want to give you. Tell you what. You hang on to them until I see you again. I'll collect them then and we'll see about that yacht ride. I promise an evening you won't forget. Soon." One last kiss sears her lips.

He turns and walks off, out the door and into the swirling fog. Diana finds words begin to well up in her but there's nowhere for them to go. The heat that burned away her clarity now forges new thoughts and something harder within. She zips her vest and digs frantically for a cigarette. It takes several strong drags until she feels she can walk steadily. The warehouse is nothing but a shell; Diana leaves through the door from which she entered.

It's a slow stroll back along the dock, the heavy feeling of the pearls swirling in her making her deliciously languorous. Stars now stare through the weakening fog. Diana discerns a tall, broad-shouldered figure walking her way. At the edge of her sight, along darkened warehouses, she sees movement, stealthy and furtive.

Detective Galbraith approaches her. "Diana Speers. Not your usual haunt here."

"Dan," she acknowledges, letting the smoke out slowly. "You already know I don't have a usual haunt, or you would have run into me before this."

His blue eyes narrow, shadowed only slightly by the brim of his hat. "You weren't meeting anyone here, were you?" At her raised eyebrow, he continues. "Well, I suspect I'll be finished here sooner than I expected. Perhaps afterward you'll allow me to buy you drink."

Diana drops her butt and crushes it under her shoe. She lets the last smoke leave her lungs. "Sorry, Dan, but I don't mix business with pleasure."

He sighs. "Well, perhaps some other time – when I'm off duty."

Diana gives a little wave as she moves slowly away from the dock and Galbraith.

◂ ▸

Dan Galbraith has been hanging around a little too regularly. Diana doesn't mind too much. He continues to bring her work and has asked her to carve handles for one of his favourite pistols. She hasn't yet relented to a drink with him; he's a little too bright. But maybe she's starting to notice some tarnish.

The shop door jangles; Johnny saunters in grinning as if he'd just seen her yesterday. He does a quick glance around but remains calm. It's been a few weeks, and he never called. She finished the handles on his gun about a week ago. They're perfect, one of the best carving jobs she's done yet. The ivy is lifelike and camouflages rather than obscures the animal on the handles.

Johnny leans on the counter and smiles at Diana, a jawbreaker clacking against his teeth. "Hi, beautiful. I believe you have something for me."

Diana pulls her hands from her pockets. "I certainly do." She pulls out a piece of black felt and places it on the counter.

"Just wrap them up. I can look at them later."

Diana is aware of Galbraith's piqued interest as he leans near the door, though nothing in his stance has changed. She hadn't counted on him being here when Johnny showed up but it works well enough. There is no danger for her here. Her back to the counter as she gets the guns, she comments, "I always like my customers to see my work before they leave, to make sure they're satisfied."

"I'd still like to take you for that yacht ride," he murmurs at her back. She hears him leafing through his bills and laying some on the counter.

"I still prefer to be paid in cash," Diana retorts and turns and lays the guns on the counter in front of Johnny. She scoops up the bills, writes his receipt and lays down his change. He frowns briefly. "Oh right. Isn't there something else you have for me?"

Diana checks her workbook. "Why, I don't think so," she says sweetly. "These are the only ones you brought in."

"But—"

"Like I told you before, I *never* mix business with pleasure. Now, was there any time you can think of where you or I have not been conducting business?"

Johnny doesn't look back at Galbraith but his eyes shift slightly. Then, as if the shadows were momentarily banished, his eyes widen. His lips pull down. "No," he says begrudgingly.

"Well then," Diana smiles, "I believe these guns are the last of our current business. I think you'll find them to your liking."

"Sure I can't interest you in dinner and a ride on my yacht?" Johnny almost pleads. Fine pearls of moistures have appeared on his brow.

"I'm sorry, but I really don't mix business with pleasure." Diana holds the guns up for Johnny. "Are you satisfied with these?"

He nods, then as she begins to wrap them he realizes what the carved animal is that's hidden among the ivy, rooting at the heart he requested. He stops her hand from wrapping them.

"You asked for an animal that represented wildness and fit in. I thought a pig did that well. Fitting into the domestic farm but wild and free in the ivy forest. I knew you'd like it." Diana hands him his parcel. He just stares at her. Briefly, she thinks anger flashes over his face and then a begrudging respect. He walks toward the door quietly, glancing briefly at Galbraith.

Not many pull one over on Johnny Jawbreaker. Detective Galbraith looks at Diana, trying to fathom what just went on.

Dan leans onto the counter. "I'm off duty tonight. How about one drink?" He holds up his index finger. "Just one."

Diana cocks her head to the side, then nods.

Once you get what you want in your sights, aim true. That's what her daddy had always said, and Diana had taken it to heart in more than aiming guns. Johnny Jawbreaker pauses at the door, then leaves, knowing that Diana's aim was true.

CHOKE THE CHICKEN

Shane Simmons

The carnival, as it always did, as it always would, came to town. It was late spring, and the air was still cool. The snow was long gone, and the mud it left behind had had weeks to bake under the sun and transform into solid ground. Solid enough to pitch the tents that would house clowns and animal acts, and anchor the steel rides that would twirl and pitch and whip riders around with all sorts of nausea-inducing contortions. The setup was long and arduous, lasting days. When at last it opened its gates for business, the fair would spend a single weekend doing its very best to pick the pockets of everyone in town before packing up and moving to the next vacant field in its seasonal agenda.

Clive Whitworth had watched the tent peaks and the high rides slowly poke up over the town's modest skyline from his classroom window. The anticipation became unbearable as the weekdays dragged on, and Clive earned himself three separate detentions for ignoring his lessons in favour of gazing out the window. Such punishment had no effect on him or his carnival daydream. He only saw the extra half-hours of after-school incarcerations as an opportunity to observe the distant construction from the slightly different vantage point offered by the windows of the detention room.

Although many of the other children in the school felt the same eager expectation for the weekend event, their interest was not aligned with Clive's. The fact was, Clive didn't particularly care for most of the spectacles that constituted a proper fairground. The rides made him sick, the candy floss gave him a bellyache. He didn't like clowns, and he cared even less for animals. What Clive liked was a challenge.

The school week dragged to its merciful end. It was late in the school year, and, with the carnival in town, only a few of the most joyless teachers bothered to assign homework. None of them expected any of it to be done by Monday. No one would be wasting a single moment struggling through algebra problems when there was so much fun to be had.

After a fitful night of sleep, Clive was up early. He could barely be convinced to finish his breakfast. Only the threat of withholding his allotment of fair money could keep him seated through his final bite of waffle and last strip of bacon. Once the go-ahead was finally issued by his parents, Clive threw on a light jacket and leapt from the front porch, dashing to the outskirts of town without ever stopping for breath or slowing his pace. He arrived at the wooden placard gates of the carnival in eight minutes flat, beating his previous record by three.

The set-up was nearly identical to the previous spring's. Tickets for the rides and the shows could be purchased at a centrally located booth. Some shows cost one ticket, others two. The same went for the rides. The merry-go-round and the Ferris wheel, the tilt-a-whirl and the pirate ship were all placed in their designated spots, spaced apart by the tents with the dancing dogs and the horse that could count. One strip along the border of the fairgrounds, stretching all the way from the funhouse to the haunted house, was where the carney booths were. Set in rows and forming an alleyway for games of chance and skill, they were ready to entrap anyone who dared navigate the gauntlet. Tickets wouldn't buy you a chance to win a stuffed toy here. Only cold hard cash could buy you a game.

The lineup at the ticket booth was long and slow. Clive didn't care. He wasn't interested in tickets and didn't plan to purchase a single one. He was there for the games alley.

Clive considered himself a master of the games. He was undefeatable at the ring toss, always on target with a dart, air rifle, or water pistol, and never failed to knock down a pyramid of cans with his three-ball allotment. Back home, stashed in a trunk in his closet, was his bounty from previous years. Plush pets, velvet posters, and plastic doohickeys of all sorts attested to his undeniable skill. He could have filled his entire room a dozen times over if his mother let him keep all the giant stuffed animals he'd won from the upper echelon of prizes. But they took up far too much space, and Clive had to admit they were garish, cheaply made, and filled with who-knows-what. One by one, he'd given them all up as they were pressed into service as gifts for birthdays and baby showers. He preferred to pore over his more compact collection of victories, often harder won. The prizes were all worthless junk, Clive was well aware, but to him they were worth far more than money. They were testaments to his skill, well honed through years of off-season practice.

Come carnival time, Clive would descend on the games alley and clean up. He would systematically travel from booth to booth, winning prizes, upgrading to bigger and better trophies, giving lesser ones away to friends who inevitably passed by on their way to the next ride or circus act. He wouldn't be satisfied until the carneys had all barred him from their individual booths for winning too much. That, to Clive, was the ultimate achievement, the one true prize he was really after. He'd made a clean sweep two years in a row now, banned for life from every single games booth. The lifetime ban was meaningless. The carneys never remembered him from year to year. They toured too many towns, saw too many faces. And Clive was still a growing boy. He hardly looked like the same kid who'd mopped the floor with them last year, or the year before.

Clive strolled the alley, checking out the games, watching the usual variety of unskilled marks lose their money as they missed their targets, failed to pop a balloon, or bounced a ball off the rim of what always seemed to be an undersized non-regulation basketball hoop. The suckers. Clive had long ago figured out how all the games were rigged. He had also figured out how this gave him an advantage, showing him the path to victory time and again. The carneys always seemed to know how to win at their own games when they demonstrated to passersby how easy they were. Through observation and training, Clive had determined what sort of counter-intuitive backspin to give his ball throws, what sort of flick of the wrist could vastly improve his odds of landing a ring around a bottle neck, and where to aim an air rifle that had purposely had its sights miscalibrated. Practicing at home with some of his own roughly recreated challenges, he had vastly improved his skills and had solved some of the trickiest deceits.

The games were his to dominate. Clive's only question was where to begin.

Are you smarter than The World's Smartest Chicken?

This question was asked in bold red paint on an arched sign over a wheeled cart. On one side of the cart was a three-by-three grid of lights randomly flashing Xs and Os. On the other was a glass cage that held a disinterested-looking white chicken. The only other prominent feature on the cart was a coin slot, yawning open, eager to be fed. Clive had never seen anything like it before. Not at this fair, not anywhere. It was a confusing, alien addition to the landscape he'd memorized over the course of his gaming adventures.

One of the carneys selling three dart-throws at a wall of balloons observed Clive's long, thoughtful contemplation of the new attraction that had joined the alley this season. The carney was old, grizzled. Clive guessed he was a long-time veteran of the carnival and at least half a dozen just like it in years gone by. He probably knew a million ways to fleece the public out of the contents of their wallet, a dollar at a time if he could, a nickel at a time if he had to.

"Give it a go, son. It won't bite," he encouraged.

"How does it work?" Clive asked.

"It's tic-tac-toe. You know how tic-tac-toe works, don't ya?"

"Of course I do. But does the chicken?"

"Sure it does. Says it's The World's Smartest Chicken, don't it? You pop a dime in the machine and you play a game. If you beat it, well then, congratulations. If you tie it, then I guess you're only as smart as a chicken. And if you lose... Well, I wouldn't go telling anyone I'd lost a game of tic-tac-toe to a chicken, that's fer sure."

Clive's eyes fixed on the chicken behind the window. It didn't look any different from any other chicken he'd ever laid eyes on in his life.

Almost unconsciously, Clive's hand slipped into his pants pocket and jingled the change nestled at the bottom. When he realized what he was doing, he removed his hand, only to find he'd come up with a single dime. This wasn't on his agenda, this uncharted attraction. Clive had a carefully calculated plan of attack. He knew which booths to hit first, which to hit last, and how long it would take him to work his way up to the top prize at each one. But this – this thing – stood in his way. There was no prize to be won, beyond the simple self-satisfaction of victory. Nevertheless, it stood as a barrier between him and his weekend loot. To ignore it, to circumvent it, would be to leave a challenge unanswered.

He reached forward, slowly, deliberately, and pushed the dime into the coin slot. It rattled and clunked its way through the inner workings of the mechanism before landing in the coin bin at the bottom. The light board reset itself and the flashing Xs and Os vanished for the commencement of a new game. Inside the chicken's glass booth, a small trapdoor painted with the words THINKING BOOTH popped open on one of the walls. The chicken immediately rose to its feet, toddled over to the booth, and began pecking at the space hidden away behind the door. In response, a bold red X lit up on the board in the upper-left corner.

Clive saw that each square of the light board had a button so the human player could respond with his own move. He pushed the one next to the centre square, claiming it with a blue O.

Again the chicken pecked at its thinking-booth and another X appeared, this one in the bottom right. Clive countered with an O in the bottom left. The chicken knew enough to block him with an X in the upper right.

Only at this moment did Clive realize he'd made a rookie error. Even little kids playing tic-tac-toe with crayons on bits of scrap paper in kindergarten knew better. You always play the corners in tic-tac-toe. It's not a sure way to win, but it's the only sure way not to lose. He'd left the chicken with two possible winning moves, and he could only block one of them.

Reluctantly, Clive chose one of his two blocks. With only one available move to win, the chicken seized it. The line of red Xs flashed victoriously, informing Clive he had lost. To his shame, he'd figured that out two moves ago. The question was, how did the chicken know?

"Tough break, kid," said the carney, who barely mustered enough politeness to keep from laughing out loud. "Like I said, that's one smart chicken."

Clive didn't respond, merely fumed. There was no recourse but to dig into his pocket for another dime. To prove a point, he ran through a second match, quickly this time, playing the corners like he knew he should have from the start. The chicken once again played flawlessly, but with Clive responding to each move correctly the game finished in a mathematically certain tie. Clive wasn't able to defeat the chicken, but at least he'd proved he could hold it to a draw – world's smartest or not.

Clive turned back to the carney, prepared to flash him a cocky grin. But the carney had already turned his attention to another mark – a teenage boy with a girl at his side he was eager to impress. There might have been as much as ten dollars to be made off him before he let the teen walk away with a fifty-cent teddy bear to give to the girl. That was much more pressing business than goading some kid into losing a couple of dimes to a chicken.

With no more audience to prove himself to, Clive nearly walked away to get on with his day. But one nagging question picked at his ego. He'd battled The World's Smartest Chicken to a draw, but could he defeat it? Against his better judgment, Clive dug for a third dime to feed into the coin slot.

And so the day went. Clive stood there as the sun crawled across the sky and the shadows grew long, pumping nickels and dimes into the coin slot, matching wits with a chicken and coming up short each time. Dissatisfied with tie after tie, Clive attempted a variety of strategies to unnerve the chicken and throw it off its game. He tried any number of nonsense moves in order to confuse and bamboozle his opponent. Each ploy failed. The chicken displayed nerves of steel and kept to its purely logical game plan. The more outrageous and unpredictable Clive tried to be on the game board, the more losses he managed to rack up, until his tie-loss ratio versus his chicken nemesis started to become very embarrassing indeed.

When the announcement came over the PA speakers that the carnival was now closed for the day and customers needed to clear the grounds, Clive was dismayed to find he'd gone through his entire bankroll without a single win to his name.

Back home, Clive picked at his dinner, hardly eating anything, not really hungry anyway. When asked if he had fun at the carnival that day, he mumbled something grumpy and indistinct and then excused himself for an early bedtime.

After dark, once the rest of the house was asleep, Clive made the rounds. There remained another whole day to bounce back and salvage the season, but he needed to replenish his ammunition. Silently he raided his father's billfold, his mother's change purse, and his little sister's penny jar. He knew the theft would not go undiscovered for long, but the consequences were something he'd deal with once the chicken was defeated and he was free to move forward with his original agenda to crush all the other games in the alley. There was still time if he moved quickly. A good night's sleep and a fresh start with a fresh perspective was all he needed. He'd come at the chicken hard in the first few minutes of the Sunday opening, catch it unawares before it had a chance to get up to speed, and then move on to a more deserving challenge.

Clive was absent at breakfast the next morning. It was the only way to be sure he was first through the gate the moment the carnival reopened for the day. He was at the chicken stand moments later, before any of the carneys had even assumed their positions in their game booths. He had to wait an additional ten minutes until someone came around to plug the cart into an extension that ran to one of the fairground's generators. Clive killed the time by staring coldly at his opponent, trying to rattle the chicken as it stared back with one profiled eye.

Once power was restored, Clive was lightning-quick with his first coin. His money from the day before had all been removed overnight, and he could hear his first dime rolling on its rim once it dropped into the empty change bucket inside the machine. He was five dimes into the rematch before anyone else stepped foot in the arcade strip. Clive played fast and decisively, hoping a sudden rapid assault of matches would afford him the advantage. Once again, Clive's strategy proved futile. A night's sleep had not improved his performance, and an early start had not thrown the chicken off its game.

After his late-night thievery, Clive had started day two with even more cash in his pockets. He went through it all twice as fast as he had previously and was bankrupt by noon. He spent the rest of the afternoon wandering the fairgrounds, hitting up any school friends he could find for spare change. He was able to borrow a few coins here and there. Close friends were willing to advance him as much as a dollar at a time. All of it was fed to the chicken in short order. Still hours away from the carnival calling it quits for the weekend, Clive was destitute. Word of his desperate fundraising had spread and no more loans were forthcoming. Even old pals turned their backs on him and hid, ducking behind thick queues of people, or losing themselves in the Hall of Mirrors, rather than get tapped by Clive again.

Any other year, even short on cash, Clive would have lingered and watched the rides and listened to the screams and laughter. But there was no joy left in it. He couldn't even bring himself to return one final time to the games in order to watch the unskilled lose their money at challenges he himself had mastered. Not with that damn superior chicken standing there, looking down on him from inside its glass box, all-seeing and all-knowing – at least in regards to anything tic-tac-toe related.

"Where were you this morning?" his mother wanted to know upon his return. When Clive didn't come down for breakfast, she had been every bit as worried as doting motherhood required her to be. But she knew exactly where her son had been – the only place he could have been – and had not called around or made inquiries of the neighbours.

"I wanted to get an early start," Clive shrugged.

"There's money missing. Do you know where it is?"

"Yeah," admitted Clive, and braced for the third degree, the disappointment, the punishment.

Sent to bed without supper, grounded for weeks, Clive felt the sting of defeat weigh on him more heavily than any loss he'd ever experienced in his softball league or at a spelling bee. This was a loss that mattered, that haunted him. Sleep would not come, and he felt certain a peaceful slumber would never be his again until he purged this loss from his troubled mind. Slipping out of bed after the rest of the house was down for the night, pulling his clothes back on, Clive knew the hour was very late, but there was still time to catch the carnival before it skipped town. He had to face the chicken one final time.

Clive was not stupid so much as stubborn. He couldn't let things lie, not where they were. Winning was no longer on his mind. The sole focus of his every thought now was revenge. It would be quick and easy as killings went. He could picture his hands around the chicken's throat, squeezing tight, choking off its air supply, crushing bones, snapping its arrogant neck.

Would his midnight act of murder be investigated, traced back to him? Would charges be laid, prison time served? It was, after all, only a chicken. But this was The World's Smartest Chicken. Surely there would be a reckoning for such a special animal. Clive supposed it would depend on just how brilliant the chicken was – if tic-tac-toe was its sole talent, or if it offered more to the world. It had been undeniably brilliant anticipating Clive's every move so far. Did the chicken foresee this one as well? Would it raise an alarm, clucking and screeching for salvation before Clive could sneak up on it and commit the deed? Clive considered all this, but recognized he'd spent the better part of two days second-guessing himself into this position. Best now to simply act, swiftly and brutally and with a violence no chicken could hope to match.

When he arrived at the fairgrounds, the tents were already flat on the ground and folded up. The staff was hard at work, tearing down all the temporary structures and packing the clapboards and canvas away in trailers that would be hitched to trucks and rolled to the next town in a matter of hours. The rides were still standing, steel skeletons, dark and imposing by moonlight. The power was out, the cables were being collected and spooled, and it was too dangerous to dismantle the big attractions in the dark. They wouldn't be torn down until morning, once all the lighter, more basic elements were out of the way and on the road.

The carnival workers toiled by flashlight and battery-operated lanterns. There was ample illumination for them to see what they were doing, but it was easy for one boy to slip by them unseen if he kept to the shadows. Clive's memory of the carnival layout helped him find his way in the dark without tripping over anything and calling attention to himself. It was a simple matter to find the games alley. The booths were empty now. Without their colourful prizes, blinking lights, bottles, or balloons, they looked uniformly nondescript. The only stand in the strip that remained unique was the chicken's cart. The silhouette of its wagon-wheel spokes and the transparent glass cage stood out in the dim light that filtered through the grounds from the opposite end of the fair.

Clive could see the chicken sitting inside its cage, unaware of his presence. He approached the cart, looking for a latch that would open the glass box and allow him access to his enemy – a clear path to a neck that needed wringing. He ran his fingers around the frame, feeling for the mechanism, but found nothing. It was too dark to see how the box opened. Clive considered shattering one of the panes, ramming his elbow through it, hoping not to cut himself too severely. But that would alert the workers, rouse the chicken, remove the advantage of surprise. He tried to calculate whether or not he would have enough time to get his fingers around the throat of a panicked and alarmed chicken before rescue was at hand.

Clive was still considering his options when he felt something underfoot. It was an extension cord. He reached down and hooked it with a couple of his fingers. Following it along its path, he arrived at a multi-socketed plug that rested at the end of a larger power line near one of the empty booths. Perhaps he could risk a little light to find his way in the dark, thought Clive. It might go unquestioned by the busy men long enough for him to accomplish the assassination and slip away unnoticed.

Clive plugged in the chicken cart and the tic-tac-toe board lit up. Freshly reset, the game blinked twice and then defaulted into automatic mode. No one was feeding change into the coin slot, but tic was matched against tac in a brutal duel that ended in stalemate each time. Clive could see that it wasn't the chicken playing at all. The machine was playing itself. And there was something else he noticed by the light provided by the red and blue Xs and Os.

The chicken was brown.

"Who's that?" said a gravelly voice from behind one row of wooden stands. It was the old carney from the dart-toss – the one who had baited Clive into challenging the genius chicken. Clive's first instinct, having been discovered trespassing, was to flee. He fought the impulse, determined to seek answers instead.

Clive walked around the left flank of the games alley and found a small campfire burning behind the stands with several wooden crates pulled up next to it. The carney was seated on one, warming himself over the modest blaze that had been invisible from the alley.

"What happened to The World's Smartest Chicken?" asked Clive.

The carney pointed at the chicken in the rig through a narrow gap in the alley's wooden façade. It remained nestled, eyes closed, dozing for the night.

"You're looking at it, kid."

"That's not the same chicken as before."

The carney considered the chicken currently residing in the glass cage, then returned his attention to the spit that was set up over the campfire. He'd been cooking up some fowl for his dinner before the boy interrupted.

"No, I guess that makes this one the new world champ."

"I don't get it? Did it beat the other chicken in a match or something?"

"You could say that," nodded the carney, tearing away a strip of greasy skin from the roasted bird's plucked breast as it sizzled over the open flame. "It wasn't no tic-tac-toe match, though. It was more of a taste test."

The carney cackled slightly to himself as he popped the loose skin into his mouth and sucked at the tips of his fingers where he'd just been holding it.

Clive noticed a small pile of discarded white feathers behind the games-alley backdrop. A slight nighttime breeze played with them, scattered them in random directions.

They'd all be blown away by tomorrow, gone like the rest of the carnival.

"You want a drumstick?" asked the carney, tearing one of the tender legs off his meal and offering it to the boy.

Clive remembered the stories he'd heard of tribes in the deepest darkest jungles of the world. Some of them would eat their defeated enemies as a way to imbue themselves with their strength, their power. It was both a sign of respect for their fallen foes and a way of stealing all they ever were and making it their own. Clive had thought that sounded kind of dumb when he first heard about it. But the way he saw things and the way he thought about them kept changing the more living he got under his belt. These days he wasn't so sure about much of anything. He wasn't even sure if that much uncertainty in life frightened or excited him.

"Yeah," he said, and sat down to eat.

GOOD FOR GRAPES

Kelly Robson

Simon wouldn't have set foot in Canada again if the harvest hadn't been late. He'd badmouthed the Okanagan all over the world, from Coonawarra to the Cape, calling it a shithouse of overpriced land, badly managed vines, and wannabe winemakers who had no business being anywhere near a ferment. Threw it off, every time.

Nothing did more damage to wine than amateurs with money.

But California was early and BC was late, and when Simon got the email from High Bench Estates, he had just finished laying a Rockpile Cabernet into new French oak barrels and he was planning to hit a Nicaraguan beach for a few months before Australia called him home to a hot February. But he had expenses, two of them, living with his ex in Melbourne. He'd emailed back with a jacked-up fee, and High Bench still wanted him.

So instead of surf and beer and stoned girls, he got a flight north and a long ride on a stinking Greyhound toward a valley full of no-hopers and vinifera trying like hell to ripen through frost.

Simon hunkered down in the bus' triple backseat and tipped airplane bottles of rum into a travel mug. Just past

Hope, the mountain pines turned from green to red. He probably wouldn't have noticed if the hippie kids in the next seat hadn't freaked out over all that dead forest. Pine beetles, apparently, killing trees by the millions. He listened to them whine about climate change for a minute or two, and then plugged into his earbuds.

The French oak back in Rockpile cost over three grand a barrel. A few pennies too much to pay for wood, but Rockpile was a professional operation from rootstock to shoot. Simon had worked twenty-hour shifts coaxing the juice through a textbook ferment and after a couple of years in those barrels, it'd bottle okay. The winery investors would be happy.

His ex had been happy too, when he sent her the money he wouldn't be spending in Nicaragua. And High Bench – well, if the old man was going to put Simon through the wringer again he just better hand over a fat cheque with a smile on his face.

◀ ▶

When the Greyhound turned off the highway, Simon punched a text into the cheap burner he'd picked up at the Vancouver airport. The red truck was waiting for him – he remembered its antique fenders and peeling paint better than the two vineyard grunts leaning on the bumper. Huey and Duey, he thought. Interchangeable. Both tanned deep brown but for the pale sunglass rings around their eyes and the white baseball cap stripes above their eyebrows.

Simon eyed the cuts and nicks knotting their forearms. "How they hanging?"

"Looking good," said Huey. "The Merlot was ready to come off three days back but they said to wait."

Two minutes off the bus and it was already amateur hour. "Who made that call? Not the old man. His Honour would never wait to put it in steel."

Huey opened his mouth to answer but Duey shoved an elbow in his ribs.

Simon tried again. "He didn't wait for winter last time. Nothing shy about him. Thought he could get a ferment from green grapes just by throwing in a pack of yeast."

Duey grunted and tossed Simon's bag in the back of the truck.

Simon watched the rows climb past the truck window as they wound up the bench. The Cabernet Sauvignon on one side was throwing out suckers and cordons and big fat watery clusters just like he expected. Bad farming, sloppy grapes.

The Cabernet Franc on the other side was only four or five years old. Nothing like the gnarled century-old Barossa vines he'd cut his teeth on, but they looked okay. Probably managed by a community college viticulture grad, doing it by the book. That would be fine until the owner decided he needed a higher yield. Then the kid would get canned and the vines would go to shit.

It was decent land, though. The slope coasted down to the lake, steep enough to create a nice breeze. Put it a thousand miles south and they might be able to make a bottle or two worth drinking.

"I bet the old man gets a gleam in his eye every time he drives down this road," said Simon.

Huey smirked. "The Franc belongs to a couple of Vancouver kids. They're going broke. And we're gonna get the lease on that rangy Cab Sauv. In a year or two High Bench will have all this land from mountain to lake."

Duey spat out the window. "Be a shitload of work slapping those vines into shape."

Simon felt a little sorry for the neighbours. Not for going broke – anyone stupid enough to put cash into Canadian wine deserved what they got. But nobody deserved the pain that came from tangling with the old man. He fought dirty.

Simon had worked a lot of crush pads. They blurred together into one cool expanse of concrete walled over with stainless-steel tanks and towering racks of oak. Three, sometimes even four harvests a year. California, New Zealand, South Africa, and Australia were in his usual rotation. Bordeaux and Tuscany now and then, just to pick up a few old tricks. Occasionally Washington or Oregon, twice Texas. British Columbia just the once. He'd sworn never again.

Most wineries left Simon alone to do his work. Only one owner had ever sat on top of him, poking him in the ribs and questioning his every move. At first Simon had ignored the old man and just tried to get on with the ferment. But it had escalated.

Duey turned the truck onto a potholed lane. Simon got one glimpse of a new tasting room building before they turned onto a farm track dividing the blocks. He twisted in his seat and watched the estate spread out below as they climbed the mountain.

The Quonset hut was still there, set deep into the rock and shaded by a row of Ponderosa pine. Even at this distance the fresh yellow paint couldn't disguise the rust around the joints. The landscaping around the new tasting room was still raw. Two cars and three motorhomes threw long shadows across the parking lot. The setting sun turned the valley rose and gold, the lake a long dark pool from bend to bend.

The vineyards stopped halfway up the mountain. A twenty-foot trailer was parked at the edge of the snake fence.

"You got the camper, that okay?" said Huey. "They said you'd want some privacy."

"It's a long climb from crush pad to bed," Simon said. Not that he hadn't slept on concrete once or twice.

"We'll leave you the truck."

Duey dropped Simon's bag in the dust. The two of them waved and trudged down the track.

The trailer groaned under his weight but it smelled fresh enough. The bed was made, the water tank was full, and someone – bless them – had put six cans of Victoria Bitter in the fridge. There was a carton of eggs too, some milk, butter and cheese, and a loaf of bread beside the toaster. He flipped the safety catches on the cupboards. Coffee. More beer.

Simon added a dozen VB to the fridge and finished the cold stuff can by can, thinking how he should be on warm sand, watching tan lines wink at him from the brown backs of girls doing yoga in bikinis. He didn't look out the windows, not at the stars overhead, not at the lake below or the mountains between, and certainly not at the grapes that waited in ranks for the frost.

◂ ▸

The rising sun turned the camper into an aluminum oven. Simon dragged a nylon lawn chair over to the snake fence and watched the light creep down the mountain. The first movement was in the campground off the highway – the harvest was worked by French Canadian gypsies, if he remembered right. Just after dawn, they rolled out of their tents and headed down the road six and eight to a car. An hour later the valley was busy as rush hour, harvesters and trucks working the wide flat blocks at the bottom of the valley, roped pickers stripping the vines on the steep slopes above.

But at High Bench, the only signs of life were the starlings squawking in the rows. Nobody working the harvest or even taking samples. Nobody around the Quonset hut. No sign of Huey and Duey. The whole estate spread out below him, so quiet it was almost spooky. He cracked a can and drained it, then got in the truck and drove downhill.

The tasting room door was locked. No surprise there – far too early to be waiting on tourists.

Footsteps sounded on the concrete behind him. A pair of big-eyed deer hopped over the fence. Simon waved them off. The deer trotted into the home block and began browsing on the vines.

"Pest management isn't my department," he said. But he ran the deer up the rows anyway, tossing pebbles at their flashing tails. He chased them over the drainage ditch and into someone else's vineyard – rows of Chardy that had been stripped weeks ago, the vines ravaged, leaves flyblown.

As he walked back down through the blocks, Simon had to admit the High Bench vines didn't look too bad. The fruit would never properly ripen, though. He plucked a few grapes, chewed them up and spat the pips into his palm. The seeds were still green. No hint of telltale brown.

When he got back to the parking lot, the winery was still deserted. The Quonset hut was locked tight, its roll-down door secured with a padlocked chain. Simon ran his hand over the deep scars at the bottom of the metal door. The rust scraped over the pads of his fingers.

Seven years ago the door had been secured with two shot bolts threaded with heavy locks. Simon had hacked them off with an axe after the old man had locked him out of the crush pad.

Simon turned his back on the hut. He should just go back to the snake fence and drink beer until the old man came to find him. But there was no point in putting it off. And he wanted his cheque.

The track continued up a steep slope bordered by Ponderosa pines, blocked by a metal gate marked *Private*. Simon dragged it open and left it swinging as he drove up the twisting switchbacks that climbed the ridge above the vineyards.

How many times had he stomped up this driveway on foot, angry as hell after a day of putting right what the old man had done wrong? The first time he had been sure of winning the argument, imagining he could beard the old man in his den. After a few more fights he began to learn that the old man never lost an argument. Nothing, not evidence, not education, not boots on the ground, or a lifetime on the crush pad meant a thing to a man like that.

At the top of the drive crouched a house sharp and cold as a razor blade, a steel and glass box cantilevered over the cliff on a pair of iron beams.

Simon flubbed the clutch and the truck's engine coughed and died. He started it up again and pulled around back alongside the old man's hunter-green Jaguar.

This house was new. Seven years ago it had been a fake Tudor pile with flagstones and flower gardens, even a bloody grape arbor. Now no hint of the old house remained, its skeleton bulldozed into landfill and replaced by this thin slice of modernism.

One kind of rich man's dream exchanged for another. When this one got stale the Ponderosa pines would see a new dream form on the edge of the cliff, if the pine beetles didn't kill them off first.

The back wall was flat zinc siding, the door a slab of black marble. Simon knocked once, waited, then knocked again. He tried the door. It swung open.

Glass walls on three sides framed a panorama of valley and mountain and lake. An eagle's nest perspective. No need for art on the walls when you're the lord of all you survey. The furniture was low, dark, modern, and uncomfortable.

The only thing out of place was the hospital bed.

The old man was on a respirator, his nose and mouth plugged into a plastic tube that snaked up from a metal bullet of oxygen on the floor. Swollen ankles puffed out above his too-tight socks, his paunch shrunken to a bib of flab under a sunken chest. The fingers of his right hand were stained yellow but there were no cigarettes, no ashtrays, no hint of smoke in the air, just a faint antiseptic tang. The old man's fingers fiddled compulsively, grasping at air.

A plate of scrambled eggs and toast sat on a side table along with a photo of the old man in his younger days, stark as a raven in his judicial robes. A plastic water bottle was tucked into the blankets at his desiccated hip. Simon circled the bed. He picked up the bottle and held it out.

"Your Honour," Simon said. "It's been a while."

The old man fiddled the bottle with shaking fingers but couldn't seem to grip it.

"Not much there anymore." A woman's voice. Simon dropped the bottle and turned. She was sharp and sleek as the house.

"Nothing left of Dad but his habits," she said.

"I'm sorry—" Simon said.

"The fiddling." She twitched her long fingers, imitating the old man's gesture. "Watch."

The old man stared out the window. He lifted his fingers to his mouth, pursed his lips, sucked on air, and then lowered his hand.

"I always thought the cigarettes would get him in the end, but it was the drinking instead. Smoking's not going to hurt him now, but I'm afraid he'll burn the place down."

Simon looked around. "Not much here to burn."

"He could burn himself to death. But maybe that would be a better way to go. Liver failure isn't pretty."

"I can see that," said Simon.

"Dad went into diapers a year ago. He would rather have died right then."

The old man lifted his fingers to his mouth again. His eyes were glazed and unfocused, his jaw slack. A bubble of spittle hovered at the corner of his mouth. Simon walked to the window. "You've got quite a view."

"You don't remember me, do you?"

He didn't, and that was surprising. She was pretty enough. But when he hadn't been fighting with her father he'd been trying to save the ferment, practically sleeping with the spectrophotometer. And drinking, of course.

Simon shrugged. "It's been a while."

"Seven years. You fought Dad hard, and you taught him a few things even if he'd never admit it."

"Did I teach him to let his Merlot rot on the vine?"

"No," she smiled. Her teeth were very white. "That's my decision." She held out her hand. "I'm Marina, the judge's youngest. You don't remember me but I remember you."

Simon shook her hand and turned back to the window. From this height he could see the big estate up the valley. Narrow orange trucks climbed the rows, tiny as ticks.

"Are you the High Bench winemaker now, Marina?"

"Not me. But I know what's good for grapes. Dad knew too, only he never applied the principle to the vines, just to his children."

"Your neighbours have the jump on you. Getting their harvest in as fast as they can."

"The weather will hold."

"The weather will hold?" Simon placed his fist against the window, clenched it hard. "You're playing chicken with winter. There's deer in your home block and starlings mowing through the rows. Get your harvest in so I can put the grapes in a fucking tank."

He said it too loud, but he didn't care. He was sick of amateurs and their magical thinking. The weather would hold, the ferment would take, and everything would work out. Well, she was paying for his advice so he'd let her have it.

"Wine is farming. It takes hard work, not luck. You're battling the elements. And you know what? The elements always win. Making wine is chemistry. It's not art. It's not an opportunity for self-expression. It's science. Farming and science. You don't leave any of it up to chance or it's not a business, it's just a rich man's hobby and a fucking waste of time."

She blinked but didn't back away.

"I'll take care of the deer, but the birds are fine. They only nibble around the edges. The grapes want more sun so I'm going to let them hang. And anyway, I was waiting for you."

"Waiting for me. Why? The old man would have hired a kid from the local college. Someone he could boss around."

"If you'll come downstairs, I'll show you. Bring that toast."

She padded down the stairwell, bare feet on slate. Simon looked around, confused, and then his gaze fell on the old man's uneaten breakfast. As he plucked the toast off the plate the room filled with the smell of shit.

Simon shook his head. "Your Honour," he said, "that's a hell of a sad way to go, even for an asshole like you."

The old man lifted his fingers to his lips.

Marina waited in the kitchen. A woman in scrubs was drinking coffee at the granite counter. At one look from Marina she put down her cup and trotted upstairs.

Marina unlocked a heavy oak door. "You're going to like this," she said.

"Is there a cellar down there?" Simon laughed. "Of course there is. Or do you call it the wine library?"

The stairwell spiralled down into a stone cavern lined with shining wood racks lit with pot lights recessed into rock. Ranks of wine bottles were filed into alcoves with brass rack labels. Decanters and stemware gleamed above a marble counter with an array of corkscrews and decanting funnels and aerators. A digital humidity and temperature gauge blinked on the wall by the stairs, and the far end of the room was dominated by a towering stainless steel fridge vault. In the middle of the room, a pair of armchairs faced off across an oak table. The air was fragrant with yeast and leather.

"I call it the cave. I don't know what Dad called it. By the time it was finished, he couldn't really walk anymore."

"You've got a private cellar dug into the cliff but you're still making your wine in a Quonset hut?"

Marina ran the rack ladder along its noiseless track and climbed up to fetch an unlabelled bottle. She looked at the slice of toast in Simon's hand and raised her eyebrows. Fair enough, he thought, as he bit into the cold toast. Let's do this right. Don't want to be tasting crap wine with a tongue fouled by VB.

Simon browsed the racks. One side was almost all Bordeaux, good labels and expensive vintages. Next to that was a rank of Barolo. Nothing wrong with the old man's taste. There were several dozen big spendy Napa Cabs further on, and then a rack of port followed by a dog's breakfast of local reds, vintages all jumbled together, some bottles past their time and most not worth drinking.

The other side of the room was devoted to High Bench wines, the bottles racked opposite the Bordeaux, and just as carefully organized. The rest of the wall was filled out with vintage Champagne. Nothing wrong with the old man's ego, either.

Marina stripped the foil from the bottle she'd chosen and eased the cork. "We're not making wine in the hut anymore. There's a new crush pad built into the hill under the tasting room. Didn't you see it?"

Simon's mouth was full of dry toast. He shook his head.

"Well," Marina said, "it's nice. Everything you'd want."

He swallowed. "I can make wine in a garage if I have to."

"But don't you like it better when you have a proper setup?" She turned her hand over and gestured at the room, a model's move, slow and elegant. "You can't tell me you don't like this. Be honest."

"Who wouldn't like it? It's a fucking wet dream. But it's in the wrong place. You can't make good wine here."

"Can't we?" Marina smiled. "Oh, I see. Tell me, what do you need to make good wine?"

Alright, Simon thought. Kindergarten time. He resisted the urge to look at his watch. "Good grapes."

"Anything else?"

"If you've got a winemaker who knows what they're doing and a hardware store within a couple hundred miles, no. A few pieces of equipment would be nice, and an oak barrel if you're making red. But Sicilians make killer red in concrete troughs. It's not clean but it's tasty."

Marina plucked a pair of stems from the cabinet and placed them on the table beside the unlabelled bottle. She sat back in one of the leather chairs and crossed her legs. "And how do you get good grapes?"

"You farm the fuck out of them. And you don't grow them in Canada."

"Don't you? Well, you're the professional." She lifted the neck of the bottle to her nose and inhaled. Her eyes rolled back a bit, an involuntary gesture of pure sybaritic delight. If this was a High Bench wine, she was putting on a show. Either that or her palate was borked.

"Let me tell you how to get good grapes." She spread her fingers again in that model's gesture, inviting him to sit.

The scent of leather enveloped him as he sank into the big armchair. "What do you know about farming, Marina?"

She leaned back and crossed her slim legs. "I used to work in the vineyards."

"Sure. The vineyards at Tiffany's, maybe."

She smiled. "Since Dad got sick I'm more in sales. But you remember me. Think about it."

Simon remembered a skinny teenager in coveralls and a baseball cap bringing in truckloads of grapes, working the sorting table, hauling loads of stems out to the compost. She had kept her distance at first, but as the fights with the old man got worse and worse she started sticking close. He remembered her hovering at his elbow as the old man shoved his shotgun in Simon's face. He thought she was being protective of her dad, but maybe she had been learning something. Learning how to survive her father, maybe.

"Okay, farmer. Tell me what you think you know."

She leaned toward him. "Vines are generous; they want to produce. If you water them and baby them and let them get comfortable, they'll throw out canes galore and give you as much fruit as they can. But it's bad fruit. No flavour."

"Sure," he said. "That's Viticulture 101."

"So you torture them. Plant the vines close together so they have to compete for water and nutrients. You cut them back hard to keep them stressed. Keep them thirsty and force them to drive their roots deep. Then you thin the buds until the vine is forced to put everything it's got into a few clusters just to please you. You don't get much quantity for your effort, but what you do get is the best quality. That's what Dad believed. Torture brings out the best. I know it better than anyone."

Simon sat back in his chair. "We still talking about grapes?"

Marina nodded. "What's good for grapes isn't so good for people. But I learned. I'm not sentimental. I don't baby the vines, I keep them scared and make them work for me. And let me ask you, what's crueller than forcing vinifera to grow this far north? They beg for every ray of sun."

"If you're going to go crazy on me, better I get my cheque now."

She laughed and poured. A ruby stream tipped into the crystal, studding the lip of the glass like gemstones.

"Anyway," said Simon, "this isn't that far north. You're on the same latitude as Champagne."

"Now you're making my argument for me. No reason why we can't grow good grapes here."

"Go ahead! Grow Riesling and Gris. Cool climate varietals make nice little patio sippers. Bottle some fat Merlot and sell it at the grocery store. Make a sparkling if you want to brag about something. But you can't grow good Cab, and that's what you need to make real wine."

She pushed a glass toward him with the tip of her finger. "Cabernet Sauvignon likes heat, and we have plenty of that. It's just getting hotter every year."

Simon sighed. "You're the judge's youngest? I bet you never lost an argument, just like him."

"Dad lost plenty of arguments. Just never admitted defeat." She lifted her glass. "How about you? Ever admit defeat?"

Simon swirled the wine and plunged his nose in the bowl. The first whiff was pure black fruit, concentrated and treacly like a Napa Cab but then all that fruit spread out over hot soil, sunk into good stony dirt. He swirled again and sipped. The fruit burst over his tongue and slid like velvet down his throat. The finish was plush with pepper.

Simon tasted wine all the time, tasted, measured, assessed, critiqued, and criticized. It had been years since he'd drunk wine for pleasure, but this glass practically begged to be drained.

He sipped again. "That's decent Bordeaux."

"It's not Bordeaux."

"Whose is it?"

"It's yours."

Simon put the glass down. Crystal rang on oak.

"Ours," she continued. "High Bench, seven years ago."

"I never made wine here. Your dad did. I just kept his mistakes from turning into vinegar."

"Yes, you did. You gave Dad hell over it, just one barrel of your own, the way it should be. The way you knew it could be. And this is it."

She sipped. Her eyelashes fluttered closed.

She could be lying. Could have soaked the label off a thousand dollar Grand Cru and poured him a big glass of bullshit. But no – she didn't just like the wine, she was proud of it. Proud like her father had been of his Jaguar and his big old house. Every sip seemed to puff her up just the way her father had puffed up every time someone down in the town called him Your Honour or gave him right of way at an intersection.

Ego, that's what he saw in her. Pure ego.

He tasted again. It was good. Very good, and after seven years starting to open up and even out. It would stand another ten years in the bottle, maybe even twenty.

He drained the glass and held it out. Marina refilled it, generously.

"Just one barrel, you said?"

"Yes, three hundred bottles. It's our Grand Reserve. We don't sell it, just give it away to wine critics and break it out for special guests. There's just ten bottles left."

One barrel. There had been one barrel. Simon had slept on the concrete beside it, kept the old man off it for weeks. In the end, he had stood over it with the axe clenched in his fists as the old man shoved the shotgun's muzzle under Simon's chin. He remembered panting with the urge to drive the axe blade through the old man's skull, his vision turning red at the edges. He had nearly done it, nearly scattered the old man's brains across the concrete, nearly painted the crush pad with his blood.

Instead, he'd used the axe handle to shove the shotgun aside and just walked away. Walked straight down to the highway, hitchhiked into the city, and had never thought about that barrel again once he was on the plane to Australia. Just wrote the whole thing off.

And now here it was, good as anything, anywhere.

"Grand Reserve," Simon said. "I bet the old man labelled his own Grand Reserve every year."

"No. This is our only Grand Reserve." She filled his glass again. "But you could make another this year, if you think you can do it again."

Simon swirled the wine. It clung to the crystal like blood and streamed into the bowl in thick rivulets.

Could he? He wasn't sure. Nothing in his experience could explain getting a wine this good from grapes like these. But he'd done it, somehow. Grand Cru quality. The kind of wine people search for, shed tears over, fight about. Legendary wine. His.

"Alright," he said. "But I still want my cheque."

Marina stood and walked over to the cold storage. "I haven't got it." Her voice echoed off the stainless steel. She opened the door. Cold air washed over Simon's skin.

"Fuck," he said.

"I haven't got the money," she repeated as she closed the door. "The new tasting room, new crush pad, finishing this house before Dad dies. And the nurses, three shifts a day. Dying at home isn't cheap. But I'm talking to the bank again on Monday and we release the new reds in November. I'll have it, just not right away."

She placed a can of VB on the table beside his wine glass. Condensation pearled the aluminum.

"The bank would be a lot nicer to me if I had a winemaker. A permanent one, not a hired gun. Someone to stay year-round, take the ferment from harvest to bottle. Especially if he was the one who made our Grand Reserve."

She was clearly crazy, Simon thought. He should grab the beer and run like hell. Go to Nicaragua and forget everything.

But there were only ten bottles left of his Grand Reserve. He would do it again, make more wine this good, or die trying.

"Stay," she said. "Forget Australia, forget France and California. Stay and make wine here. I'll make it worth your while, eventually."

Simon settled back in his chair and lifted the glass to his lips. "What the hell," he said. "It's just getting hotter."

A SQUARE YARD OF REAL ESTATE

Steve Vernon

In order to make this whole system work, you've got to learn how to break a few rules. That's one of the first things you figure out when you go into business for yourself. The government never wants to know the whole truth. I've owned this used bookstore for over seventeen years. That's a success in some people's eyes. I'm not so certain.

There's a guy out there who sits on the sidewalk nearly every day. Well, actually there's quite a few of them. They've got the whole downtown Barrington Street area divided up by street corners. You can find one of these guys on pretty near every street corner leaning their back up against a telephone pole. I think in some ways they're holding the whole damn city together.

They used to call them bums. For a while they were called the homeless or the out-of-doors. Some folks are polite and refer to them as houseless. The bureaucrats have named them transient populace. Romanticists call them pilgrims of the road or, more poetically, the walking wounded of society's endless battle against poverty. I once heard a social worker refer to them as the disenfranchised. All of those labels with way too many syllables. Do you know what I call them? I call them people, because they just don't look all that different from you or me.

The funny thing is you never see them fighting over who sits where. They've got a pretty good system worked out, I guess. They sit there, usually on about a square yard of cardboard, shaking a Tim Hortons coffee mug and saying those same words over and over again: "Spare-sum-change?"

I saw a show on television once about this holy guy who spent his days squatting on a prayer mat somewhere in Alberta or Alabama, one of those A-places. It seemed he had it figured out that if he sat there for long enough saying special secret words over and over to himself that he would be transported to a better reality and perhaps even a higher tax bracket.

I don't know what those words were. Maybe he was chanting nothing more than a lead pipe confession from Professor Plum, or whispering the Cadbury Caramilk secret or intoning Colonel Sander's eleven herbs and spices. But part of me figured that all that his secret incantation amounted to was some form of the panhandler's never-ending mantra: *spare-sum-change?*

I hear that mantra a lot these days. When I go into the bank the tellers sit there and rattle tin cups against the banker bars and mutter in coordinated unison – "Spare-sum-change?" Telemarketers phone me every night and whisper in dry, crackling, static-bound tones – "Spare-sum-change?" George Bush sends me telekinetic messages from a WMD site in some spun-dry-desert-kingdom, Arabia or Albania, one of those A-places, and asks me if I can "Spare-sum-change?"

Like I said, I run a small business here on Barrington Street in Halifax, Nova Scotia. I sell used books and cigarettes and soda pop and lottery tickets. I sell an awful lot of lottery tickets. The money goes to the government. They tell me that the government does good things for us, but all I know is they seem to be the number one panhandler out there on the street.

I pay taxes on my bookstore. I pay taxes on my business license. I pay taxes on what I earn and I pay taxes on the cigarettes I sell and I pay taxes on my tax deposits. I even pay taxes on the awning over my store window that people stand beneath when it's raining and they're waiting for a bus. It's called encroachment tax. As near as I can figure, I have to pay a tax for the wear and tear that the shadow of my awning inflicts upon the sidewalk.

They've got themselves a new angle now. Do you know those sandwich boards that sit outside restaurants advertising the special of the day? Or outside beauty salons, letting pedestrians know how much it will cost to paint their nails in shades of neon? They've decided that businesses need a license for each sign they own.

Last week the sidewalk-sign inspector showed up. That's what we call him. He's got a little uniform like a doorman and he's been given the job of making sure that all of the sidewalk signboards in the city of Halifax are legitimately licensed. I've got a sign out there advertising the lottery tickets that I sell. The sign occupies about one square yard of real estate. I told the sign inspector that the lottery sign made money for the government with the lottery ticket sales, and as such, ought to be exempt from the tax, but he told me that it didn't matter. I had to pay to apply for a license for my sandwich board or else take it in.

So I took the sign in. I taped a handwritten sign in my window that read *Welcome to Halifax, Nova Scotia, leave your wallet at the door*. Of course, there isn't a city of Halifax any more. Back in 1996, some chowder-headed bureaucrat decided to amalgamate the four adjoining municipalities – Bedford, Sackville, Dartmouth, and Halifax – and give them the name Halifax Regional Municipality, or HRM for short.

I'm not sure where that leaves Halifax these days. Maybe we ought to start calling ourselves the city formerly known as Halifax. It worked for Prince, didn't it? Of course everybody still called him Prince, except if they were telling a joke or were being paid to be polite. Everybody here still calls the city Halifax, and when we take the ferry across the Halifax Harbour we're headed for Dartmouth.

Halifax has had a few names over the years. The local Mi'kmaq called the area Jipugtug, which was mumble-slurred into Chebucto and is now a name for a road that leads into Halifax – or should I call it HRM? – from the Armdale Rotary, which we are now supposed to call the Armdale Roundabout, which sounds a little like something you might ride on in a carnival midway. The new roundabout looks a little like a pentacle from the air, and I sometimes wonder what sort of a spell the road designers had in mind when they redesigned it.

They've decided to widen Chebucto Road by plowing a few feet from the front yards of the folks who live along Chebucto Road. Nobody's really happy about that; petitions were signed but the road is being widened all the same. The folks whose front lawns are being taken have signs out reading PEOPLE, NOT CARS. I don't know if they have to pay a sidewalk-sign license fee for them or not.

Jipugtug is a native term that means "the biggest harbour," which Halifax Harbour is. Halifax Harbour is kind of toilet shaped, which is probably why we've been flushing our city's sewage system into the Harbour since the Second World War. I don't know if we pay a poop tax or not.

That's how it is when you live on a peninsula like Halifax. There's just nowhere else to go but down to the sea. Only the water is too dirty to fish in so we settle for whatever we can bum from all of those fat American tourists smelling of toilet water, limes, and eagle feathers. All of us sit down by Pier 21, a pack of cargo cult cannibals lurking in commercially designed kiosks festooned with state-of-the-art price tags, shaking our booty for the tourists and saying those three wonderful magic words – "Spare-sum-change?"

Some folks in the HRM have figured out a better plan. They greet the tourists with brightly painted Nova Scotian plaid tour buses that whisk them away to a wonderland of Walmart and folk art. Bagpipers lure the tourists away from the ships, as the kilted bus drivers tap their toes to a hypnotic Riverdance rhythm, the tassels on their sporrans swinging in a Svengali-like state of instant mesmerism.

As a result, the tourists bypass Barrington Street. We're becoming a street full of closed-up shops. Our windows are covered in butcher paper and old newsprint. You can read the obituaries across the street in the window that used to be Sam The Record Man's. The art gallery on the corner of Barrington and Prince has moved down to Pier 21. The Dooley's Pool Hall has closed down, and the street is lined with demolition trucks that haul trash from closed-down stores like an army of trained looters. The only businesses that seem to be flourishing are the telemarketers, who have opened up three offices directly above three of the closed stores. They sit up there at their telephones, the dials spinning like so many Buddhist prayer wheels (alright, so they don't use dials anymore but I like to imagine they do), and you can hear them whispering into the airwaves, over and over – "Spare-sum-change?"

Nobody comes into my store these days. The silverfish are having a fine feed on all of those used books on the rusty shelves and the words on the pages are forgetting their meaning. I've torn up the lottery tickets and smoked the last pack of cigarettes, refusing to pay taxes on every single butt.

Now I sit outside my store, on the spot where my sidewalk sign used to stand. I'm wearing an overcoat that I found in a dumpster behind a closed-out Frenchy's used clothing store. My boots are two different sizes and two different styles, and I have to stuff newspaper in one of them for a tight enough fit. They both leak when it rains. I have a dirty fedora that I found blowing down the street one morning like a forgotten Leonard Cohen lyric. I wear the fedora with a seagull feather poked into the hatband for luck. I figure it didn't hurt the seagull any.

"Spare-sum-change?"

In the old days, I would have been a fisherman or maybe a hunter. Working a stream or a trapline, trying to fish something out or snag some beaver by its flat waffled ass, standing on snowshoes or moccasins or a pair of mismatched hip waders, probably whispering to myself – "Spare-sum-change?"

Every morning I move one telephone post closer to the waterfront. I'm just a transient drifting on down the street. I don't know what I'll do when I run out of telephone poles. That harbour is looking better every day.

I figure the change of scenery will do me good.

JACK WON

Edward McDermott

Just after 2:00 a.m. my phone rang. I shook the sleep out of my eyes and picked up, expecting a wrong number, but the caller ID showed *Beecham*.

"Yeah?"

"Frank," he said, his words slightly slurred. "Frank. My ship has come in. I'm flush and I need some help."

I didn't have the faintest clue what he meant. "So tell me," I said.

"Five grand," he said. "Five grand for you to pick me up, take me to an airport, and put me on a plane to Charleston."

"Legal?"

Beecham didn't wave five grand around for nothing.

"All legal. I'm at the Seminole Casino Immokalee. I won big but I think someone has ideas."

"So take a cashier's cheque, mail it, and drive away."

He laughed. "They want that money. Think how they'll react if they don't get it."

Jack Beecham stood six foot one, with all the muscles twenty years on the offshore rigs as a roughneck could build. Not a good man. Too quick with his fists for friends or family. He had broken everything that meant something to him. That's the type on whom God's good fortune falls out of the heavens.

I looked at my watch. Lake Worth to Miami and along Alligator Alley. Call it two hours. "I'll be there in three. Stay where you'll be safe. And stop drinking." I hung up before he could start yammering at me.

I didn't like Jack Beecham. I respected the hardness of his fists and the way he'd laugh if you gave him a hard shot, but I didn't like his angry destructive race to the end. Still. Five grand.

Augie was up for a ride in the middle of the night, for a big one. He'd been in the Marines and *Semper Fi* was tattooed into his soul. I could trust him to keep his head when things got hairy. Besides, he had a car and knew how to drive.

After I dressed, I slipped into a little spot in my boat, the *Pelican*, a place under this and behind that and pulled out a sealed plastic box. Inside was a Colt Police Positive with a short barrel and chambered for .38 calibre. The Colt is for needful times. It's small, light, and doesn't toss brass all over the place.

I put on a jacket and slipped the gun into a pocket. I walked out of the marina into the parking lot, where Augie picked me up.

Ten minutes later we were onto I-75 heading south at seventy miles per hour, in the black of the night.

◂ ▸

"Beecham," I said as he answered. "We're in the parking lot. Red Ford Taurus."

"We?"

"I can't drive and protect you at the same time. We'll pull up to the front. You walk out the doors and into the car as I step past you. Understand?"

He did. Beecham had four inches on me, but he knew when I put my mind to it, I am like that Natalie Grant song. I will not be moved.

Augie pulled into the sweeping driveway before the casino and rolled up to the entrance. I stepped out of the car and put a ten spot in the doorman's hand and told him to open the rear door. Next, I started for the entrance.

Beecham saw us and came out at a fast walk, not a panicked run. Behind him trailed a couple of hard boys, just getting ready. I was walking slowly. The thugs didn't even notice me. I kicked one in the balls and thumped the other with the roll of nickels in my fist. I turned and sprinted back to the car. Augie pulled out sharply, making the tires squeal.

Beecham was shaking in the back. The adrenaline in his system had him so wired he practically bounced out of the car.

I turned. "Money."

He handed me an envelope. Hundreds. I peeled ten off and shoved them into Augie's breast pocket. I put the envelope inside my jacket.

"Smooth," Beecham said. "You made that smooth. I'll bet we're home free."

"Frank," Augie said. "Lights behind us, coming up fast."

"Lose them."

His Taurus wasn't exactly factory and Augie liked nothing better than speed, except cooking. He just pushed the pedal down and it felt like we were in a rocket on the Bonneville Salt Flats.

We left them behind but not as quickly as I would have liked. We flew down FL-29 toward I-75. Should we go along 75 through the big cypress swamp to Miami, hook back into

Fort Myers on 75 North, or drop down to the Tamiami Trail and head for Miami? I didn't like any of these routes.

"Can you lose them?" I asked Augie.

"I have an idea," he said.

He killed the car's lights. Now we were flying blind. Then he put the car into neutral and turned off the engine. Now we were flying in a rapidly slowing car without power for the breaks. In a newer car this would have locked the steering.

He pulled hard to the right and slid us off the road into a little fruit-stand lot. He stood on the brakes and pulled us into some bushes coming to a stop, with the green waving around our windows.

Thirty seconds later the pursuing car raced by.

We waited. We waited some more. Ten minutes later the same car roared by on the far side of the road. After they had passed, Augie started his car and we headed off once more.

"Route?" Augie asked.

"You're driving. You choose," I replied.

"There's a non-stop flight from MIA to CHS on American Airlines at 2:45 p.m.," I said to Beecham. "Unless you want to fly charter."

"No," Beecham answered after a second. "I don't think we'll need that." How wrong he was.

As we drove, he told us how God's fortune had simply fall-en into his lap.

"I'd been playing pretty much the whole evening. Blackjack went nowhere. The dice at the craps table were cold, so I wandered over to the roulette. I'm not much for the wheel, but something told me to stay.

"I started with a couple chips. Alternating red and black and the pile began to grow. I was up a thousand when I decided to go for a corner bet. Something or someone must have moved my pile. When the wheel stopped on 24, I saw my entire stack sitting firmly on the number. It paid off thirty-five to one. Even after the 35 percent withholding, I was up more than fifty thousand."

He paused. The car rolled through AlligatorAlley in the night and silence. Neither Augie nor I spoke. It was his story to tell.

"Well, when you win that type of money people notice. And I guess I was a bit loud. They took me for a dumb redneck and I could read what they planned in their eyes. If I'd taken a cheque, they would've just picked me up immediately and before they'd finished with me, I'd be begging to sign it over to them. No, I thought. This goes to Darlene. So I called you, Frank."

I nodded. Darlene was the only good thing Beecham had made in his entire life, the only thing he hadn't ruined. She would be seventeen now. He'd shown me her picture more than once. A shy-looking skinny blonde with her mother's features and her father's size. First string in girls' basketball all through high school.

"She's in Charleston. I'm going there and I'm giving her this. It'll pay for four years of college. Darlene's brighter than me or her mother."

The flight was scheduled tomorrow afternoon. Where should I stash him until then? Did I believe his story about the roulette wheel? Stranger things had happened. Beecham had spent more time in casinos than in churches. I always thought he was punishing himself for something. Perhaps he just needed to lose every cent before he could go back out to the rigs in the gulf, the one place he really felt at home.

"Lots of hotels near Miami International," I said to Augie. "Think of anything better?"

"I have some friends from the Corps down there. Might find something further off the radar if you want?"

"Do it."

He didn't find us five-star. We spent the night in the car in a garage at the back of a property in Homestead. Around ten we picked up breakfast from a hamburger drive-thru.

"So we drop you off at the entrance?" I asked Beecham.

"No. I want you to take me through to the gate. I want you with me until I walk into the plane."

"Going to need a ticket to get past security."

"You have your passport?" he asked.

I could have said no but it didn't sound like much. Augie could wait for me in the short-term parking until the flight was in the air. I took my pistol out of my pocket, showed it to Augie and slipped it into the glove compartment after he nodded. The TSA wouldn't approve of it.

Augie pulled up to Departures and I stepped out first and opened the door for Beecham. There are two ways to cover a man. You walk in front of him, but then everyone behind you is the black zone. Alternately you walk behind him, in which case he can walk into trouble. I chose the second. Why? At least I could keep an eye on Beecham.

We strode up to the counter. He bought two refundable tickets from Miami International Airport to Charleston International Airport, nonstop. No baggage. He paid for them with cash. Maybe they see a lot of that in Miami. Nobody blinked.

We walked to security, where they asked questions and scanned us with wands.

Then we waited, drinking bad coffee and thinking our own thoughts. Thirty minutes and I'd be shut of him. When they announced his flight was ready to board, Beecham wanted to use the airport facilities.

"I just don't fit well into those airplane bathrooms."

So I let him.

As he entered the bathroom, I noticed something from the side of my eye. I didn't know what it was but I knew Beecham and I had made a mistake. Whoever wanted the money knew about Darlene and Charleston and this flight.

I raced into the bathroom.

Two of them. Beecham had one by the coat lapels, whapping him in the face with all his might, while the other smashed his fist time and again into Beecham's kidney. I saw blood.

I took the second one with a straight open-handed blow that caught part of his jaw and rattled the dust out of his attic. He turned to me. He had blood on the shank in his hand. I didn't wait. I kicked him in the shin, the kneecap, and the groin – bang, bang, bang.

The first fellow was taking the punishment Beecham was handing out and whipping him with a homemade sap. I stepped in, keeping clear of the sap, and rabbit-punched him in the back of the head. As he turned all sloppy eyed, I grabbed the arm with the sap and dislocated his elbow.

Beecham sank to the floor, blood from his back turning the tiles a burgundy red.

"No," he said. "No. We have to make that plane."

"They won't let you on; if they did, you might bleed out before it lands."

"No. Have to get the money to Darlene. You don't understand. Have to do the right thing."

"Dying's not the right thing."

Someone walked in.

"Call an ambulance," I snapped and turned back to Beecham.

He tried to stand but didn't make it. He looked surprised, as if his body had never betrayed him before.

"Damn," he said under his breath.

"Here," he continued, taking off a money belt which was bloody in places. "Here's her address. Tell her Daddy wanted to give her this stuff himself but he couldn't make it. Can I trust you, Frank?"

I smiled. "You have to decide that yourself."

"Damn you," he said. "Always was a hard case. Now go."

I got out of the bathroom seconds before the airport security arrived. The money belt was stuffed into my armpit, held there by keeping my elbow in tight. I caught the last call for the flight. Inside the cabin, I called Augie and told him what had happened and hung up.

Buckling in, I noticed blood on my hands. The flight attendant noticed too.

"Bad paper cut," I said and asked for a wipe. She brought one but gave me a disapproving look.

I had one hour and forty minutes to figure out how to stay alive at the other end of the flight.

After the plane was in the air, I used the washroom. I checked the money belt and opened each packet of bills, looking for a homing device. Nothing. The mugs knew Beecham well enough to know where he planned to go. There was more than the big fifty Beecham had mentioned. Enough to kill a man over.

In Charleston, I ducked into a washroom. They knew about the flight to Charleston. Did they know where Darlene lived? I hadn't seen anyone and I hoped no one had spotted me. Sometimes the bull wins and sometimes the rabbit wins. When the wolves are on your trail, it's a call you have to make.

A new rush of people into the bathroom meant another plane had landed. Time to exit with the crowd, and I did. Down where the cabs waited I took the next in line.

"Where to, Mac?"

I gave him a fifty. "A FedEx store."

I bought two boxes and packed them myself. I addressed one to Augie, with a note for him to hold it for me. If I didn't make it, he might as well have the rest of the five grand. The second went to Darlene with fifty grand in it. I just wrote a note.

"Your father wanted you to have this. Keep it quiet for a while."

I sealed both packages and paid for three-day deliveries. When I came out, the cab was still waiting. I gave him the address and he took me there. The money belt was still comfortably full.

I had the cab wait as I knocked on the door. When Darlene opened the door, she looked older than her father's picture. I waved to the taxi and he took off.

In my pocket, I had my phone open, with the speaker turned down to nothing.

"Darlene," I began. "I had to leave your father in Miami. He wanted to come but he had an accident."

She led me into the house. Someone pushed the muzzle of a gun against my neck. It felt cold. I didn't move. My hand in my pocket dialled 911.

"Yes, Jack's sick. Trouble was he didn't have the money, did he?" the second thug who stepped from the dining room said. He had a gun as well. "We figured you might be coming here."

"So you're robbing us at gunpoint," I said. "What if I hadn't come?"

"The ladies would have told us who you were, eventually," he replied. "Now, where's the money?"

Slowly, I lifted my shirt and unbuckled the money belt. It fell to the floor.

The nasty one started toward it, looked at me and said to Darlene, "Sweet pea, pick it up and give it to me."

She picked it up. "There's blood on it."

"Damn right, probably your father's blood. Tough guy. Most guys get a shiv in the kidney and they're down for the count. Not him."

He herded us into the living room, where Darlene's mother sat. "Sit down over there. Bennie, get the car."

He stood over us, the gun in one hand and the money belt in the other. He was weighing something. He wanted to get clean away but he also hungered for more, to mix his type of fun with this business.

"Mr. Hotshot, let's see what's in those pockets."

Airline ticket stubs, a paperback book. Some tissues. My wallet and, last, my phone. If he checked the call history, I was dead.

"Buddy, Beecham didn't pay you?"

"When we got here. That was the plan."

"Sucker."

With taking his eyes off me he said, "Benny, go and get the car started. I'll be there in a bit."

Benny went out the door. Suddenly I felt cold. I was sweating. What did this thug want to do that he didn't want Benny to see. Nothing good came to mind.

I waited. He wanted something more. What could I give him? Desperately I said, "Yeah, Beecham never thought you guys would come to his daughter's place. Didn't think anyone but him was at risk. Last I saw, he was bleeding like a pig. I wonder if he made it to the ICU."

Darlene gasped. She clutched her hands together. I turned to her. My left leg was off the couch and under me.

From outside, a loudspeaker began, "This is…"

I didn't wait. He had turned toward the front door for only a moment but that was enough. I drove in low, my chest at my knees, and came up a little to smash my shoulder into his stomach.

The air burst out of his lungs with the sound of a pricked balloon. I didn't stop. My left hand hammered blow after blow into his balls. I grabbed the gun and twisted it out of his grasp, breaking a finger. Then I hit him with it three times.

"Darlene, go and open the front door. Keep your hands up and in front of you. Move slowly,"

I dropped the gun. The cops stormed inside in seconds. All helmets and bulletproof vests, with assault rifles. As they forced me to the ground, I relaxed and smiled. No one would die today.

BURNT OFFERINGS

Hermine Robinson

Dale handed the joint back to the girl – a girl of unspecified age because he never bothered to ask and she never offered – probably not underage, but with a name like Chelsea you never knew. *If* that was even her real name. Ryan had vouched for her, but lately Ryan's judgement left a lot to be desired. The dumb shit had passed out in a corner of the bar halfway through the evening, leaving Dale to pick up the tab and deal with the girl.

Chelsea seemed okay. She had propped Ryan up in the booth, pulled a ball cap over his eyes, and dropped a twenty on the table for the bar owner to call a cab when Ryan woke up. Then she offered to go home with Dale. He had not planned for her to stay overnight, but who was he to question the fates, and the whole thing seemed like a sweet deal until now, when she started asking too many questions.

"Come on, I want to hear about the fires you set," said Chelsea.

Was she really begging to hear this shit? "I don't know what you're talking about."

"Bullshit. That's why Ryan introduced us. He said you knew something about fires."

Ryan, the fucker. Dale should have known better than to trust an idiot who liked spreading tales to any young girl willing to give him the time of day – or night.

"Knowing about fires isn't the same thing as setting them."

Dale could not get a read on the girl. He watched Chelsea inhale deeply and he felt better – smoking up made it less likely that she was a cop.

"What are you staring at?" she asked, squinting through the blue haze. Chelsea sat cross-legged on the end of the bed across from Dale. He could not sit like that anymore; his knees and hips would not take it. Maybe that was what bothered him about her: girls her age thought men in their thirties were ancient, and Dale was pushing a hard-fought forty.

"Are you a cop, Chelsea? A snitch maybe?" It was a stupid question to ask but Dale could not help himself. Paranoia.

Chelsea laughed and leaned forward across the bed. "Do you wanna check if I'm wearing a wire?"

Dale looked past the gold locket dangling from Chelsea's neck, down the V-neck of her top. A pink bra, probably the push-up kind, gave her more cleavage than a girl her size deserved. No sign of a wire from here either.

Chelsea smiled as he stared. "Why would you think I'm a cop?"

"Because you ask a lot of questions."

"Blame my grandmother. She's the one who told me that polite girls show an interest in other people and don't only talk about themselves all the time."

Dale leaned back against the headboard, still enjoying the view. "Tell me about your grandmother."

Chelsea crawled forward and handed over the joint before fumbling with the locket and pointing to the photo inside.

Dale barely gave it a glance. Maybe it was his eyesight, or the crappy light from the bedside lamp, but all those grainy old portraits looked the same to him.

"My grandmother raised me until I was eleven."

"Where was your mom?"

"Are *you* a cop?" asked Chelsea.

Dale choked as he inhaled. It made him feel like a rookie – hacking and coughing. The girl looked concerned, but not about Dale. She slapped at the glowing cherry melting a hole in the cheap nylon bedspread where he had dropped the joint. She made an old lady tsk-tsking sound while she snuffed the ember and put the remnants of the joint on the saucer Dale kept beside his bed. "You should be careful," she said when he finished coughing. "You could start a fire."

"I thought you were into setting fires."

"Setting fires is easy. Any idiot with a match can commit arson," said Chelsea. "I'm more interested in how you get away with it."

"Who said anything about arson? Can't a guy have a couple of bad breaks?"

"Not really. One fire is unlucky, but more than that and someone's going to figure it out."

Dale shrugged. No one had figured it out yet, and right now the only thing he wanted to figure out was how much of Chelsea's cleavage was real and how much was padding. "Mind if I check you out for that wire?" He pulled her toward him.

Chelsea ran her hands up under his T-shirt and said, "Me first."

The girl did not act like any kind of cop Dale knew, undercover or otherwise. Afterward, Chelsea lay propped up on one elbow beside him, her clothes strewn at the side of the bed, except the panties she had put back on, along with his grey T-shirt. Dale was not a big man, but on her his shirt hung loose like pyjamas. There was not as much padding to her bra as he had suspected either – and no scars from surgery that he could see. Some girls were lucky that way, all skinny and tight but with a nice rack. Lucky her; lucky him. Dale lit a cigarette.

"You shouldn't smoke in bed. It's dangerous."

First the conniption about the joint and now she was lecturing him on smoking in bed. The girl definitely had an issue with fires. Dale butted his smoke after another couple of drags. Fuck it, he should quit anyways. Chelsea played with her locket, flipping it open to the grainy picture inside before closing it again and winding the chain through her fingers. Dale said, "So, you never told me why you were raised by your grandmother instead of your mom."

Chelsea looked relieved to talk about it. "My mom was only fourteen when she had me and took off before I really knew her. Then, after Grandma died I got bounced around to foster homes because Mom was too strung out to have custody."

"It sounds like a tough kind of life for a young girl," said Dale. "So, how long ago was that? How old were you when your grandmother died?"

"I know what you're trying do." Chelsea laughed. "But it's a bit late to try and figure out if I'm jailbait." She sat up, and pulled her hair back. "Okay, you tell me. How old do you think I am?"

Dale guessed eighteen – a safe number because the underage girls liked to think they looked "old enough" and the older ones liked it when they looked young enough to still get carded. He could not remember if the bar where they met held to such formalities – probably not.

"Hah! I'm twenty-three."

Dale played along. "You barely look legal. I thought I was guessing high."

"Everyone thinks I'm younger. It's because I'm a tiny thing and people underestimate me."

"I'll bet they do," said Dale. "But even twenty-three is kind of young to hook up with an old man like me. So what's your angle?" Chelsea considered the question a moment too long; Dale waited for the lie.

"I like older guys," she said, "and Ryan told me you only smoked good pot and didn't mind sharing for the right price."

Halfway to the truth, thought Dale. It did not explain her earlier interest in the fires. "That's selling yourself kind of cheap, isn't it?"

"Maybe, but you know that's not the only reason I'm here." She tiptoed her fingers down the line of hair below his navel toward his shorts. "Tell me about the fires."

"Okay, but it'll cost you." Dale's body responded to her touch; he reached under the grey T-shirt to slip it off her. Afterward, he lit a fresh cigarette and offered Chelsea a drag, but she declined. "Why would you smoke pot, but not cigarettes?"

"My grandmother hated cigarettes. She couldn't stand the smoke because of her asthma, and ever since I was little she drilled those anti-smoking messages into my head."

"But not the ones about drugs."

"Maybe if she'd lived long enough." Chelsea played with the locket again, snapping it open and shut.

"Did you get anything else from her besides a locket and advice about not smoking?"

"This." Chelsea showed Dale the gold band with a tiny diamond she wore on her thumb. "It was her engagement ring."

It would barely pass as a promise ring nowadays, thought Dale, but maybe back in the day it was adequate. His brain felt too tired to do the math and figure out how long ago that might have been. He lit another cigarette. "Grab me a beer."

"Only if you put down the cigarette while I'm gone. One burn hole in the bedspread is enough."

"Are you scared I'm going to burn down the place? Because I'm not into that anymore."

"That's not what Ryan said."

"Ryan doesn't know shit and should keep his fucking mouth shut," said Dale. "Now go get me a beer."

Chelsea shrugged herself back into Dale's shirt before padding out of the bedroom. She came back with a single can, popped the top and took a swig before holding it out to Dale. The girl had some nerve. "Hey, get me a fresh one. I don't need your backwash."

"Last cold one." Chelsea wiped the top of the can with Dale's T-shirt and handed it to him. "You afraid of girl germs?"

Dale grabbed the can, peered into it, and used a corner of the bedspread to wipe the top again before draining it. It tasted like backwash. Fizz and spit. Dammit. The girl was getting to him. He glanced at the alarm clock on his dresser across the room. It was not too late to get rid of her. Maybe he could kick her out and get a good night's sleep.

"So I got you the beer," said Chelsea. "Now tell me about the fires. Not just setting them, but the secret of getting away with it. Pretty please." She sat cross-legged near the end of the bed again, elbows on her knees and chin resting in her hands like a kid waiting for a bedtime story.

Twenty-three years old, my ass, thought Dale. How had he gotten hooked up with a teenybopper? Fucking Ryan, that's how. "Nothing to tell," answered Dale. "Fires are terrible accidents and even the stuff that doesn't burn is ruined by smoke, so you lose everything."

"But just the stuff you don't care about, right?"

"No, important things too, because it looks suspicious if all your photo albums and the new television just happen to be at a friend's house."

"So then, what's the point? Why burn down a house for no good reason?"

"I didn't say there was no reason. It just can't be about stuff," said Dale, "or money."

"So you just burn them for fun?"

"Hell, no!" Dale grabbed Chelsea's arm, pulled her forward, and twisted her around to pin her on the bed with his hand across her neck. "Is that what Ryan's been saying? That we set fires for fun?"

Chelsea jerked her head side to side as she kicked to get free. Dale pressed harder, and her eyes grew wide before he let her go. Fire was one thing, murder another. The girl rubbed her throat and gasped a couple of times before using the grey T-shirt to wipe away her tears. *His* grey T-shirt, and Dale wanted it back before he sent her packing. Chelsea moved warily around the bed, just out of reach. Dale leaned back against the headboard, biding his time. Her clothes were right beside the bed; he reached down to pull them closer. He liked the fear in her eyes as he stroked the lace of her cute little pink bra.

"It was just a question," she said. "You didn't have to try and kill me."

"I don't kill people," said Dale, "and I don't set fires for fun, no matter what Ryan says."

"That's not what Ryan said, but it doesn't matter because Ryan's a fucking idiot and you need to get rid of him before it's too late. I'll help you."

Whoa. Dale kept the leer frozen on his face as he stared at Chelsea, but his fingers hesitated in their travels over pink lace. "Ryan's my friend," he said.

"No, he's your stooge," said Chelsea. "A dangerous one because he talks too much, and the first time he gets caught setting one of your fires he'll talk even more."

"Ryan knows shit."

"If you say so."

"Whatever he's told you is all hearsay – nothing that anybody could prove. I had some bad luck with fires a few years back but that's all it was." Dale could still see the impression of his hand on her neck, and the locket twirling at the end of its chain glinted yellowy-orange in the incandescent light from the bedside lamp. But the glint in Chelsea's eyes as she crawled across the bed was from something else. *Holy fuck, she's getting off on this fire thing*, thought Dale.

"So tell me about those fires." She ran her hand up his leg. "How did it start?"

"The first fire was an accident. I was crashing on a friend's couch for a few nights while I was out of work and some bonehead dumped an ashtray in the garbage after a party. I didn't lose much, but everyone still felt sorry for me anyways. I got new clothes, job offers, and some agency found me a place to stay until I was back on my feet."

"Oh." She sounded disappointed. "Were you the bonehead who dumped the ashtray?"

"No, but everybody I met had stories about stuff like that, and the whole thing got me thinking about all the accidental fires that happen. I set up a little side business, helped a few people out of some jams and did them some favours. It was all good as long as they followed the rules. No padding the insurance, or moving valuable stuff out of the house at the last minute."

"That makes sense," said Chelsea. "It's all good so long as nobody gets hurt."

"That's the first rule, nobody gets hurt."

"Except things don't always work out that way, do they? I heard that someone died because of one of your fires."

Dale stared at Chelsea. What the fuck had Ryan told her? "It wasn't the fire. A neighbour lady died of a heart attack. Nothing to do with me, but it's what I got for breaking rule number two." Chelsea did not ask about the second rule. Had Ryan told her that one, too? She played with the locket. Dale felt like ripping it from her throat so he could throttle her good before doing the same to Ryan. "I promised myself to never start a fire for my own benefit – that was rule number two – but then I hit on some hard times and I figured 'what the hell' and did it anyways."

"How?"

"Paint rags," said Dale. "I was staying in a rental house for free while I helped fix up the place, except the fucking owners reneged on the deal we made. Suddenly they were accusing me of stealing tools and demanding next month's rent after they had promised I could work it off in trade. They knew I didn't have a job, the assholes. So I got a bit careless with the paint supplies and left some oily rags too close to the furnace."

"Spontaneous combustion."

"An accident," said Dale. "I lost everything I owned, but it didn't matter because I was headed for the street anyways. I got a fresh round of sympathy, and the fire covered up the fact that a bunch of power tools were missing from the basement."

"So no one suspected?"

"They could suspect all they wanted, but nobody could prove anything. There's all kinds of solvents and chemicals around when a house is getting renovated." Dale closed his eyes. God, he felt tired. That fire was the riskiest one he ever set because it connected directly to him and he knew – *he fucking knew* – everything had to be exactly right. And still, he had not anticipated every possible circumstance. It was supposed to be small, confined to the basement, but it grew too fast. Something flammable in the walls maybe. Dale barely made it out before the whole place lit up. The flames blew out a side window and spread to the fence. Totally out of control. That was when the lady next door ran out screaming about her house going up in flames next. In the middle of her freak-out she grabbed her chest, started gasping for breath and collapsed on the lawn while Dale stood there shivering in his underwear. All before the first fire truck arrived.

Afterward, the owners of the rental gave him no end of grief even though they were insured and should have been grateful to him for burning down their firetrap. Yeah, he learned a lot from that fire.

"Cops aren't stupid," said Chelsea, "and insurance companies are buggers for paying out if they suspect arson."

"I personally never collected a cent from insurance, and the arson guys know a lot of fires are accidental – especially when there's no obvious motive like money."

Chelsea did not look convinced. "Not everyone has paint rags lying around."

"Grease fires, candles at Christmas, careless smoking," said Dale. "It's like the holy trinity of arson, and that doesn't include crazy shit like towels soaked with massage oil if the client happens to be a masseuse."

"Client?"

"Ryan has a knack for finding the kind of people interested in fires," said Dale. "It's not a crime to talk about it, and that's what we're doing right now. Just talking. But there hasn't been a direct link between me and any fires in over a decade."

"You're wrong. Ryan is the link," said Chelsea. "That makes him dangerous. You have to get rid of Ryan."

She was right, and if some young punk girl like her could figure it out, it was probably already too late, but cutting Ryan loose was risky too. It might give the shithead even more reason to talk.

"Do you want me to get rid of Ryan for you?"

"What?"

Chelsea repeated the offer. She stood at the end of the bed, wearing Dale's T-shirt, the one he wanted back. Twin pinpoints of pain behind his eyes made the room spin when he tried to focus on her face, to see if she was serious. Dale could not think straight and suddenly nothing made sense – not Ryan, not the girl, nor the fact that sitting up was too much effort. He barely managed to wave an arm toward the door. Chelsea turned and left the room. Good. He needed her to leave.

"My grandmother didn't die of a heart attack, you know. She had an asthma attack from the smoke of the fire you set – from the panic of seeing it spread to her house. Our house. I lost everything that day." Dale dragged his eyes open. The girl was back. He could not tell if it was Chelsea's voice or something else that had pulled him out of his stupor. She blathered on about smoke and fire until it filled his senses. Only then did he realize it was real. Acrid smoke rose at the side of the bed as the first lick of flame spread from her pink bra to other clothes, to random tissues and his pack of butts. Dale tried to roll away from the fire but his body did not respond. He looked helplessly at Chelsea as she tossed some pills on the bed.

"In the beer," she said by way of explanation. "I slipped a couple to Ryan at the bar too, so he probably won't remember too much about introducing us." Chelsea popped a pill in her mouth before she dragged Dale partway off the bed, leaving him hopelessly tangled in the bedspread as smoke billowed across the ceiling. She stayed low the whole time; Dale wondered if her grandmother had taught her that, too. Toxic smoke killed more people than the fires.

"Oops – almost forgot," said Chelsea as she crawled toward the door. "I'm supposed to lose something important." She yanked the locket from her neck and tossed it back at Dale.

CIRCLE OF BLOOD

Simon Strantzas

I'd been staying at the Y for a few weeks, trying to keep a low profile. I signed in under the name "Robin Littlejohn" not only because the name made me laugh, and sometimes laughing was all I had left, but also because Detective McCray was on the warpath and the name *Owen Rake* on the register would have stuck out. McCray was built like a solid wall, and wanted me like I was the one who put that scar on his face. Sometimes I think he and Mrs. Mulroney had something going on and that was why he was so mad at me. Other times I think it's just because my screw-up got her killed, but either way, the cop was gunning for me. For some reason, it seemed like the best way to avoid the law was by turning tricks in the dark of the YMCA.

Jake Rasceta was the kind of suited douchebag you see on the street all the time – a Bluetooth earpiece in wherever he went, speaking at a volume one decibel higher than everyone else. He was about a foot taller than me and a foot wider. When he approached me as I smoked by the emergency exit I'd propped open, I thought he was there to kick my ass. Instead, already sweating, he looked me dead in the face and said, "I'm looking for a blowjob." I told him I knew where he could find one.

Afterward, things were awkward. He wanted to leave but had to get dressed. I wanted him gone so I could gargle for a million years but I couldn't leave him alone in my eight-by-eight. The last thing I wanted was anyone going through my stuff and finding something they shouldn't. So I waited while he put his suit back on, noticing how much more he was sweating than before. He was silent, especially compared to the shit he'd been saying to me only ten minutes earlier, and in that silence I heard the traffic outside my closed window and the coughs and gags of my neighbours. It was a peaceful Sunday morning, I thought. Not at all when I expected to see something bizarre. It caught my eye as he opened his thick wallet to pay me for services rendered. There, tucked within a clear plastic envelope, I saw his gigantic face mugging for the camera, behind him some cheap department-store backdrop. He stood with his wife and what I assumed was his kid, but the photo didn't show all of that – at least, not clearly. It showed him and his wife, and something else I wasn't seeing right.

Most people don't notice these sorts of things – Rasceta hadn't – but I've been around too much crazy shit in my years to let it go. Rasceta was fixing his tie around his throbbing throat when I got out of my chair and went to investigate what I saw. Rasceta immediately hid his wallet from me, glaring, and shoved me away, hard. His skin was red from overheating, but he continued to add more layers of clothes. I wondered if my ass-kicking hadn't been so much cancelled as delayed, and started babbling small talk in hopes of avoiding a confrontation. If I got thrown out of the Y, I had no idea where I'd end up.

"Hey, take it easy. I just wanted to see that picture. Was that your family?"

He seemed startled by the question. He wasn't really paying attention. I saw it in his glassy bloodshot eyes.

"In your wallet. The photo?" I said again, louder in case he hadn't heard me the first time. "Do you mind if I take a glance at it?"

He looked at his pocket, then at me strangely. "Why, ah, why would... No, I don't—"

He was trying to protect them, I respected that. But it was clear something was seriously wrong with Rasceta, and I suspected that photo would give me an idea of what.

"Seriously, let me see it. I'm trying to help."

For a second he hesitated as though he was going to do it. Maybe he knew, subconsciously, he needed help and wanted to reach out, but I guess his programming kicked back in because his face scrunched in anger and he increased a foot in size. At least, that's how I remember it.

"Fuck off. You have your money."

Which I did but that wasn't the point. I would have explained if he hadn't stormed out of my room without even a thank-you, slamming the door hard enough his cash lifted up and floated around the room. It was probably a good thing I'd closed the window.

Here's the thing: people don't always know what's best for them. They know what they want, but there's a difference between *want* and *need*. I saw what Jake Rasceta needed, and all he could see was what he wanted. There was little I could do to stop him.

I should have let things go and forgotten about the guy. He'd almost taken my head off when I tried to help him, but that photograph in Rasceta's wallet wouldn't stop haunting me. Whenever I closed my eyes, I saw his child squirming like some deformed reptile breathing slowly while mucousy black eyeballs rolled in its head. I knew if someone didn't do something about it there would be dire consequences. And I was the only one remotely qualified for the job.

Nowadays it's amazing how much information you can find about people using the internet. But what's equally amazing is how much is available off the internet, and always has been. My life would be a hell of a lot harder if it weren't. It's there for anyone to dig up if they know where to look and aren't afraid of getting their fingers dirty. Or taking their time, too. A whole lot of time. Luckily, I met all the qualifications. Jake Rasceta didn't try too hard to hide who he was, but guys like him, guys who help me pay my rent when I have rent to pay, they don't usually plan their actions too carefully. I make my money in more of a spur-of-the-moment fashion. Kind of like that chocolate bar at the cash register you don't know you want it until it's in your face, and less than an hour after you've swallowed the thing you start to regret it. But, oh, during that time nothing tastes better. At least, that's what I imagine. For me, it was just a means to an end. And I knew Jake was going to come close to his if I didn't get to him soon.

Finding where Rasceta lived and getting there were two different stories. At the time I was travelling lighter than usual, and the price of two buses – one out of the city, the other through suburbia – ate up more of Rasceta's money than I wanted. I would have hitched it if I could, but few drivers are interested in picking people up anymore. Still, I made it to Collingwood in only a few hours. Everything was so quiet and still, and the trees on the streets weren't in tiny concrete planters but in a long string along the side of the road. I felt horribly out of place, as though I were wearing a neon overcoat and marching to the beat of a bass drum. Those few couples I passed on the street stared at me like I was from Mars, and they were right; we were from different planets.

Rasceta's house was one of those split-level ranch houses you see being built along the highway north of the city. It looked like every other house on the block, its bricks painted a godawful fake terra cotta. It was still early in the day, so I figured I'd catch him before he left for his sales job. I knocked on the door and waited. It was a nice morning out, which made it strange that I couldn't hear any birds. Maybe they were avoiding the place? I rang again, then knocked.

When Rasceta answered the door he only had enough time to say, "What the fu—?" before the door slammed in my face. That half-second was enough to see the guy already looked worse. His face was sallow and sweaty and his shirt was plastered to his chest. I hoped he wasn't dumb enough to call the cops; the last thing I needed was any cockeyed company. I rapped on the window when he didn't come out and then looked inside. There was a dark-eyed woman there, terrified, hair plastered to her sweating face, holding tight to a familiar little boy. I was terrorizing them, which wasn't something I normally liked to do. I would have felt worse about it if I hadn't realized too late they were trying to distract me long enough for Rasceta to slip out the back door and sneak up on me. It was a stupid mistake, and I paid for it when his sweating hands reached around my neck and choked me. Everything went light and wishy, and in my oncoming daze I saw the face of that little boy in the window staring out at me. It seemed impossibly big, flickering as it filled the pane edge to edge, and it slowly turned. Then I realized it wasn't the face that was turning but the world. In the distance I heard a voice cursing me, calling me names, telling me to stay the fuck away from his family. It was a normal reaction, considering. Weird how you can have a guy's cock in your mouth but never really know him. I'd had enough of what he was dishing out, mainly because I knew that if I lost consciousness I'd probably never wake up again, so I did the only thing I could think to do. I grabbed hold of his balls and squeezed as hard as I could. He let go instantly, and as the blood pumped back into my head, my skull felt as though it were on fire. I coughed, my eyes a river of tears, and I knew better than to stick around long enough for him to recuperate. Instead, I stumbled down the driveway and out into the street. I half-expected him to follow me, and if he had there wouldn't have been much I could have done, but he stayed away and I was able to find a backyard overgrown enough to hide in. Needless to say, the whole intervention could have gone better.

I licked my wounds and wondered what I was going to do. I would have liked to hop on the next bus out of there but that thing was stalking Rasceta, and I wanted a better look at it. Besides, the way that kid had looked at me – maybe it was a choked-out hallucination but it didn't seem right. The kid was *flickering* when I looked at him, for fuck's sake. That sort of thing wasn't normal, and it was worth investigating. I stayed in those overgrown bushes for a few hours, though, just to make sure neither Rasceta nor his wife called in any sirens. I didn't hear any, but I haven't survived this long without being careful. Once I was sure no one was looking for me, I straightened myself out as best I could and started walking back to the Rasceta house. The road was quiet in the middle of the morning, and when I got closer to their place, I saw there was still a car in the driveway. If he was smart, Rasceta would have taken his wife and split, but something told me the guy was too big to think straight. He probably felt invincible, probably told his wife I'd never come around again. Probably told her lots except about how he met me. I bet the last thing he wanted was for her and me to talk. As for me, I wanted nothing more. At the very least, I wanted a piece of their kid. But when I got back to the house, it looked empty. I peeked in as many windows as I dared, but Rasceta and his wife were gone. What passed for their kid was nowhere to be seen.

Normally, in the city I pretty much disappear on the street, which makes life a lot easier for me. I can get around and watch people that need watching or get into places to look around when they need exploring. Or I can simply wander, trying to understand all I've seen. The city is like an open book to me – its secrets are my secrets. The suburbs, though, are like another galaxy, one where I'd stand out less if I wore an actual astronaut suit and scowled at the primitive Earthlings as I strutted around. I felt people peeking out their windows at me from behind their silk curtains. All curious who I was and what I was doing there. I didn't think I could stand the scrutiny for very long, so I did the thing I do best: I gave up and went to find somewhere to sit and ponder.

There was a park not too far from the Rasceta house, one big enough that I wouldn't be too conspicuous. Suburban parks are little oases, filled with green grass and flowers. Just the sort of thing to make you forget about cockeyed cops and weird things that look like children but definitely aren't. I almost felt normal sitting there, listening to the kids on the playground close by, ignoring the mothers henning it up on the benches around me. Had I found a bed there, I might have lain down and taken a nap. As it was, the day was getting to me and my eyes were already feeling heavy. I wanted to close them but I was afraid of what might happen if I slept. I shook myself to keep aware and once I did, I realized something was wrong. There was a lot of noise, as though the volume on the world had been turned up two notches. I heard the kids louder, and the birds were kicking up a storm. I half-thought I heard ants crawling across pavement because there was the sound of footsteps moving quickly, but I couldn't see anyone around who might be walking. I might not have noticed it if I hadn't run into crazy shit like that before, but I *did* notice it, and whatever it meant I knew wasn't good. As though on cue, as soon as that thought had formed, the sound dropped out. And this time it was noticeable, and not just to me. Even the hens stopped henning and looked around.

The birds were dead silent again. Have you ever seen a bird when a snake shows up? It was like that. Eerily silent, waiting for the predator to move on. Then I saw the Rasceta kid standing in the middle of the playground, staring right at me, his worn-down mother and sweating father not around. That did not inspire hope in me for their safety. Why else hadn't they called the police after I showed up at their door? Why else had the house looked so empty when I went back later? The kid didn't say anything or react at all to me. He simply stood there watching, and damn it if I didn't see something other than a boy in his place. He looked at me with a sort of soulless gaze, an empty vessel steered by something malignant, and part of me wanted to go over and take the bait he was trolling, but before I moved I heard voices clucking behind me. The hen party had made me their concern.

"Excuse me, but is one of these your child?"

I only barely paid attention to her. I wanted to keep my eye on the Rasceta kid.

"I said, do you have a child here? Sir?"

When I looked at her, at her fat rubbery face, I almost said something vile but noticed the lineup standing at her back, all in pecking order. Suddenly I didn't feel as inconspicuous as I'd hoped. Even the kids had slowed their games to watch me…except for that Rasceta kid. He didn't do anything at all but stare. Things were suddenly worse.

"Why are you looking at our children? Who are you?"

"I'm just relaxing in the park, lady." I hoped my indignation allayed their suspicions. The Rasceta kid went back to playing, but it was calculated. He wasn't watching me directly but he knew exactly what was going on.

"I'm not relaxing until you tell me your name and why you're watching these children."

"Goddamn it, will you back off? I didn't—"

"I will *not* back off," she said, and I knew I'd slipped, that I'd made too much of a spectacle of myself. It was time to get gone.

"Fine, fine. I'm leaving, see?" I held my hands up and turned to walk away. She clamped down on my arm to stop me while her hens advanced.

"Oh no, you don't. Not until the police get here."

This wasn't going to end well for anyone. Especially anyone around that Rasceta kid when he started feeling murderous again. I had to make a choice: fight now or fight another day. As usual, it wasn't much of a choice at all.

I have many faults, but not being aware of all the tools at my disposal isn't one of them. I know what I can do and I have a good sense of how far I can push things. This woman who was grabbing my arm, for instance: I knew how far I could push her. I could push her right the hell over. She was a sight, falling backward after I shoved her, throwing her into the grass and dirt, stunned like I'd just slapped her across the face. It shut her up, and her hens too. Long enough for me to hightail it out of there, but not before I gave them all the stink eye. I hoped it would be enough to buy me some time. I didn't know for certain if they'd called the police when they said they had, but if they hadn't they sure were going to once I was out of sight, so I had to make myself scarce until things blew over. It was back to the bushes for some cover. My home away from home.

Things were a mess, and I wasn't sure why I was bothering. No one had asked for my help; even if Rasceta had, it wouldn't exactly have done much for him or his wife. I wasn't completely sure what their kid was, but I suspected it was what I like to call a cuckoo situation – something had managed to finagle a flesh-and-blood suit and use it to infiltrate this world. It was probably just biding its time, and my unfortunate appearance caused it to escalate its plans. That, or once again I was in the wrong place at the right time. If I were smart, I'd have left Collingwood right then and there. I was already a suspected thief. Last thing I needed was to be accused of being a child molester, too. I needed to get back home. I even missed Detective McCray, that righteous bastard. But I couldn't do it; I had to stay. If not to keep that thing from destroying Collingwood, and afterward probably the world, then at least to satisfy my curiosity.

Two things happen when you hide out in bushes for a long period of time, listening to sirens and chatter from somewhere outside your vision. First, you get bored. I used to carry a paperback in my pocket to read when I was just sitting around doing nothing, but I'd read everything I really wanted to read and couldn't find anything new. It was all just trash, really. Instead, I ended up drawing over the tattoos on my arm with the stem of a leaf. For some reason, tracing those wards relaxed me. That led to the second thing: you fall asleep. I'm not quite sure when I slipped out, but I know when I woke up. It was when I was being dragged into the open by the scruff of my coat.

It took me a few seconds to figure out what was going on wasn't good; by then I had received a few kicks to the ribs to clue me in. Around me stood a circle of men, screaming at me to stay out of their neighbourhood. For a brief moment I wondered if I could suck my way out of the situation, but I didn't think they would go for it in front of each other. So instead, I rolled up into a ball and tried to cover my face and my balls. I didn't get kicked more than a few more times though, and when it stopped everything went quiet. So quiet that I didn't really want to uncover my eyes and see why. But I did, because I realized that was *exactly* what I wanted. One of my eyes was already swelling shut, so it wasn't as easy as I'd hoped, and I hurt like a son of a bitch, but I managed to stand up and look at what awaited me on the lawn: about a dozen men, all lying in pieces on their backs, dead eyes wide, staring at the empty sky.

Across the lawn, I saw the Rasceta kid. He was crouched down over one of the bodies, doing something to it I had no desire to see up close. His tiny arms were covered in gore, but not nearly as much as his face. For a second, I forgot that beneath that little boy suit was something old and soulless, until he looked at me with a gaze that made my nuts crawl up into my chest. He ran right at me, those smiling teeth getting sharper with every step.

Imagine being charged at by a vicious dog. Then imagine something worse, all long teeth and crazy eyes. The kid was practically on four legs and moving quicker than he had any right to. He leapt at me – and my brain finally kicked in and my closed fist connected with the side of the kid's face. He fell, but it only knocked him off balance temporarily; I'd done no real damage. So I dropped down and wrapped my hands around his blood-caked throat. His jaws opened and closed, revealing at least three rows of the craziest teeth I'd ever seen; his tongue darted out, short but seriously forked. His eyes were cloudy to the point of white, but they focused on me while I struggled to stay on him, although not at the same time. Like a lizard's, those eyes moved independently of one another, while the kid hissed and spat and tried to push me over. I felt the muscles in his neck as I squeezed – they were like rock. I couldn't even dig my thumbs into them, which did not bode well. There was nothing I could do to contain the kid and yet I was stuck on top of him. If I let go and ran, how far would I get? No more than a few feet before he tore me open. If I stayed, could I really outlast him? Already my strength was leaving me, but his bucking and thrashing did not seem to be slowing down. I'd put myself in bad trouble and I had to quickly figure out a plan to get out of it. Otherwise, I was going to end up on the menu. But I didn't need to bother worrying; the kid's bucking made the decision for me. With a final jump, he threw me into the air and I careened forward over the dead men on the ground. The kid watched me like a hunting dog watching a wounded duck.

I was better prepared when he charged at me again. I'd already removed my coat and when he got close, I tangled him in it, then dropped him to the ground. He was strong, but I didn't need to hold him forever. Just long enough to cinch the belt tight and form a makeshift straightjacket. He still bucked with unheard-of strength, so I put my knees right into his ribs, where I knew they'd be weakest, and put all my weight down on them. I heard the thing's muffled screams as it died in agony, shattered bone cutting though flesh like a thousand razor blades. Beneath me, my coat turned the darkest shade of red, and though the bucking stopped, the gurgling didn't. It took the kid a lot longer to die than I expected, even after I jumped on his chest a few times to make sure, digging my knees in deeper with every jump. Eventually, I had to stand to prevent a cramp, so I stomped his head a bit. That ended things a lot quicker.

I wiped my forehead. There was no way I was getting my coat back. I reached in the pockets and took out whatever I could. The rest couldn't identify me anyway. Still, to be safe, I lit the kid on fire. Then, for kicks, I took off the pants of some of the dead guys lying there. I figured it was better for all involved if it looked like some crazy circle jerk that had gone horribly wrong. At least people would understand that. I felt bad for them, but I felt worse for Rasceta. He hadn't wanted my help, and in the end it probably got him killed sooner. At least I did a favour for the rest of the people in Collingwood. They'd never know it, but I saved their lives. More or less. Still, I wasn't going to wait around for a ticker-tape parade. Instead, I got myself to the station as quickly as I could and then caught the first bus out of there. It wasn't until I saw the WELCOME TO COLLINGWOOD sign fading in the rear window that I began to calm down. To be on the safe side, I needed to lie low for a while. I checked my pocket for the rest of my money before realizing I'd left whatever I had in my coat pocket, the same coat I'd burned along with the kid.

I knew a way I could make some more cash, at least enough for a room at the YMCA. This time I vowed: *no more small talk*. It wouldn't be the last time I had to remind myself of that. I ought to get it tattooed across my fucking chest.

ROOKER

Laird Long

It was a dive off B Street. A dingy, dirty bar filled with sweaty, stinking men yelling and laughing and swearing, drinking copiously. Where there's water, there's booze.

Voltumus had plenty of water, deep beneath its sun-seared surface. Thanks to an ancient ice age that had long ago melted into the planet's cracks and crevices. And now Voltumus had plenty of "drips," the roughnecks shipped out from Earth to drill and pipe and tank the cool, crystal-clear water, barge it back to an increasingly parched home planet. Watertown was the centre of it all, a boomtown in the middle of a vast and desolate nowhere, a rugged oasis.

My drip, Kit Misker, was crowded up against the brass-railed bar that ran the length of one side of the stifling room. He was shoulder-to-shoulder with other broad-shouldered cohorts, yet strangely alone. He'd take a sip from his shot glass, then fling the lethal moon mash down his throat. Like he was building up the courage to do something out of character, perhaps out of bounds.

I watched him from a tiny round table in the corner. My table rocked with the bodies of men stumbling or shoving against it, so I held my drink in my hand, untouched.

Misker finally set his latest empty shot glass down and pushed away from the bar. He elbowed his way through the raucous throng, to the saloon-style swing doors, out into the night. I followed, getting challenged to more than one fight as I muscled my way clear of the room. Voltumus was a hostile environment.

The street was almost as packed as the bar. It was Saturday, pay had been distributed, and the drips were sloshing their money around before they returned to the dunes and the underground on Monday. Misker made his way along B Street to the canopied entrance of the Hotel Largo. He glanced right, left, stared straight ahead at the heavy, frosted glass doors.

The Hotel Largo was five storeys of sandstone brick and pulsing pleasure. The ground floor was lit up neon-bright and noisy, the other floors sporting shade-drawn windows that leaked just a little light, but throbbed with excitement. It was a brothel, thirty rookers or so inside to choose from.

I leaned against an undertaker's storefront window and waited for Misker to make his move, one way or the other. He at last gulped his protruding Adam's apple and walked forward, pushed through the front doors of the brothel.

"Pleasure dreams," I murmured, mouthing the Hotel Largo's blazing red signage.

I cooled my heels while Misker heated his loins. I'd have to break the bad news to his jealous wife back on Earth. She'd hired me to find out if her drip was cheating on her way out in the galactic wastelands. And she hadn't differentiated between real women, of which there were few, and rookers, of which there were more. She was the possessive type, a rooker as good, or bad, as the real thing.

For most, it was a fine line: was having sex with a robot-hooker actually cheating? They weren't humans, after all, just shrewdly crafted along those lines. I pulled a deck of cigs out of my jacket pocket, shook one out, getting all philosophical. Never a wise thing to do in Watertown.

Sure enough, a beefy hand slapped my cig away, another huge mitt jarring the deck down to the ground. My arms were clasped in twin vises. "Tony Galanto wants to see you, Diamond," one of the thugs growled.

They were big men, even for Watertown. They walked me over to a vehicle waiting by the curb, and we all got in as a threesome.

"I'm not swilling enough moon at Tony Galanto's joints, that it?" I cracked, when the vehicle hit zoom.

Their faces were as cool and blank as the sky.

◀ ▶

"I don't give a damn what your business is! You're working for me now!" Tony Galanto jabbed a sausage finger down at me for emphasis, blowing smoke and garlic.

The notorious business, brothel, and bargain game owner-operator towered over me in my chair. His round face was filmed with grease and sweat, like everything he touched, his corpulent body encased in a tuxedo that strained its stitching and his credibility.

"You don't have any right to hijack me off the street and into your operations," I protested. "I—"

"Shut your hole! Two-bit gumshoes don't tell me what I can't do – not on this or any planet!" His beady blue eyes glared down at me out of his fat-laden face.

I sat back in the chair, waited. At least I was still alive. Many of those called upon for conference with the galactic gangster never surfaced again, or so I'd heard. The sands of Voltumus ran deep.

Galanto barked, "One of my rookers' been stole!"

I raised an eyebrow.

"Ebony. Cost me a cool million! The latest and greatest model – fully functional." He gestured obscenely with his hands. "I can't get a replacement from Earth for another six months. I'd use the missus but, unfortunately, she's a real woman." He hacked out a phlegmy laugh.

Prostitution was legal on Voltumus, but only if robots were employed.

"What do you—"

"I want you to find Ebony, get her back! Then I'll take care of the asswipes who stole her." He turned and rumbled around his desk, sat down in his shiny brown leather chair in a whoosh of stale air. "I hear you're pretty good at jobs like that. And since you was on Voltumus anyway..." He hefted his ham hocks and grinned.

"Who do you—"

"Bim Starrett or Sedge Mackey. They run the other joy houses in town." He pursed his mouthflaps. "Tough part's going to be making sure it's her. See, with these newer models, you can easily change their eyes and hair and skin. Their tit size, too, of course. Even their body shape and length."

He grunted, his pig's eyes gleaming with obvious fond remembrances of Ebony. Then he pointed at me again. "But that's your job – to figure out how to find her and get her back. Hedge'll help you."

He looked at the screen on his desk. Our meeting was over.

◀ ▶

Hedge was a house mechanic. Every brothel had one – a computer and mechanical whiz who kept the machinery of commerce functioning, maintaining and repairing rookers. Some of the customers could be a little rough on the merchandise, and there was always normal wear and tear.

Tony Galanto's number one mechanic was a gnarled gnome of a man with a twisted grin. "Maybe you should test drive 'em all, huh?" he quipped. "There're only about five hundred spread out in fifteen different houses."

"Did Ebony have any tells? Pull to the right or anything like that?"

Hedge chortled. "Naw. That's old-school, early-model. Ebony had eight distinct personalities, from shy to sultry, all designed to give pleasure. She didn't have any flaws."

That was the thing about rookers, the way they were built: their personalities had to be friendly, accommodating. They couldn't pout or mope or get angry or murderous. In that respect, they weren't like real women at all.

I glanced around Hedge's workshop. It was in the basement of Tony Galanto's brothel on F Street, the Okay! Corral. The claustrophobic room was cluttered with computers and tools, pornographic holograms projected all over the place. Against one wall, six rookers were lined up, five females and one male, naked and turned off. Their unseeing eyes glittered obscenely in the light, their bodies shining so.

Hedge scuttled over to an ivory-skinned, big-breasted brunette with wide violet eyes and lips as red and plush as rose petals. He grinned perversely at me, then pointed and clicked a remote control. The rooker shuddered to life, her long, dark eyelashes fluttering and sensual mouth opening, her body softening, breathing.

Hedge's stumpy fingers danced on the remote, and the rooker's hair went from black to blond to red, long to short, eyes brown and then blue, skin pale to olive to black, breasts pumping up huge, body rising up taller. "You'll never find Ebony," the mechanic drooled. "Their Business Identification Numbers are easily removed and replaced. That's so they can be easily stolen – so the manufacturers can sell more units. But their software – what really runs them – is proprietary, of course." He frowned like a petulant teenager. "Even I can't hack into it, to make 'em really unique."

The rooker was now caressing Hedge's face, and other working parts due south.

"We're going to have to wait for them to steal another one, then," I grated.

Hedge looked at me, his expression sublime. "What'll that accomplish?"

"In the old West it was called rustling. Know how they stopped it?"

Hedge nestled into the rooker's arms, settling his head down on her rising and falling breasts. "Hanging?"

"Branding."

◂ ▸

Two weeks after I'd been shanghaied by Tony Galanto, another of his rookers turned up missing: Angelica, a blue-eyed pixie-faced blonde. Also going missing at the same time, perhaps coincidentally but probably not, was Galanto's wife.

I went on the prowl.

The Filly Ranch was located on the outskirts of Watertown, where the dust met the desert. It was one of Sedge Mackey's brothels. The western motif shot straight through to the white cowgirl hats the rookers wore, the silver six-shooters slung seductively from their bare hips.

Clementine was a bubbly, fun-loving redhead. I crowded her up against a wall of our pen on the second floor before she even had a chance to unlatch her chaps and unholster my gun. I thrust my tongue into her open mouth and swirled it around inside, scouring her gums in back of her front teeth with the curled tip of my sticker. My oral explorations yielded no small *T*.

That's what Hedge and I had come up with: a small *T* branded just above the upper gumline in back of the rookers' front teeth. We knew whoever was rustling Tony Galanto's joy toys would go over the sophisticated stolen equipment with a fine-tooth comb, or get his mechanic to do so, looking for any distinguishing exterior marks or under-skin identifiers, eliminating moles, birthmarks, and giveaway signs of stress and strain as required. And a rebuilt remote control would render the rooker sufficiently changed in other physical appearances for their camouflaging purposes. But it would have to be a really thorough, or kinky, house mechanic who searched behind the upper front teeth for a tiny identifying brand.

I let go of Clementine and sat down on the bed, flared a cig.

"Why, honey, I hope that ain't all you got to offer a gal?"

Her teeth shone like a constellation. She dropped the white leather chaps, eager to please, built for it in the truest sense of the phrase. All rookers were programmed to be willing and able, compliant with any human desire, all of the time. Only this time, her considerable charm was wasted.

When she strolled over to me in her cowgirl boots, her breasts bouncing like overstuffed saddlebags, I switched her off. The room remote wasn't just for working the bed and screen.

◄ ►

I worked my way across town, from west to east. By the time I hit the Hotsheet Motel on Pipeline Road, the plastic chit Tony Galanto had given me was running dangerously low on credit. I'd probed more females with tongue or finger in three days and nights than a gynecologist does in a month. It was a dirty job, but someone had to do it, I guess.

And I'd like to say that I carried my part off strictly professionally, testing the merchandise for markage and then moving on. But if I left a room in under the thirty minimum bought and allotted minutes, suspicions would be aroused. I had to kill time somehow.

So, when I pushed through the roadside glass office doors of the Hotsheet Motel, I was more than a little worn out.

This place was owned by Bim Starrett. It was done up low-track sleazy, a one-storey horseshoe loop of twenty rooms connected to the front office. The flaky paint scheme was yellow and red, the rooms threadbare, the beds creaky, the sheets hot as advertised.

Taylor was tall and skinny and tan-lined, dressed for cheap thrills in a purple tube top and pair of pink shorty-shorts. Her blonde, black-rooted hair was a fluffy mess, her war paint garish. Her mouth hung loose as her joints. She was everything you'd expect to find and pay for in a motel like that, open for business all hours.

"So, how you want it, big boy?" she slurred.

I grasped her arms and pulled her close. She groaned when I kissed her, moaned when I thrust my tongue into her mouth and curled it upwards.

I groaned. Nada.

I headed for the door, getting suddenly weary of the grind.

She grabbed my arm and spun me around. "What the fuck! Is that all you got?"

I stared at her. Taylor's heavily made-up face had darkened with rage.

"Sorry, sweetheart, but I've got miles to go before I sleep with yet another rooker."

I shook off her claw and exited, bumping into Cindy on the sidewalk outside. She was placidly bringing some dirty sheets to the front office. When we touched skin, she went into full seduction mode.

Her shtick was little girl lost, her overripe body on shameful display in a white shirt tied up at the front and a ruffled plaid skirt that barely came down to her thighs. She toed the concrete with a patent-leather shoe tip, her brown pigtails bobbing, eyes and braces glinting softly in the harsh light as she glanced up at me.

Eschewing the preliminaries, I stuck a finger in her mouth. She eagerly sucked on it. And I touched pay dirt – the small *T* brand! "We're going home, sweetie," I rasped.

Cindy blinked her liquid-brown eyes. "Back to my room, sir?"

It wasn't in her programming to go anywhere else. I manually switched her off, slung her over my shoulder. The door to room 20 opened up and Taylor glared at me. I blew her a kiss and spun around and strode forward. Right into the broad waiting chests of two male motel employees. "That's the guy," Taylor sneered.

"Takin' little Cindy for a walk?" one of the men asked.

"Dine-in only, pal," the other man growled.

They formed a solid wall of muscle, blocking my path and seriously jeopardizing my future.

I did a slow half-turn and dumped Cindy up against Taylor. "Okay, okay," I said, nice and easy. "No harm done." Yet.

I clenched my hands into fists and whirled around, hit the man on my right full in the face, knocking him backwards. I sunk a left hook into the other guy's gut, doubling him over. Followed that up with a kick to the jaw, toppling him onto the pavement. His cement head cracked on the concrete.

The other man charged me with open arms. I avoided his crushing embrace with a well-timed foot to the groin. Then I brought up my right fist and shattered it and his chin. I'm the only one who cried out, though, because my assailant was out cold, joining his buddy on the ground.

I scooped Cindy back up onto my shoulder, preparatory to rushing her over to my vehicle and zooming back to the relative safety of Tony Galanto's office. But a pointed boot-tip tripped me up. I staggered forward, spun around.

"Mrs. Tony Galanto, I presume?"

"Taylor" confirmed my suspicions by spitting in my face, trying to claw my eyes out. I clicked a short left off the point of her chin and her eyes flickered like candles. I caught her up, draped her over my other shoulder, and shuffled fast and furious for my vehicle.

"You helped Bim Starrett steal the rookers?" I said more than asked, when we were all safely zooming away from the battleground and stolen property depot known as the Hotsheet Motel. Tony Galanto's wife was in the front seat with me, Cindy in the back.

"We were going to be partners!" she retorted, rubbing her jaw. "Which is more than Tony would ever let me become."

"Then why were you working the rooms?"

Her eyes glittered defiantly. "For compassion, for empathy, for love! What a woman needs!"

I stared at her.

She shook her head. "You wouldn't understand. In a world of rookers, what chance does a real woman have? All females are property, objects, as far as men like Tony Galanto are concerned – not people." She brushed a couple of fingers under her nose. "And he'd rather get his pleasure from a rooker. They don't give him any backtalk, or demand anything of him. And there's more variety."

She blinked, tears in her eyes. "So I take my feelings where I can get them. The customers give me tenderness…and longing."

She almost had me crying. But then her voice changed. "And they give me money."

I snorted.

She suddenly pressed against me. A warm, slim arm coiled around my neck, a soft, slender hand sliding up onto my chest, then lower, where the crux of the matter lay with most men. "Don't take me back to Tony," she breathed in my ear. "He'll kill me." She squeezed the growing interest in between my legs, her body hot and inviting, like her parted lips. "We can be together – knock off Bim and take over his operation!"

She was a woman, alright: scheming and manipulative, and very, very restless.

I clipped her on the chin again, the bruise I raised there branding her as off-limits.

All I wanted to do was deliver unto Tony Galanto what was his. And then get the hell off this wild desert planet where the waters ran too deep for the likes of me to fathom.

THE LAST GOOD LOOK

Chadwick Ginther

Old Town gets practically medieval after dark.

When the trolls come out from under their bridges and the suits are made of armour, not by Armani. The old gods were long gone, or long dead, but what they'd left behind could still cause a body grief.

Case in point: the cyclops giving me the stink eye from across the tavern. Maybe he had a score to settle. Maybe I'd killed his brother, his sister, his mother, his father. Hell, maybe I'd killed them all.

I've done a lot of killing in my time.

"What're you looking at, troll?" The cyclops brayed a laugh. He sauntered closer. "Shouldn't you be under a bridge?"

The same smartass remark, time and again.

He was big, but I wasn't worried. So am I. Bigger'n most. Bigger'n him. I stood and straightened my suit jacket. I cracked my knuckles and it drowned out the jukebox.

◂ ▸

I dragged my monocular pal outside, leaving him to cool down in the biting Winnipeg winter. He should've remembered that cardinal rule: *There's always a bigger guy.*

He'd called me a troll, and he was right. But I want to set one thing straight, I *don't* live under a bridge. Pile the joke on enough times and even a troll's shoulders drooped under the weight.

It got dark early this far north – making Winnipeg a desirable vacation spot for the discerning monster. Didn't hurt that the city was perennial champ in the murder capital of Canada contest. Pick the right victim and no one's going to look for you too hard.

Out in the alley in the heart of Old Town, I heard her steps before I saw her. Light from the streetlamp and the fog of car exhaust obscured her in a halo. Her perfume smelled like wood smoke and sizzling meat. She wasn't dressed for the weather, but that didn't seem to bother her. Her lack of concern for a killing cold imbued her with a sense of casual danger. She had two-toned hair – dyed black and blue, that reminded me of the chump snoozing at my feet – and a jaw set for business. She stopped within my shade. I could feel her, a bonfire in the cold span between me and the Old Ways. I shifted my shadow.

"You're Neal?" she asked. Pupils dilated, searching for light in the darkness, melding into her smoky eye makeup, as if she were looking at me with ravenous sockets. Neal – Neelak Trollborn. Wizard of Runes. Muscle for Hire. Champion – when it suits me. Which it doesn't, these days. Step into my shadow and you'll catch a glimpse of what I've done.

"I need your help."

"My kind of help gets people hurt." When I wasn't trying to pass myself as human, my speech came out as a rumbling growl. She caught my meaning.

"Maybe I need someone hurt."

I grunted. "Who doesn't?"

She stepped back into my shade. Persistent, I'll give her that. She didn't flinch. Gave me a faint smile.

"You're dressed differently than I'd expected."

I shrugged. I knew a cheap custom tailor. Nice thing about a well-fitted suit, it can intimidate as easily as a cocked fist or a growl. Hides what you don't want seen, shows off what you do.

One last look of appraisal, and she said, "But you'll do."

Whatever she wanted, she wanted it bad – and she needed a monster to get it. Needed me. Too bad I was out of the monster business.

"No, I won't."

"Don't you want to know what I want you to do?"

I shrugged. "Does it matter?"

She didn't lean in or try and tempt me. I wondered if she knew that the sight of skin would only get me hungry. Tempting the troll inside the man was not the best way to do business.

"I need somebody found," she said, each word sharp, like steam hissing from a kettle.

Her long, manicured fingernail played with a golden hoop that bisected her lower lip while she waited for my response.

"And then what?" I asked. "If a person *only* needs someone found, they don't ask me to do the finding. They ask me when they want to turn somebody into some *body*."

She flashed me a toothy grin. Whether she appreciated the pun, or she figured I was game, I couldn't say. I didn't know what dirty deed she wanted done, but I felt the thrill, the rush, bubbling up from my marrow. The old times. The Old Ways.

I choked that thought down.

"I don't do that anymore."

◀ ▶

If she was disappointed, she didn't show it. Didn't press her case, either. Surprising. She struck me as the type who was used to being obeyed. When I got back inside, the waitress had left a drink at my table, and it wasn't alone. Someone was in my booth. He was short, squat and bald. I could smell his fear, and followed his eyes to my shadow.

"Hello, Armin," I said.

"Neelak Trollborn, as I live and breathe."

I was a popular guy tonight. I didn't like that. I'd been left alone since after the Calgary Affair.

"I mostly go by Neal, these days."

"I don't need Neal," he said. "I need your old self. Your wild self."

"You're asking a lot." I asked, "How'd you find me?"

"Does it matter?" A slight smile, playing at nonchalance, and then, "You're not too hard to spot."

I returned his smile, just as slightly. "You'd be surprised how easily Neelak Trollborn can slip through the cracks when he wants to."

"Those must be some big cracks."

"There are cracks in this city large enough to fit a linnorm through. You know that. You used to live here."

Armin drew a handkerchief from his pocket and daubed at his sweating pate.

"I need your help. You owe me that much."

And more.

"I do." Not that I was happy about the debt.

"Will you help me?"

Anyone else, I would've turned down flat. *Had* turned down flat. I slammed my drink. "Let's talk upstairs."

◀ ▶

I led him to what used to be the pub's stage. The owner gave me the space, and I kept the worst of Old Town from coming knocking on a Saturday night. I motioned for Armin to sit on the leather couch – he didn't. I poured us each a two-troll-finger tumbler of whiskey.

"So, whaddaya need, Armin?"

My old fight manager stared at his feet; antsy, by the way he was shifting his weight.

"I need you to get in the ring again, Neelak."

My surprised face looks a lot like my angry face. Armin blanched and took a step back, eyeing the stairs and ready to bolt. I stared down at my giant mitts. I hadn't realized I'd clenched them into fists until I saw the fear in his eyes.

I could see every old crack and split along those knuckles. They'd healed, but still ached sometimes when my blood got up and I remembered who I really was.

"I'm done with that," I said. "I thought you were done too. 'Bigger scores than fight stakes,' that's what you said."

"I was done, but…remember when I found you?"

I nodded.

Armin smiled. "You were trapped in a golden box. Fenced in with the bones of dead children."

"I didn't kill them," I muttered.

"I know," Armin said. "They were sacrificed to keep you in your prison. You were mostly dead yourself when I pulled you out of there."

"What's this got to do with the fight?"

"The guy who tipped me off to you – Toone? He said he had a tip on a binding ring. I found it."

Armin held up a rune-marked golden ring, rolling it from knuckle to knuckle before palming it. I couldn't tell for certain it was what he said it was. Binding rings were rare, made in the Inquisition days of Europe to bind a beast into human form, and I'd already been sleeping then. Judging from its runes, this ring could be legit.

He sighed. "Toone didn't know that the bound subject was still alive."

"They want the ring."

Armin nodded. "And they want me dead. Can't touch me personally while I hold the ring. But they don't need to. They've already killed Toone. Strong-armed everyone I've ever owed. If I don't place another fighter, I'll have to forfeit the ring."

And any safety it offered.

I asked, "Are you calling in my debt?"

He looked up at me, eyes watery. "Can't we call it a favour?"

"I don't do favours, Armin. You know that. If it's the old days and the Old Ways, I have to get paid. I can't buy whiskey with favours."

A shake of his head. A pleading look in his eyes. Strange to see on Armin's face. "I'm tapped out. I don't think I can afford your old rates, even with the friends and family discount. Not until I get this handled."

"You managed other fighters," I said. "And you're owed other favours. Call one of them."

"There's no one else." He was talking fast – desperate. I didn't like it. I'd never known him to be desperate. "Debt or no debt, haven't I respected your wishes all these years?"

I felt my head bobbing in agreement. One might call what Armin had done respect, one might also call it keeping an ace in the hole.

"Where's everyone else?"

"Dead."

Now it was my turn to take a step back. Armin had managed some tough customers. Mel – one of the Gorgon sisters – and Billy-Danny – a two-headed, three-armed ogre – came to mind immediately. Shit, he'd even had a flock of harpies on his roster for a time.

"What happened?"

"One last fight," he begged, dodging my question.

"Let me guess." Anger curled up my lip to show a little fang. "They went up against the guy you want me to fight."

"Yeah," he said, eyes alternating between his shoes and my fists. "Sorry, Neelak."

"Hypothetically, what would I be up against?"

"I don't know," Armin said, and I didn't buy it for a second. "Someone old. Older than you."

I drained my glass. "You don't fuck around when you make an enemy."

My voice was a rumble of anger, but I felt it inside, that old thrill. *A challenge*. It's been a while since I'd faced someone no one else could beat. There's always a bigger guy.

I'd grown used to it being me.

I shook my head. "Goodbye, Armin."

◀ ▶

I woke up in flames. Smoke filled my room to the top of my fourteen-foot ceiling. Sirens rang, but I knew it was a lost cause. This fire burned too hot, spread too fast, for it to be accidental. I grabbed my suit bag, cradling it to my belly to protect it as I burst through the flames and out the window. Glass shattered, scraping my arms, and then I felt a blast of heat at my back and a slap of cold at my front.

My momentum carried me across the alley. I pinballed off the opposite building wall and back into the fire escape. Rusted rivets were torn from brick, and the whole thing followed me to the ground. A dumpster slowed my fall by trying to snap my spine. I bounced to a stop under the twisted iron of the fire escape.

Somebody wanted to make a point. Somebody who knew this probably wouldn't kill me. If pissing me off was what they were aiming for, they'd succeeded.

This place was my home. And it's been a span since I felt that way about anywhere.

Watching the fire department try to control the blaze confirmed it wasn't jake. Only a few things could cause a conflagration of this scale, this quickly.

Somebody woke something up. Elemental, efreet, devil. Hell, maybe a dragon.

I thought they'd all been hunted to extinction. I shook my head and muttered "Armin" under my breath.

Big power also left a big signature behind, something that would be impossible to hide from me.

Wizard of Runes isn't a title I throw around much, and I have less cause to use those gifts than my mitts, but it looked like it was time. I may not smoke, but I always carry a lighter. There are a number of runes that deal with fire. I called to one that would speak to that primal, uncontrollable fire. Getting too close to that kind of blaze, that's the sort of thing that could take a guy back to a part of him he felt was better left buried.

I flicked the Bic. The smell of butane was absorbed immediately by the larger fire. Flames coalesced, forming a serpentine beast, curled up catlike in the shape of a crown. It glowed against the smoke of my burning home. *Dragon.* I shook my head. Worst of a bad lot. The conjured residue flew off and disappeared. It could've gone anywhere. I couldn't track the one responsible for the fire, but they'd stand out to my sight should our paths cross again. I had a feeling that wouldn't take long.

My breath misted, blending with the smoke and steam from the fire, and I got dressed. I slid a rune-marked washer into the first payphone I could find, tricking it into thinking I'd offered coin of the realm, and called Armin.

"Didn't expect to hear from you again."

Bullshit.

"Since everybody wants the old me to come out and play, may as well oblige them."

A pause. The line crackled with static. "What changed your mind, son?"

I bristled at the "son," but Armin had been a father in a way, teaching me how to get around in the world outside Old Town. "Someone burned down my place."

"I'm sorry. I never thought they'd go that far."

"Hrrm. Not as sorry as whoever did it is gonna be."

"So...you'll fight?"

"This is the last time," I said. "And you'll clear my marker, or I'm coming for you next."

A sigh. He *really* hated the idea of giving up that power over me. "Do this, and the marker's gone."

Armin must be in serious trouble. He'd held onto that bargaining chip for decades. But he also knew it was the only thing that would pull me out of retirement. He was desperate. I had been his get-out-of-anything-free card for the last twenty years; knowing Armin, his line of enemies could circle the city.

I didn't want to leave him any wiggle room. "Make it official."

A deeper sigh. "Neelak Trollborn, Wizard of Runes; Neelak Trollborn, Reaver of Cardiff; Neelak Trollborn, Shield-Breaker, Sword-Taker; Neelak Trollborn, fight on my behalf this last time and I will release your debt."

I could feel a chain going slack and being lifted over my head.

The moment before I said, "Agreed," Armin blurted, "After the fight."

The chain of debt was pulled tight again.

I growled.

Armin asked, "Do you remember—?"

"I know where the fights are." I hung up the phone.

◀ ▶

The Fighthome was in an abandoned train station, laid out in years past when the city had considered installing a subway. That station had gone from fact to myth, and been absorbed into Old Town. Through these tunnels a guy could walk to any Old Town in any city in the world.

In the audience were manitou and djinn, kumo and kami, and unless I missed my guess, more than a fair share of humans. All eager to see monster get it on with monster.

Normally, I don't like being the centre of attention. Here, under the torchlight, I felt at home. There was no neon, no fluorescents. I could stretch my shadow, and no one would run screaming. I paced the ring, cracked my neck from side to side, threw a couple quick jabs. My shadow filled the ring.

"Neelak Trollborn!" the announcer called out, rolling the *r* in troll and holding the last syllable longer than a whale's breath.

Only a few voices called out my name in response. I would've thought my return to the fights would've been enough to get me top billing, so Armin must not have lied. There must be a new big bad. I glanced over my shoulder and I could see the sweat glisten on Armin's bald head. Even with the torches, it wasn't that hot in here. He was worried about something, and it wasn't my health.

I folded my jacket over my forearm and passed it to Armin. The crowd was here for the old Neelak. That troll didn't wear a custom suit. Didn't wear much at all. In lieu of a loincloth made from the faces of my vanquished foes, my Joe Boxer would have to do.

Loosening the knot of my tie, I slid it over my head, straightened it and laid it on top of my jacket. Never wear a tie to a fight unless you're planning on strangling someone.

When I finished undressing, I said to Armin, "See this gets no blood on it."

The announcer called out my opponent: "Halftone!"

It was the woman from the alley. The one who'd wanted someone found. She looked at Armin, and that look told me all I needed to know.

A halo of fire runes shone atop her head like a crown. She was also the dragon who'd burned my home. She was the one after Armin. Unless I missed my guess, she was trapped in human form. Her eyes were burnt coals, embers smouldering behind thick lines of her eye makeup. She stomped out of her alcove, and the crowd scurried away like rats.

I didn't let the fact that Armin's heavy was a woman throw me. Go three rounds with a Valkyrie and you won't be cracking wise about "hitting like a girl."

Drums boomed, bouncing off the stone walls. Halftone's head was bowed, ever so slightly, and her eyes bored through me from under the scowl she directed at Armin.

She wore a gauzy white dress and army boots. When she reached the ring, she kicked aside her boots and stood slightly pigeon-toed while the announcer went to work. Halftone didn't primp or pose as some fighters did, didn't play to the crowd like a fake television gladiator.

I say things like *ring* and *fight*, but we're not talking boxing. There's no Marquess of Queensberry rules in Fighthome. It's maim or be maimed. Kill or be killed. Eat or be eaten.

From the crowd's chants of "Halftone. Halftone. Halftone" I knew I wasn't the favourite. There were only a few folks still shouting "Trollborn."

"Your name's Halftone?" I asked.

She smirked. "You couldn't pronounce my true name… Neal."

The announcer yelled, "Round one!" and it was on.

I threw my shadow at her, full of Hyperborean winter and fell deeds, wanting her to whimper, to drop, but it didn't work. Tossing your shadow only works if the person is scared of who you are and what you've done. Halftone wasn't.

I was in trouble.

She'd seen what I'd done, and wasn't impressed. Which meant she'd done much, much worse. I hadn't thought such a thing was possible. But here we were. There's always a bigger monster. As our shadows scrapped, I knew, impolite as it was to mention, that she was older than me. Meaner. Stronger.

Debt to Armin or not, I considered throwing the fight. But this wasn't money stakes. Not for me. To the victor go the spoils and I was back on the food chain.

Halftone moved slicker than whale shit, and she was on me too fast to dodge. I tensed, my gut waiting to take the punch. Her fist opened up and she sank her nails into my hide. She got in there good and deep. Her hand clenched and she tightened her grip as if she were going to tear out my ribcage. She walked her feet up my legs. Her toenails dug into my thighs. I grabbed at her left hand to try and jerk her off me but she twisted it out of my way, jabbing it at my gut as if she was stabbing me with a knife.

Those talons she had for fingernails came in rapid-fire. Tiny knives stabbing again and again. Turning my chest into a cribbage board.

Her assault slowed. Must've thought I was done. I caught her mouthing "You're next" at Armin.

Instead of trying to knock her off, or throw her, I wrapped my arms around her. If I turned that spine to powder, she wouldn't be dancing so lightly.

"You burned down my home," I growled.

"Done worse," she gasped. "So have you."

She squirmed in my grip. Something tore in my leg, and I dropped to a knee. I was low enough for her feet to touch the ground. I heard a crack. I thought I heard her cry out, though that might've been wishful thinking.

And then I heard the goddamned bell.

"Corners," the announcer yelled.

I had to drag myself there. But I made it.

I don't know why they break the fights up, but they do. Anything goes, but I figure you've got to give the audience a chance to get drunk before the end. I also figured Halftone was playing with me.

"You're losing," Armin said, more concerned for himself.

"No shit." I could feel the words slur out, my tongue fat in my mouth.

"Fight harder," Armin suggested, as he daubed a burning poultice over my shredded chest.

"You want to fucking tag in?"

I'd barely got my breath back, and Armin was still searing my wounds shut when the announcer yelled, "Round two!"

Round two went even worse than round one. But I hung on until the bell rang. Halftone practically hurled me toward my corner. Armin wasn't there.

Bastard.

Knowing what I did of Halftone, running wouldn't help him.

"Round three!"

Armin's desertion meant that Halftone was no longer distracted. She landed a shot to my throat. My vision flickered. Her shadow fell over me like never-ending night. The only light came from her flickering crown of runes. My eyes closed as the roar of the crowd became a white blur, and then was gone entirely.

◂ ▸

I woke up on a bed that was too small for me, surprised to wake at all, and my head hurt worse than the time I'd stumbled into a train. Halftone stood over me. She still wore that simple white dress. My blood was liberally splashed all over it.

Her hair was blonde, still not natural, but *more* natural than it had been. I wondered how long I'd been out.

She dropped my suit down on the bed. "It's been laundered. Smelled a little smoky. I still need you to find someone for me. I'll even pay you."

"Why do you need me, when you can beat me?"

She smiled. "Why should I do my own dirty work?"

Armin had her binding ring. She wouldn't admit it, but she *couldn't* go after him. I grinned back. The fight was over. He'd released *my* bond.

◂ ▸

His eyes went wide when I came knocking.

"But...but...you owe me."

"We're square, remember? The fight cleared my debt."

But I figured I'd give him something for old times' sake.

My shadow stretched from the doorway to envelop him, and I gave him a last good look at what was coming to him.

NUNAVUT THUNDERFUCK

Dale L. Sproule

I was chillin' solo at the club, three hours before opening, when I heard the brap of an iron dog on its last legs and went out to find Anyu Kigutaq sittin' on his Ski-Doo in the middle of an ice storm. So I grabbed the hood of his parka and dragged him in the side door.

"What the fuck you doin' out there, kid?"

Tell the truth, I knew Anyu was coming and had an idea why. Thanks to my bro DJ Crispy Kay, we got taps and spy-cams at three separate police detachments. He got access working security for Baffin Hydro when they were running the power lines from Jaynes Inlet. Even designed and installed our industrial perimeter harpoon rig round the welcome mat at the old lab. Durin' the long darkness, if somebody we didn't like came snooping – *presto*, they were on an instant fuckin' ice cube floating into Hudson Straight. Smart motherfucker, my brother. But he's a polar bear, so his employment options are limited.

After he stopped opening and closing his jaws to thaw out his facial muscles, Anyu said, "Nice to see you too, Tulok."

I didn't make a habit of consorting with humans, but Anyu's old man, Karpok, and I went way back. When I was living with my sister on the fringes of Dorset City, he was yard supervisor on the nightshift at the dump. Turned a blind eye when Manny the Fox and I put some heat on a gang of lemmings to honeycomb under the bear fence, so we could run a big culvert, eh? That was some concession we had – moving upward of eighty kilos of meat scraps every day all summer long. Karpok even gave us the heads up when the Nunavut Sanitation Authority twigged to our scam and came to plug the hole.

So I liked to help out his family when I could. And Anyu was always kinda special. True that half the humans in Cape Dorset who can hold a hammer end up sculpting, but he's one of the truly talented ones. Previous summer he came out on a mission, telling me, "All the sculpture galleries want dancing bears these days, eh? Walking bears – dime a dozen – but dancing ones are the shit. Problem is, I've never seen a bear dance. I need live models, and I heard there were a couple sows out here who could boogaloo like nobody's business."

"Whoa, whoa, round here you don't call 'em sows unless you wanna wear your nanooks as a necklace."

"Wha—?"

"Sedna's an equal partner in the club and she thinks the word 'sow' is misogynist bullshit. 'Bear-assed bigotry' she calls it. And that don't cut no ice with her, eh? As for the dancing, ask her to boogaloo she'll tell you to watch *The Jungle Book*. But she'll be happy to freestyle for ya. Maybe throw in a little lockin' and poppin'."

Turns out my warnings were unnecessary, because Anyu and Sedna got on like a house on fire. Last I heard he was making a killing with his dancing bear sculptures.

"What brings you back here in the middle of winter?" I asked this time, in a considerably less friendly tone than I greeted him with in the summer. "Got some heavy duty ursine kink going on, kid?"

"Lemme lubricate you, Tulok. You drinking Canadian?"

"Blood," I deadpanned.

He gave me a gap-toothed grin. "If it were blood, your muzzle would be covered with it, 'steada just foam."

I grabbed the front of his parka and pulled him up real close. "Polar bear foaming at the mouth ain't no fucking joke, kid. We can smell you from three glaciers away."

I licked my teeth for emphasis. "Come evening, there will be twenty starvin' bros in here. Think it'll be a cakewalk keeping you off the menu?" I got straight to the point: "Nobody comes out here for a joyride in minus fuckin' fifty." I leaned forward menacingly. "I know for a fact you're working for the Dorset Metro Police. I was told they caught you and Gilbert Etok with a kilo of sour diesel at the airport. That little cooler is crawlin' with po-pos – what were you thinkin'?"

"Thought the jar was vacuum sealed. It's Colorado hard goods, medical grade. One of your bear buddies musta sniffed it out." I raised my eyebrows skeptically, but he didn't miss a beat. "My uncle's sitting in the territorial legislature. He's gonna introduce a Medical Marijuana bill. Maybe we can change the law before my conviction comes down."

"Good luck with that," I said.

Anyu held up the palms of his sealskin mittens. "Hey, you can't lecture me about selling pot while you're running a meth lab. Look, I don't deny that the Mounties busted us. And told me they'd let me off if I helped bust your operation. But I'm not here for that. You're my *illamar* – my buddy. So I actually came to warn ya."

"Spill!" I growled.

"When I was at the cop shop, there was another guy there, sittin' in the captain's office. An elder with one arm. I asked about him, but nobody answered. Just traded these spooky stares like the guy was freakin' them out. When they put me back in lockup, my buddy Gilbert's there, eh, and he asks me, 'Did you see him?' 'See who?' I says. And buddy says, 'Torngasuk.' And I say, 'Fuck you. Torngasuk's not real.'"

As Anyu was telling me his story, we heard a voice from somewhere inside the club, "Oh, but I am."

"Who's there?" I shouted, kickin' my chair outta the way as I stood up. How could I have not smelled him?

"It's me – Torngasuk," and this feeble old one-armed man steps into the light.

"How'd you get in here?" I demanded.

"Rode here on the back of Anyu's iron dog and followed you guys in. But I was invisible, so neither of you could see me. The Mounties didn't know where your base was, but they figured Anyu here would come to warn you. And they were right."

"So *that's* why I ran outta gas!" exclaimed Anyu. "Carrying the extra weight."

"No, you ran outta gas because you forgot to fill the tank," says Torngasuk. "You're always too stoned."

I gave him my steeliest glare. "Okay, so you're here. What now?"

"I'm supposed to bring you to justice, eh?"

"For what?"

The old shaman shrugged. "Breaking the taboos."

"Whose taboos? The Mounties? Whose side you playin' on?"

"A taboo's a taboo! You're cooking crystal meth and sellin' it to our children."

I shook my head. "I just run a nightclub. Welcome to Sedna's Dance Emporium. Feel free to look around, eh? You wanna drink?"

"Don't usually drink. But I been livin' up on Ellesmere Island by myself for so fuckin' long..."

"Got Polar Ice Vodka," I said.

He shivered visibly. "I'm thinkin' a hot toddy. Or maybe a mai tai?"

"Our bartender comes in at two-thirty. But I can get you a coconut rum." I poured him a double and brought the bottle to the table.

Torngasuk sat down. We debated the word taboo and talked about the white man's hypocrisy.

"*If* I *was* cookin' meth," I said, "who could blame me? Seal hunting is all but impossible. They say in the old days, you could stack bowhead whales eight deep before one of those ice floes would crack. That true?"

Torngasuk shrugged. "I never stacked any bowheads."

I rolled my eyes and carried on with my rant. "Anyway, ice like that is rarer than auk feathers these days. Try to get close to a breathing hole, guy my size would pop through the ice like a card slidin' into a cash machine. Sneak up on a seal, my hairy ass! Might as well go krumpin' on plate glass. And nobody can outswim those fuckers in the open water."

Torngasuk pushes his empty glass toward me, so I pour him some more and keep talking. "So there's half our food supply gone, eh? What's a bear supposed to eat these days? They shoot us if we go into the dumps, get all pissy if we compete with 'em for the caribou. Woulda loved to get in the family business – kill seals and pretty much anything else I can sink my claws into. But it's not viable, eh? So now I run this joint, and I make lotsa cash, so I don't need to do anything 'taboo.'" Don't know that I was convincing him of anything, but it felt good to get that shit off my chest.

"The Mounties intercepted a package to your cousin," said the old shaman.

"Which cousin?" I asked. With just thirteen subpopulations in North America, I have more than a few cousins. So I can believably plead ignorance. It's not like I put on a return address on Zed's packages.

Zed used to be a popular attraction at the Chief Saunooke Bear Park in the Carolinas. A little undignified for sure; he couldn't go for a shit without some little kid pointing and laughing. But to tell the truth, he loves all those insecure townies marvelling at the size of his dick. When they shut the place down, he put in for a transfer to that Danish zoo, figuring he'd be in line next time they decided to feed a giraffe to the predators. Never tasted giraffe. But instead they shipped him off to some little game farm in Two-Farts, Saskatchewan. He got depressed and started hibernating with the brown bears – till he heard rumours that there was some pussy wagon action going down with the locals and fucking roofied polar bears was a thing. He swore never to sleep again. When he asked me if got anything that can keep him alert, I sent him a freebie.

'Course I didn't tell any of this to our friend Torngasuk. But I did keep refilling his glass. He was still there when the customers started coming in, and it was nearly midnight before he passed out.

We sat around the table looking at the shaman flopped unconscious across the table. Sedna had joined us by that point and she wasn't impressed. "Why don't we just eat him?" She suggested.

"He is a god. So it could backfire."

"So what are you saying? He'd give us gas or diarrhea?"

"At the very least," I nodded. "He might even repeat on us in other ways. Possession. Smiting."

"He doesn't look that powerful to me. Couldn't even grow back that arm," said Sedna.

"And he has been marinating in coconut rum," I observed.

"Oh, come on, guys. That's gross," said Anyu. "And not a good idea. Might even be a trap. That may be exactly what he wants you to do."

"You got a better suggestion?" With all this talk about a late-night snack, Anyu was looking pretty tasty.

"Might be better to just imprison him somehow. Build a tomb out of ice and set him adrift."

"What with global warming, he could be melted by April."

"By which time he'll be a long swim from anywhere."

I gave Sedna a side-eye and saw her nodding. "Okay, fine. Let's get it done before he sobers up."

The igloo we built was like a bank vault. Took six bears to push it out into the open water. We watched until the current picked it up and it started moving faster. We were just about to go back inside when Anyu nudged me. "What's that? Got any binoculars?"

"No," I said, "But your camera has a zoom lens."

"Oh yeah!" After a minute, he says, "Holy shit" and starts snapping pictures like crazy.

"What's going on? Let me look." Sedna and I bugging him.

Anyu says, "He's working some old time transformation mojo! He just turned into a narwhal, and he's using the tusk like a jig saw. Cutting a hole in the top of the vault."

At which point Sedna grabbed the camera from him. "Sonofabitch! Now he's turning into a bird!"

"Press the button. Take some pictures!" cried Anyu.

She scowled at him, but I could hear the click, click, click.

"I think it's a snowy owl," Sedna said. "No, wait. It's w-a-a-ay bigger. Some kind of white thunderbird or something."

"Whoa," I said, suddenly able to see it with the naked eye as it flew our direction. "We could be screwed now."

But then I noticed something else. I said to Anyu, "Do you know Gilbert Etok's brother?"

"Christian?"

I nodded. "Didja hear about the trouble he got in when he was a kid? Animal cruelty. He soaked bread in booze and fed it to the gulls and terns down at the harbour."

"What's so cruel about that?" asked Sedna.

"Well, birds and booze don't go well together, eh," I said, as we watched the big white thunderbird swerve erratically over the water. "They kept flying into the rocks..."

As I explained, Torngusuk swung abruptly toward the ice cliffs. Unable to slow down or stop, he smacked headfirst into a wall of ice, splatting like a gorged mosquito on a windshield.

"Ewww," said Anyu.

"Told ya we shoulda ate him," said Sedna. "What a waste."

The blood poured down the jagged cliff face, forming an arrow pointing straight down at the entrance to our lab.

I shook my head. "We'd better get that place cleaned out before the Mounties show up or we could lose the whole batch."

"I can hook you up with my pot dealer, eh. They got a new strain called 'Nunavut Thunderfuck.' If ya swim down to pick it up, we can avoid the airport altogether."

And that's how Anyu and I became partners. We've been doing pretty good. If you want to see his transformation sculpture *Torngasuk Intersecting with the 21st Century*, it's on permanent display in our new ice hotel up at Iqaluit. I'm the one who came up with the inscription on the base: "The old Gods ain't nothing to be afraid of. It's the new ones you gotta look out for."

FERN LEAVES UNFURLING IN THE DARK-GREEN SHADE

David Menear

Is that really my buddy Allan's mother in some shabby motel room somewhere, naked and on her knees with her head resting on an ottoman, smiling back at me gleefully being photographed while she's being fucked doggy-style by a drooling Irish wolfhound? It can't be, can it be? Yet it seems it could be her, maybe. I don't know if it is her but I do know that it's somebody there being dog-fucked and merrily photographed, acting like it's an ordinary everyday hobby or pastime like doing macramé or jogging or frying eggs wearing pyjamas. It is somebody's mother or sister or wife or daughter and it's somebody's dog. It's weird, alarming, chilling, and it's troubling. The dog doesn't care and can't. She doesn't seem to care and should. And yet they both appear to be enjoying themselves enormously. Turn a few crumply pages on and it's a possibly pretty girl lying on a wooden bench in a barn with her mouth wrapped around a massive horse cock. Her mouth is forced wide open, deformed like she's having some serious dental work done. She's looking straight at me all gleeful and proud. We don't see the face of the horse. The next page she's splattered in his cum. It covers her face and she's rubbing it all around on her huge tits. Again she smiles back at me, lustily licking her lips. Jesus. There are pictures of incestuous families all at each other, mothers and sons, fathers and daughters, grandpas and kids, all doing sex things together. If these images are intended to be erotic and sexually stimulating then why is my dick now rubbery limp and shrunken to the size of a thimble? My balls are hard and hidden far away in self-preservation and dread. I freeze, shivering in the hellish heat of the high-rise furnace room, mortified in my confused understanding of love and family and limited knowledge of sensuality, intimacy, and sexuality as a boy/man of sixteen. I'm no virgin and I trust and welcome the burning bilious acid that rises up into my throat, revolting against this twisted shit to puke at the idea of these ideas – and I do. I barf. I barf up my bran flakes and bananas big time. I hear the rats rustling.

Riffling through all these magazines scattered across the floor like the unburied dead after some battle, what troubles me greatly is that this is what these people no longer want or need. These are what they throw away down the chute into the building's garbage room, where I am. What is it that they covet and keep up there in those solemn locked apartments? Up to fifty magazines fall my way in a day into the my 8x12 cement holding cell where I labour with a heavy steel snow shovel scraping up the trash, turning and taking the seven steps to heave it up into the inferno of the furnace, where an appetite for chocolate or creepiness is converted and disguised as black smoke and grey ash. I'll sometimes find an innocent copy of *Readers Digest* with the address label removed as if this were a doctor's office waiting room, maybe a kid's scrolled-up *Archie* comic selling sea monkeys, or an ancient issue of *Canadian Living* with some recipe pages torn out. But the majority of the publications are of the supreme smut porno-erotica-dementia genre.

This is a "government-assisted" low-income high-rise rental accommodation deep in the largely unpopulated hinterland of this suburb. Here, we are further financially and geographically impaired in our ability to integrate with those beyond our social strata. It's a prison camp for the poor. Isolated and surrounded by the barbed wire of poverty and ill health. The ruthless guards are the other inmates. The twelve-storey building is architecturally austere, a bleak palette of rusts and greys. The lobby is a no-man's-land wasteland of litter and graffiti and fear. There are maybe eight to ten units per floor and so 100 to 120 apartments in total. Your rent is income-based and so people are returning to the government the money given them by the government. Out in the parking lot there is a black shiny Cadillac with a 40-foot speedboat hitched to the back of it. To the east of the parking lot are two always busy basketball courts and then, beyond that, an almost always abandoned kids' playground where swings don't swing and little kids don't run and laugh or dangle with their legs flailing from the monkey bars, shouting out, "Mom, look at me!" Mothers keep their children away from the broken glass and dirty needles.

No one knows I'm down here. That someone sees what they don't want to see again. They shuffle or stride unseen down the hall in socks or slippers with random trash or tightly cinched little plastic bags to the garbage room and then, alone inside, they pull down the heavy metal door to the chute in secret. They feel the rising heat and smell the staggering stink but still they bend over into it, pinching their lips and nostrils, looking down inside the tight square black tunnel, and listen to the sound of their garbage thumping or whisking at each floor below and then fading away to a mysterious silence somewhere else.

I wonder at the source of all these creepy magazines. Is it all the singular detritus of just one excessively obsessive twisted guy who blows his entire welfare cheque on this perverse obsession, pulling his dick to a rosy scabby pulp, or is it half the tenants here? I'm not certain what's worse. More is much worse. But these are my neighbours from down the hall or even next door. We pass each other all the time nodding or saying hello. We ride together in the elevator, commenting on the weather or most often with our heads bowed as if in silent prayer. Maybe it's the remarkably alert elderly woman that I often see with her walker in the hallway eternally in her quilted floral robe, thumping after her blind cat, calling to it in a hissing whisper? "Freedom-Freedom, come here." Maybe she is saying *Frieda*? She explained that her cat escapes by climbing from her balcony to the next apartment, where it is less than welcome and so tossed roughly out into the hall accompanied by various threats of death that include drowning, poisoning, and balcony hanging. I once heard him yell out in his rough Jamaican accent: "Pudit down de trash hole anudder time, Mutter!" Maybe it's him then? There is a strange stranger, though, I sometimes see sitting on a bench out next to the basketball courts watching the black kids perform their athletic magic tricks. He is tragically obese and forever sweaty. He seems to be struggling through cold porridge to walk anywhere. His long dark hair is greasy and tied back in a ponytail. He can spend hours there in his filthy XXXL Nike tracksuit smoking cigarettes, swilling his Pepsi, and crunching his way through a party-size bag of Nachos. I think he is watching what he wishes he were. Cool power and grace. They ignore him when he calls out to them excited about a great shot or a bad foul, but are never rough or unkind. If he is sitting asleep on his bench speckled in crumbs like a sated Yogi the Bear, when they are finished for the night they will shake him gently on the shoulder to wake him as they pass by. I imagine he sees them in his dreams as magnificent friends so big and so beautiful.

There is this woman, though. She is sort of sexy in a sleazy stripper kind of way. I see her coming and going with a lot of different guys. She has a dog that she treats very poorly. She pulls him along, screaming at him, dragging him along even as he tries to crap. I saw her try to kick him once and her high heel flew off high into the air. I laughed at a distance. She chased after her shoe like a hobbling cripple but the dog got to it first and brought it to her smiling. She smacked him in the mouth with it. He yelped and just lay down before her, whimpering. I wanted to hurt that woman then and take the poor dog home. I think it's her. She's the freak. But, why do I care who it is? They can't touch me or hurt me.

Some images and ideas, both good and bad, are carved so sharply and deeply into the headstone of your memory forever enduring well past even your death. Distant voices from faraway as faint as fern leaves unfurling in the dark-green shade fanning out like the wings of newborn birds. Tiny tremors like earthquakes of our ghostly soul sometimes shiver through us touching our hearts and taking our breath. Why, is what matters. The rats scurry boldly everywhere through the garbage now because I am too quiet and still for too long. I stand roaring like some barbarian warrior swirling and slamming the metal shovel down hard on the cement floor. This scares them away squealing. They know I'm scared too, is what they're saying. They smell it in my sweat.

THREE-STEP PROGRAM

Alex C. Renwick

Jimmy the Woof had always liked the francophone girls, ever since his folks moved to Montreal when he was a kid. It'd been a rough transition in school, what with Jimmy being American and never having learned French. But there was no drinking age in Montreal, at least none Jimmy had ever noticed, and that had seemed like a fair trade for not fitting in so good. Hell, back then kids were still sent to the dépanneur to pick up beer and smokes for their parents like it was milk and bread.

Something furry brushed past his legs and Jimmy froze, flattening against the peeling paint and red dust of the crumbling brick wall. Typical Montreal apartment: second storey, balcony in back, wrought-iron railing that had seen better days, corkscrew staircase leading up from a tiny backyard choked with weeds and old scraps of litter blown in off busy Rue Saint-Denis. The cat at Jimmy's feet looked up, eyes glinting in hard moonlight, tail swishing. Must be Nathalie's, coming from the door propped slightly open with an empty flower pot. More typical Montreal, this casualness, this feeling of safety so deep a girl leaves her door open even at 3:00 a.m. Even a pretty girl, like those francophone girls who wouldn't give Jimmy the time of day back in school. Even a beautiful girl who for some reason did, like Nathalie Beauville.

Jimmy reached to pet the cat and it skittered from his touch, disappearing down the exterior spiral stairs, a whisper of fur against iron. He pushed lightly on the door and it swung inward on silent hinges, opening into a kitchen striped with moonlight coming in the tall narrow windows. The envelope with the cash weighed down his shirt pocket, solid, off-kilter. All he had to do was put it on the counter and leave, and the last bit of Jimmy's Three-Step Program would be complete.

It'd been a year and three weeks since Jimmy had touched booze. He'd been a horrible drunk – stealing, lying, getting into fights, letting his fists fly even when he didn't mean to. He'd hurt some people: his folks, his kid brother, his boss at the pizza joint where he'd regularly helped himself to a little extra from the till – never more than it took to buy a bottle of Jack, but still. When he finally had enough of himself, got so disgusted with the forever bruised and busted stubbled slob looking back at him in the mirror each day, a guy without a single thing in his life worth a shit in this world, he made himself a three-step program. Right then and there in the bathroom, wrote it on the mirror with a shaky finger in the steam from a shower that could never clean away all the fucked-upedness that was Jimmy's life:

1) *List everybody I done wrong.*

2) *Make good.*

3) *Find peace.*

Three simple steps. Jimmy was proud of that. He knew most people wanted to quit the bottle, they did twelve. Fuck that.

His folks were dead, so all he'd done there was apologize to the sky and move on. His baby brother was grown, moved back to the States. Their parents hadn't left much but Jimmy signed it all over, every penny of his half, such as it was. His old boss from the pizza place had a kid, a nerdy boy who got picked on at school every day by the kind of kid Jimmy had been himself. He took care of those bullies, scared them off, figured he'd made good as best he could in that quarter. All he'd taken from his boss had been money anyway, but Nathalie…

He'd heard Nat was seeing a new guy, another American. He was glad. She deserved more than he'd ever given her, and a lot less of what he had. He'd never meant to hurt her, never wanted to, but after a bottle of Jack it was like the whole world turned red and black at the same time, red over black over red, until Jimmy couldn't see straight, couldn't see anything. Couldn't even see kindness like what Nat had given him, all she'd ever given him no matter how much he took.

The envelope dug into his chest through shirt fabric. Heavy with cash, inadequate. The liquidation of everything he owned, which hadn't been much, not nearly enough.

Jimmy pushed the door a little wider and stepped into the kitchen. The metal baseball bat crashing across his back was a surprise, as was the little noise from his own lips, a soft grunt disproportionate to the thunder of his spine crunching under the blow. Sprawled on his side on the chipped linoleum, Jimmy watched the man holding the bat flip the kitchen switch.

The guy stepped over, smacked him a couple more times, a whack to the kidney, one across the back of his skull. Not as hard as the first blow, but unnecessary, mean. Jimmy wanted to reach into his pocket, pull out the envelope full of cash, but his arm wouldn't move. A soft white shape padded into his line of sight, a girl in a thin white T-shirt and a familiar pair of pink panties with blue stripes, somewhat faded now. "Jimmy?" she said.

The way she said his name, with the French lilt, pierced Jimmy to his gut. He tried again to reach for the envelope, failed. The guy with the bat was staring at Nathalie. "This is Jimmy?" he said. "That fuck who hurt you?"

After living in Montreal so long, the American accent sounded hard to Jimmy, rough and angry. Nathalie's voice was so much softer, even her cries and shrieks as the American lifted his bat again and again to bring it crashing over Jimmy's face, cartilage and bone splintering with each whack, blood turning the spun metal red and wet. He'd known a pathetic wad of cash wasn't enough to make up for the pain he'd caused Nathalie, so maybe this was the real Step Two, making up for what he'd done, paying for it like he should.

The bat fell again across Jimmy's face, shoving hard parts into soft, and Jimmy recognized the arrival of Step Three, coming sooner than he'd expected, and not in any of the hundred ways he'd tried to envision it, tried to figure and to plan for it to come.

His vision swam, and Nathalie's cries faded in the rushing sound in his ears, and Step Three arrived and it was good. It was good.

A NOTHINGALE

Patrick Fleming

The new guy comes back from the storage room with a sign-in clipboard in one hand and Tara's backpack in the other. He glances at the faded ID I'm holding and flips through the sheets until he finds her name on the shelter's resident list.

"We almost lost hope," he says. "Another day and you'd be looking for it in the dumpster."

I take the clipboard and sign her name the way I've seen her do it. I'm not much of a forger, but it hardly matters. He doesn't know Tara or what her writing looks like. He doesn't know me, either; doesn't realize I'm not her. Not even her sister, despite what everyone says. He's too new to know anything about us, which makes what I'm doing here so much easier. As far as he's concerned, I have blond hair like what's on the ID and I look like I could use a break. Who else would I be, right?

"So, what was it?" he asks. "Picked up?" He means, was I held overnight and is that why I didn't keep the spot they'd been holding for me? It's a fair question but he makes it sound accusatory, like I should feel bad about not making it in until now.

But one thing about being a street kid is that you stop feeling bad about things you've done real quick. I hardly feel bad about anything these days, and that goes double for some unused shelter bed that has nothing to do with me in the first place. I'm only here because I promised Tara I'd do what I could, and this is where I thought to start: the place we always ended up when we had nowhere else to go.

"No, not picked up," I mutter as I slide the clipboard back to him. I flash the admission bracelet on my left wrist and say, "Hospital." Tara's name is on it, if he bothers to look. I doubt the nurses realize it's gone missing. Even if they have, they'll probably assume it came off during her transfer to Palliative Care and get a clerk to do a new one.

"Now can I have my backpack, please?"

His eyes go a bit cold as he shoves the bag across the counter that separates us.

"Next time," he says, "we won't wait for you to wander in like this. Next time it's gone the minute you don't show up for check-in."

I sling the pack over one shoulder and tell him there better not be any panties missing from my bag. It's exactly the kind of talk that gets you a temporary ban, but so fucking what? Tara's never coming back anyway.

◀ ▶

There's a park nearby that a lot of us guttersnipes go to when we want to get high. It has a concrete picnic table that's nice when the sun is out. I head over to it and put the pack down so I can look through what's inside. There isn't much, considering it was everything she owned: some spare clothes, a toothbrush, her old Rudimentary Peni tape (*Cacophony*), a plastic baggie with a few sticks of incense in it (sandalwood), some perfume sample vials (Dior Poison), and a black plastic lighter. Near the bottom, I find a book on the occult she apparently stole from the library. A few pieces of jewellery have settled underneath it, mostly rings and cheap bangles, along with three or four safety pins and a little sewing kit. That's about it.

We shared a lot of this stuff when we ran around together, terrorizing the hangouts, being crazy. Like I said before, everyone called us sisters, and that kinship became a mythic thing for us. It tied us together, like conjoined twins. People acted like we were a force of nature. You could see it on their faces when we really got each other going.

I go back through the clothes in her pack and dig out a tattered black hoodie. It's musty and reeks of cigarettes and old sweat, but her unmistakable sweetness is somewhere in there too. I bury my face in it and breathe deep, closing my eyes against the fabric and the tears that are suddenly welling up.

"Promise you'll make her give it back to me," she'd said when I last saw her. "Tell her I need it, tell her it's mine."

I said okay because I couldn't stand to see her suffering like that. I didn't think it was going to amount to much, so I just went with it. I had no idea who she was referring to or what any of it meant, but she seemed so grateful to hear me say I'd do it. She cried from relief, saying between sobs that she was sorry. For everything.

It was unreal how much she'd wasted away by then. "Failure to thrive," a nurse had called it, although I got the feeling they weren't sure what exactly was killing her. Cancer, maybe? Or was it the drugs? Had her PTSD finally hollowed her out? Nobody knew what it was, not even me. I was as clueless as the rest, couldn't do anything about it but watch her get worse and worse until she was spectre-thin.

The picnic table is warm from the sun but I slip the hoodie on anyway. I zip it up and use the sleeve to dab at my eyes until I'm sure the tears are gone. Having it on makes me feel better, like she and I are communing in some small way. It's intimate, and I hug myself to keep that feeling close, but something in one of the pockets is poking into my side and it distracts me. I dig around and eventually fish out a folded-up wad of paper. I flatten it on the picnic table and find myself staring at two prescriptions nested together, one for Valium and one for Darvon.

Both were written several months ago, prescribed by different doctors (*surprise surprise*). Neither one is for a particularly high dosage, but if taken together... My heart breaks all over again. She kept these scripts secret, even from me; walked around with them tucked safely away in case she ever found herself in need of a surefire fatal interaction.

Ah, Tara. What happened to you? I don't realize I'm crying again until I see droplets staining the tabletop.

Embarrassed, I glance around to make sure no one's seen me. But of course you're never quite alone these days, especially during low moments like this. I spy Jeremy not a hundred yards off, sitting on a bench with some other people I sort of recognize. He hasn't seen me yet, but I know it's only a matter of time before he comes over to see what's up.

Jeremy comes off as nice, but he always wants to get real buddy-buddy with me, always wants to touch my clothes or share my cigarette when we're hanging out. It never used to bother me much, but he got me alone at a party once and he...well, he wasn't exactly taking no for an answer. That was the night I first met Tara, actually; she stormed in and nearly took his head off with a beer bottle.

Now she's little more than a pile of bones on a gurney. The thought kills me all over again, and I feel myself getting frantic for someplace quiet and peaceful and safe where I can just be alone for a few minutes. Someplace where I can mourn my best friend without anybody coming up to me. Without worrying about the cops either hassling me to move on or else failing to show up when the creeps start sniffing around. Christ, what I wouldn't give for a place to disappear to for a while.

I'm about to stuff the prescriptions back in the hoodie when I notice something funny about the one on top. Her basic info is printed out on one of those patient information labels. It shows her last name as *Ragana*, which is something I haven't seen before. We usually coordinated that kind of thing so we didn't accidentally fuck up each other's little pharmacy scams. Not that I'm surprised she used a fake name to get these, mind you; it's just that "Ragana" definitely isn't ringing any bells with me. It makes me wonder what else she's been using it for, and for how long.

There's an address under her name as well. It has an apartment number and everything. It's also new to me, and I feel another twinge of betrayal at the exclusion. *So full of surprises today, sis*, I think. *So many secrets*. I feel myself getting worked up about it but try to keep the anger from showing. Jeremy's still too far away to see what I'm doing, but he gossips as much as everybody else, and they're all dying to hear the latest sordid details about Tara's condition and how it's turning me into a bitter fucking hag. They're all so *concerned* about me.

The address under Tara's name is on Oke Street. Everyone knows that's part of Suzerain Park, right in the middle of all that public housing war-zone shit. Not a great part of town, but right now I don't have much else to go on. Hopefully I can steer clear of those SP Crew gangster assholes on my way to this mystery address of Tara's.

◀ ▶

I walk up Church Street until I get to Dundas. There's a streetcar stopped at the corner, and I have just enough time to scrounge an almost-expired transfer from the garbage. I flash it at the driver and get a lot of shit about this not being a valid transfer point. But neither one of us cares that much, so he closes the doors mid-argument and resumes his route east.

A drunk guy sitting near the front pats the empty seat beside him and tries talking to me. I ignore him as I head for the back, but he keeps going anyway, mostly slurred vowels and filthy hand gestures. He's obviously been making everyone on board uncomfortable for some time, and his unwanted attention transfers their unease onto me.

He eventually gives up on the sweet nothings and resorts to just whistling at me. And I have to give it to him – he's a pretty good whistler, in a birdcall kind of way. Maybe the missing teeth actually help in this case. He warbles on, stopping every now and then to laugh and nod at me. I pull out Tara's library book in the hope that it'll discourage him.

It's a history book about witchcraft in the Baltics, with lots of old engravings reproduced throughout. We used to go through this kind of stuff a lot because we were obsessed with what we liked to call *The Dark Shit of History*. This must've been real dark if Tara was interested enough to actually steal it.

Stuck in about halfway through is a piece of scrap paper, probably what she was using for a bookmark. On the paper is a carefully drawn skull. A number of birds are flying out of it. Strong black lines attach their bodies to its empty eye sockets, making it look like the skull is tied to the birds and they're dragging it. I assume she was using the book's illustrations for a new tattoo, but I can't find the original image on any of the pages I flip past.

The Parliament stop is announced and I push the drawing into my pocket while I wait for the rear doors to open. I want to keep it handy for further scrutiny, to see if I can figure out where it's from or what it might've meant to her. If nothing else, I can think about where to put it on my own body, a kind of secret memorial to remember her by.

Oke Street is just a few blocks up. It opens directly onto the western edge of Suzerain Park, where a series of X-shaped buildings are spaced out evenly along a stretch of muddy "green space." It's not a proper street, really; more like a concrete path branching off Parliament in order to wind through the centre of the housing development.

As I leave the safety of the main streets behind, I hear music filtering down from the frayed mesh of a thousand loose window screens. Small groups of men are standing together here and there, spitting in the dirt and watching me as I search for the building number that's printed on Tara's prescriptions. I glance up and see a baby on a nearby balcony, naked except for its diaper and watching me with serious eyes. Behind it, the faint glow of a cigarette tells me someone else is up there too, out of sight but keeping tabs all the same.

I'm pretty far into the housing units before I start to hear whistles bouncing from one building to the next. They're quick little chirps, probably meant to alert people that a stranger is walking through. The buildings are too close and the path is too winding for me to tell if I'm being followed or not, so I just keep moving forward. *As long as I don't hit a dead end*, I reason, *I'm fine*. It's pretty clear that getting back out won't be nearly as easy as getting in.

Up ahead, I see a woman standing off to the side of the path. She's dark-skinned and so thin I can't help but think of Tara. *They could be sisters*, I say to myself. She looks like she's waiting for me, and the realization fills me with unease. There can't possibly be any good news for anyone in this place.

"Ten-fifty?" I say as I approach, but she doesn't seem to hear me.

"Is this ten-fifty? Ten-fifty Oke?" I point at the building and then hold up Tara's scripts, but she still doesn't respond.

"I can't find ten-fifty," I say, speaking slower this time. I reach out to touch her arm but stop when I see a tear spilling down her cheek. She turns her head just enough to indicate that I should keep walking east.

"Ten-fifty is over there," she says. I follow her gaze and see that the housing development continues on the other side of River Street. There are a few very tall buildings over there, easily twenty storeys apiece.

"Tell them Eshu needs to see you," she says. "Tell them until they take you."

I nod my head, trying hard to keep my confusion from showing. Am I supposed to know who that is?

A tear rolls down her other cheek.

"Don't go with them to any other buildings, no matter what they say."

She stops talking, and we both stand there looking at each other for what feels like a long time. Her mouth is moving like she wants to tell me something else, but no more words come out. Uncomfortable with her odd silence, I say thanks and move on, my legs suddenly heavy with dread. What the fuck have I gotten myself into? The question has me knotted up inside. I reach the intersection of Oke and River and take a quick look back when the traffic light changes. She's still standing there, watching me cross the street.

◂ ▸

There's a little white sign by the sidewalk with the words "Suzerain Mews" printed in the standard Community Housing style. I keep on the sidewalk as it curves past the sign and find that it leads to the space between the three immense buildings.

Despite the size of the monoliths around me, the sun has managed to slip in and cast most of the inner square in a comforting glow. The covered entrances to the buildings still cast shadows, but a soothing light falls on the middle part of the square, where an empty public fountain languishes in disrepair. It looms up from a wide circular basin, its central spire supporting wide bowls that get smaller as they go up. People have obviously been climbing into them or trying to knock the whole thing over, because the bowls are lopsided and the main spire leans over to one side. Time and exposure to the elements have coated it in a dusty, green-blue tarnish.

There's garbage everywhere, and the benches near the fountain look busted and filthy. I pick out a low concrete wall to sit on instead and slip off my backpack, taking in the eerie silence around me. While it's quiet, I pull out Tara's drawing of the skull. I want to study it some more, but end up staring at that massive fountain instead. It was built to match the size of the apartment buildings, so it's huge as well – at least twenty feet tall.

The colour and shape of it reminds me of a gigantic flower, and the thought gives the whole place a kind of bizarro fairytale vibe. Sitting on my concrete perch, I feel like I've found a few outsized headstones hidden away in a remote clearing. The strangeness of it all is so rich it's almost intoxicating. There's a dreaminess to it that makes everything feel suspended, like this place has been waiting patiently for me to arrive.

Eventually, a shape detaches from the darkness inside one of the buildings and steps out into the square. It's a young guy in baggy clothes and work boots, still barely more than a shadow beyond that, even when he passes through the afternoon light on his way toward me. When he gets close, he puts his hands in his pockets and mumbles something I don't quite catch. It's a single word, spoken like a question. It sounds like *Want?*, maybe. Or maybe *So?* or even just a grunt to let me know I should explain what I'm here for.

His eyes are bloodshot and looking into them makes me nervous, so I let my gaze slip away. It settles just above the corner of his mouth, where I find myself staring at the rind of dried snot that rings one of his nostrils.

"I have a sister..." I start to say, but don't know how to finish.

He leans forward anyway and points at something. I look down to find the drawing of the birds and the skull crumpled slightly in my claw-like grip.

"Eshu," he says. His teeth are yellow, nestled in pink gums. The name lingers in my ears as he motions for me to get up and follow him.

I stand and reach over to slip on the backpack. He's already turned around and is heading back to the building he came out of. Am I doing the right thing by following him? Is he leading me to the right place?

I catch up after fumbling for the prescriptions. I hold them out as we walk and point at the address under Tara's name.

"Ragana," I say. "I need to find Ragana."

"Yeah, yeah, Ragana," he says as he waves off the papers. But then he says "Eshu" again, this time more sternly, and I get the hint that finding the Ragana residence is not going to happen right away.

We go in through the front doors and I breathe in uncirculated air laced with roach poison and stale piss. Directly in front of us are three elevators all in a row; stencilled signs on either side of them indicate the presence of stairwells tucked away to our right and left.

The stairwells in these big buildings are notorious corridors of violence and raw predation. Crews often run flights like street corners, enforcing their own tolls at all entry and exit points. All while slinging their particular product to anyone they manage to trap in there with them. And if you happen to be a girl coming home alone or trying to go out unmolested? Good luck to you, sister.

I glance over at my guide to gauge whether he's steering us in that direction, and am relieved when he moves without hesitation to the elevators instead. He punches a button and we wait for the car to arrive, which gives me time to think about my odds here. Can I take him if he hits the car's STOP button once we're between floors? Will anyone hear me if I yell for help?

The middle elevator dings and we head up to the sixth floor in a very tense silence. The doors finally open and I see two more young shadows hanging out in the hallway. They're standing by what looks like a reinforced door. My guide waves at them and they wave back.

"For Eshu," he says as we approach, and one of them nods and knocks on the heavy door. I'm ushered in quickly and don't even have time to see my guide turn back down the hall before the door is shut and locked behind me.

The room is surprisingly bright, and I find myself squinting at two big windows on the far wall across from me. There's a third window as well, but a boxy contraption full of little birds almost completely obscures its existence. Those birds are happily chirping away, apparently content to hop around in the little cages that subdivide the box in the window. I quickly count three rows of five cell-like pens, with each bird tethered to its cage by a slender silk ribbon. The ribbons are a deep red, like a burgundy I guess, and are affixed with little clasps on each end.

The other two windows offer a view of the stagnant Don River and the slab of parkway that flows along beside it. It's not much to look at, really, but I'm guessing "Eshu" doesn't live here for the view.

There's a couch and a glass coffee table nearby, and also some chairs and a big TV. I can tell music is playing, but the noise from the birds pretty much drowns out everything. The murmurings of a bassline bubble up here and there.

A couple more man-shaped outlines are sitting at a little round table near the windows. I can't see their eyes well enough to tell whether they're watching me or not. There's also an old guy in one of those motorized wheelchairs, like the kind they give to paralyzed people. He's parked near the birds and has the chair reclined a little so he can stare at the ceiling. A blanket is spread over his chest and lap. Malformed hands lie on top, his oddly splayed fingers twitching every now and then. Drool has been trickling out of the corner of his mouth and is starting to pool near his neck. He looks pathetic and I feel like I'm gawking, but his eyes are clouded over in milky blue cataracts so I don't worry about it too much.

I don't see the other person in the room right away. He's sitting on the far end of the couch. Hash smoke hangs in the air around him and, set aglow by the light pouring in from the windows, acts as a floating blind spot that has only now begun to dissipate. Behind it sits a big guy in an expensive tracksuit. There's a SPC tattoo on his neck, the letters done up in ornate blackletter. He sets down the video-game controller he's been gripping and gives me a big smile.

"Well, come on in, little Miss Room Service."

I don't say anything. I don't move a muscle. This makes him smile even bigger.

"Somebody send you over?" he asks. "You got a man owes me a favour or something?"

"I don't do that," I say. I try to sound stern and confident, but I can't quite keep the nervousness out of my voice. "I'm just looking for someone who lives here. I don't want any trouble."

He smiles some more, then nods in a way that's supposed to be thoughtful.

"Yeah, we get that a lot. People coming through, in need of safe passage and all that."

"I need to go to the twenty-first floor," I say. "I won't go anywhere else or bother anybody."

"But the thing is," he interrupts, "it's bigger in here than you think. More of a maze, too. You could get turned around if you don't know where you're going, know what I'm sayin'? Maybe end up in the wrong place."

"I can find my way. I already know the apartment number." I hold up the scripts as proof, realizing my mistake a second too late; his eyebrow arches at the sight of them.

"Lemme see those?" He extends his hand in my direction, beckoning me to come closer.

I tell him they're fine where they are and his smile wavers a bit.

"Up to you," he says. "Getting out's just gonna cost you something else, then."

I start to panic when I realize he's done talking and is now waiting to see what I offer him. I know the longer things stay quiet, the more he's going to assume he can dictate the terms. At this point, that can only be a bad thing for me.

Music burbles up again from under all that bird chatter. It's distracting me, making it hard to think. I doubt I can unlock the door behind me quick enough to get out into the hall. Even if I could, what then?

We're both startled by a thin, ragged voice that says, "She can go up."

We look over at the old man in the wheelchair. His blind eyes are still staring at the ceiling, but his face doesn't look as slack as it did before.

"She can go up," he says again.

The guy on the couch looks annoyed. "Eshu, man," he says, "this is my building. I should be the one who says—"

"Give her a bird to take," the old man says. "You play your games some other time."

The big guy doesn't like this but motions for someone to go to the cage anyway. One of the dark figures gets up from where it was sitting and carefully pulls out a bird from a wire compartment, along with the ribbon attached to the thing's leg. He walks over and silently hands me the free end of the ribbon. I grasp it numbly and the bird hops onto the sleeve of my hoodie. It seems so natural for it to perch there, but its closeness freaks me out a little and I have to fight the urge to shake it off me.

"They're nightingales," the old man continues. "She likes their songs. Give it to her, or she won't let you in. Tell her it's a gift."

His instructions must be for me, but he makes no effort to acknowledge my presence in the room. It makes me feel like I'm not really there, like I can still escape this whole shitty scenario if I leave quietly enough. I turn to unlock the door, hoping the spell will hold and they'll somehow forget I'm here.

But I hear the guy on the couch say, "See you on the way down, bitch," and I know he still sees me all too clearly. And the flat way he's speaking makes me think he won't be giving me any more of those big smiles the next time we meet, either.

◀ ▶

The elevator stops and I step out into a quiet hallway. Beige apartment doors line both sides of the corridor. I follow their progression until I find the one that matches what's printed on Tara's scripts. It's unremarkable like all the rest of them, which surprises me for some reason. I stand in front of it for a while, going over what I should say. Eventually I knock.

Nothing happens at first, but then I hear an old woman's muffled "Yes?" from inside.

"Is this the Ragana residence?" I ask.

She's understandably suspicious and wants to know who I am. I tell her Tara asked me to come by. After a handful of seconds, she cracks the door enough to get a look at me.

I hold up one of the prescriptions close to the opening for her to see Tara's name next to her address. The longer she squints at it, the more disapproving her expression gets.

"So much trouble," she says. Her mouth compresses into a hard line and she shakes her head.

"She's in the hospital," I say. "She's very sick."

Her eyes flick up to mine and I can see she thinks I'm probably scamming her. I get the feeling she's about to slam the door in my face. But as her eyes continue to scrutinize me, her attention is caught by the little bird quietly perched on my forearm. Her eyes go wide, and she looks up at me with a sly grin.

"For me?" she asks.

I nod uncertainly and tell her it's a gift, like I was told to do. Nearly clapping with delight, she coos at my little companion. She pulls at the door a little to undo the security chain, then opens it wide to welcome us in. *Thank fucking God*, I think, and exhale the breath I've been holding this whole time.

I'm barely through the door when she takes the ribbon from my hand and quickly carries the bird deeper into her apartment. I follow behind at a respectable distance, giving her time to get the bird into its new cage while I look around for signs of whatever I might be here to pick up.

Most of it is typical old-lady stuff – doilies and porcelain tchotchkes and an old china cabinet full of fancy plates. Everything is tidy and clean in a way that brings back memories of childhood visits to my own grandmother's house. My nana cleaned a different room every day of the week; I wouldn't be surprised if this Ragana lady did the same thing. Grandmas the world over must do that.

She eventually comes back for me and we move into the living room.

"Sit, sit," she says. "I make tea." She disappears into the kitchen while I sink into a recliner sporting leaf-patterned upholstery. It's very hushed in here, even with the birds and all. She has them tethered to a stand with branches like a tree, but they aren't moving around on it very much. It's a little darker in here as well, so maybe that explains why they hardly make a sound.

"You are good friend of Tara's?" she calls from the kitchen. Her accent strikes me as Eastern Bloc, but with a lilt I can't place.

"We're very close," I yell back. "More like sisters."

I hear a faint "That's nice" while she clinks around with the teacups and saucers in the other room. Any further small talk is cut short by the kettle's moaning whistle.

She finally comes back in with a tray full of dishes, and I move a candy jar from the nearby coffee table so she can set it down. On the tray are little plates of thick crispbread crackers with some kind of moss-like garnish on top. I take one and briefly consider the tiny bowl of pickled fish, but decide not to risk it. She leans over to pour tea for the both of us, then takes a seat across from me in a high-backed wooden chair. I drop a sugar cube in my tea and leave it to cool while we smile uncomfortably at each other.

"So, she is not well," Grandma Ragana prompts. Her eyes are scrutinizing me again as she blows on her tea. This makes it harder for me to read her, because she keeps the cup hovering protectively near her mouth while she waits for me to respond.

"The nurses think it won't be long," I say. I take a sip of my tea to settle my suddenly shaky voice.

"She's pretty out of it by now," I continue. "But the last time I saw her, she asked me to come here and see you. She said you had something of hers and that she needs it back."

Grandma Ragana doesn't say anything. The teacup still obscures part of her face, but her eyes are twinkling in a way that makes me think she knows what I'm talking about.

"Did she say what it is I have?" she asks quietly.

"No," I say. "I'm not really sure if she knows herself. I think it might have to do with you, though. I think maybe she's desperate for something that will make her feel safe, now that the end is so near. I think she wants to have that feeling close to her again, and I'm guessing you must be tied up with it in her mind."

"Ah," Grandma Ragana says, and cracks a compassionate smile. She takes another sip of her tea.

"That is very touching," she says. "Very sweet of you to say. But forgive me when I say that does not sound like the Tara I know. To me, it sounds like what *you* are feeling. Being safe must be something *you* want. And I am glad for you to feel safe here, in my home."

We smile at each other and I find myself feeling almost grateful for the understanding she's showing me. It puts me at such ease, and I'm surprised to find that I actually do feel safe in here with her, safer than I've felt in ages, despite the dangers of the building she lives in. Relief floods over me, a real contentment that makes me feel almost woozy.

Grandma Ragana notices this change in me and nods approvingly. There is a long pause where both of us are happy to just sit and enjoy a peaceful moment. Finally, she says, "I do have something of Tara's. Now that you have come, I am happy to give it back to her." Then she puts her teacup down and stands up. She takes a few steps over to where her birds are kept, and clicks her tongue at them to get their attention.

"I was born near a place called Cēsis," she says. "Do you know where that is? I lived for a long time in the forests there. It was so lovely, and I could be alone as much as I wanted. The birds always kept me company."

I smile at the image this paints in my head; it's like something from fairytales.

"But then the Germans came," she continues. "And the Poles. There were the trials, and many people were burned. The Russians came, and with them so much blood spilled. Then the Germans came back and made their massacres near Riga. After that, more Russians. No place was safe, even for someone like me, alone and hiding in the woods for all those years."

She picks up a bird that had been sitting near mine, and holds it up for me to see.

"I am like you; I want to feel *safe*. So I learned a trick, to survive."

Holding the bird out, she says, "This is what Tara sent you for." Keeping her eyes on mine, she whispers something to the bird. It stops moving, and she opens her hand to let it roll off her palm. Her eyes are still on me as it falls to the carpet, dead.

"Now I share my trick with you," she says with a tight smile, and picks up my bird. I try to tell her I don't want to see whatever it is she's about to do. But the woozy feeling has come back, and I can't seem to draw a breath. I can't move. I'm horrified to find myself trapped in my own body.

Grandma Ragana holds up her thumb for me to see, then carefully digs her nail into the bird's body. It screeches in agony, and she smiles as she continues gouging away at its innards. She finally gets ahold of some wet piece of organ, something long and bloody, and pulls it out of the shivering bird. She lets it dangle for me to see. Then she puts the bird back on the perch it had been sitting on.

Still smiling, she returns to her chair. She's watching me intently again, her eyes blazing in a way I haven't seen before. It scares me and I try to scream, but no sound comes out. My limbs won't move, either. I can't even look away. It takes all my energy just to moan in disgust.

She takes a deep breath, one that flares her nostrils, and I feel something in me wither. Something collapses, perhaps turns black. I know it means I've begun to waste away.

"There now," Grandma Ragana says. "That will do nicely."

She picks up her teacup again and sips at it while she watches me struggle to breathe.

"You're scared," she says. "But don't worry. They can live for quite some time this way."

There's blood on her teacup now, blood staining the sleeve of her blouse.

"But I wonder if she will become lonely in this place, here with me."

She leans forward like she wants to confide something in me.

"I wonder," she whispers, "if she would like a sister."

I want to cry but nothing happens.

"Wouldn't that be nice? Maybe you can find her one for me."

LADY BLUE AND THE LAMPREYS

Ada Hoffmann

Lady Blue likes everything just so. Second table from the far window at Old Benny's Pub, the dark wood shining clean and the drapes half down, an Electric Lemonade in a frosted highball glass just off-centre. No menu, no salt shaker. This is Lady Blue's spot, and Benny saves it for her every Wednesday, Thursday, and Saturday night, with a second chair pulled out discreetly for Lady Blue's dearest husband, whether or not he arrives.

He is here tonight. The latest model is a Jason, young and clean-cut, with gym-rat muscles and a mischievous little beard. His eyes are hazel. The girls at the bar can tell he's Lady Blue's property from the way he hangs on her gestures. That, and the bright silver key on a bright silver chain round his neck. Lady Blue's husbands get keys, not rings.

That's the tableau. Lady Blue impeccably neat, in a sky-blue evening gown, with her hair up to bare a slender neck. Jason, in the half-light, leaning in to her whispers. Men in old brown coats around them, drinking and drinking, and girls in a little less than that. Everyone's huddled together, night like tonight. Benny says there's a sea-storm coming.

"Hah," says a girl all in red: the hair, the lips, the dress, the heels. She's playing cribbage with the boys, two tables down from Lady Blue, and she's just won two nob points for dealing a Jack. "Clear sky, not a drop. Anyway we're tens of miles inland."

"Doesn't matter," says gap-toothed Shaun, who's been at Old Benny's Pub longer than a girl like Red can remember. "Benny's never wrong."

"Nobody's never wrong," says Red. She snaps down a card. "Five."

Then it comes.

It's a wind that whips through Benny's half-open windows. A visible wind, a dirty brownish-blue, smelling of brine. It leaves a scuff on Jason's glass, like someone's rotten-tooth breath.

"What'd I tell you?" Shaun hollers. He points to the frigid swirl at the centre of the room, which grows more visible by the second, thickening into something like limbs. Shaun loves it when Benny's right. Benny just shakes his head, keeps washing the bar.

The wind thickens and thickens, and then the howl isn't wind through branches but an unearthly trill in the throats of what's standing there.

They're men from the solar plexus down. Above that, something slimy and finned twists up and up to a blind head. Each one gapes with three black lamprey mouths.

Lightning flashes, flickering off of their thousands of teeth.

Everybody's looking now, even Jason. Bloody Tom Jackson with the long sideburns, fingering the switchblade in his back pocket, is the first to rise.

"This ain't your town," he says. "Get going, you."

Bloody Tom stares down the lampreys. The lampreys, eyeless, gape back at him.

Jason edges a little closer to Lady Blue.

Then there's a lunge. Nobody's sure if it's Bloody Tom who strikes first, or the lampreys. There's just a whirling howl, a wet smacking noise, then Bloody Tom lies limp in a lamprey's grip, his knife knocked out of his hand. The creature dips its mouthy end as if about to kiss him. One sucking mouth latches on to the hollow of Bloody Tom's cheekbone. One at the base of his jaw. And the third, the largest one, at the base of his throat, between the collarbones.

There is a sound like a child sucking a milkshake through a straw. Bloody Tom's body shrivels.

Jason clutches at Lady Blue's hand. He's shaking, poor thing. Lady Blue trails a fingertip along his knuckles. She is not fool enough to interfere, but she rather wants to stay and watch. Lady Blue is not afraid of anything.

The lamprey drops Bloody Tom's body to the floor. Its mouthy end looks different now, rounder, with something rough at the edges, like a parody of sideburns.

"My name is Bloody Tom," it says, all three mouths speaking in unison. "Everyone knows I beat my wife. Nobody knows I beat my children. I want them to be tough enough to get *out* of here, see? But they fuck up and I lose control. Then I beat myself. I think I never really had control, not in my whole life."

The other men, poised at first to defend Bloody Tom, back away.

"My name is Bloody Tom," says the lamprey again. "Does anyone else have a problem with me?"

And no one's dumb enough to say they do. The lamprey stomps to the bar and orders a Jim Beam, Bloody Tom's favourite. Benny's the kind of bartender who doesn't say anything. Just slides the glass across and takes his money.

The other men make excuses and leave: some with terror in their eyes, some saving up murder for later. Lady Blue would like to watch the lampreys a little longer. The one taking Bloody Tom's name looks like his head is imperceptibly unrounding, gradually losing Tom's features. She'd like to see how that works, what it means. But Jason is practically in her lap now, clinging to her, though he's man enough to pretend that's not what he's doing.

"I got to get you home, honey," he says. "I don't think it's safe for you here."

◂ ▸

Lady Blue's house is the biggest in town. There are rooms for breakfast, rooms for lunch, pantries and dining rooms, bathrooms, shower rooms, hot-tub rooms, guest rooms, storage rooms, linen closets, wardrobes, rooms full of appliances, rooms for television and board games and stacks on stacks of books. There is the one little room where Jason must never go, and there is the big bedroom, the mountainous canopy bed where he waits every night, naked but for the key round his neck, the way Lady Blue likes. If he were a dog, he'd be wagging his tail.

Tonight when he gathers her up in his arms, his forearms quiver. "What *was* that tonight, honey? Where do things like that come from? Do you know?"

"Not a thing," says Lady Blue, which is the truth. "Smart men learn not to look too hard for answers."

Jason has an adorable way of multitasking when he's drunk. He tugs at the buttons of Lady Blue's dress while he talks. "God, when I think of anything happening to you – when I think of you in the same room with those things, I just get…" He reaches the last button. The thick blue silk falls away, and he falters midsentence. Falls to her creamy skin instead of talking, kisses and bites the curve of her breast.

Lady Blue smiles indulgently, weaves her fingers through his short hair. "You get frisky, honey?"

"No! No, that's not it, I just get—" Whatever he gets is lost in another set of incoherent noises. He clutches her waist, pulls her closer and kisses his way up to her mouth.

She leans in over him, hands at his shoulder blades, makes him lean back. Lady Blue doesn't talk back because there's no need. Jason knows just how to please her. She tells him sometimes, when they're done and lying puddled together, what a good boy he is. How he makes her shine from the inside out. But she will never admit the other thing she feels. The way she looks down at him sometimes and dares to believe that he's perfect. After all these years and all these husbands, this one will stay good to her. This is the one she can keep.

If anything ever scared Lady Blue, it would be the way she gets that feeling every time, even knowing better.

◂ ▸

The lampreys don't go away. They skulk on street corners gaping at passersby. Working mothers pull their children close to cross on the other side of the street. Men glare at the lampreys and growl.

On Sunday, three of Bloody Tom's friends jump a lamprey, figuring three men with blades drawn are a fair match for three mouths. The lamprey doesn't think so. There's a whirling of wind. Now it's three men and seven lampreys. No one sees those men again, but everyone hears their voices in snatches of three-part harmony.

"My name is Lou, and I'm so lonely I sleep with my arms wrapped around the radio."

"My name is Cal, and when my sister died, I knew who'd taken her. I never told. I was a kid. I thought he'd come for me next if I said anything."

"My name is Mack. I was lying when I said I wanted to stab that lamprey. I was drunk, I just wanted to sound tough, and didn't think – please. I don't give a shit about Tom. If I hadn't lost that factory job, think I'd be here? You think I'd care about you lowlifes? I hate you all. Please. God. Please, let me go."

Some folks look at the lampreys with pity when they say those things – though the pity is not for the lampreys. Most folks, even the ones who thought they loved Cal and Mack, draw away. Most don't want to know the things at the bottom of a dead man's heart.

On Monday there's another fight, and no one in town agrees which side started it. On Tuesday, the lampreys take the local seamstress and her baby son. When a lamprey crosses town declaring that its name is Ollie and it misses its mama, the game changes. Conquest now, not vengeance. Families hide in their cellars. Leave the window open a crack, or a knothole unguarded in the wall, and there's a chance they'll come shrieking in on the wind.

On Wednesday night, Lady Blue slinks into Old Benny's Pub and takes her usual seat. The pub has been unofficially divided, with lampreys to one side. A few of the shabbiest regulars, still alive, huddle at the other and nurse their cheap liquor.

Benny raises an eyebrow as Lady Blue enters. "Where's the husband?"

"Safe," says Lady Blue. Benny puts down the usual Electric Lemonade, and she raises it to her lips. "Doors weatherstripped, windows shut, snug as a pin. I mean to keep this one a good while yet." And she means it. Poor thing – when she suggested going out, he said yes, but he shook like a trapped rabbit. It's a good enough reason for missing their date night, she thinks. This once. As long as he's waiting for her when she returns.

"Yet you're out here."

Lady Blue takes another sip. "I want to understand what's happening. A lady doesn't do that by hiding at home."

"So what's your grand plan?"

"Observe."

Lady Blue looks away from Benny. The man's seen a lot, and there's a wariness in his voice when he talks to her. He avoids looking straight at her, even while he's setting out the highball just the way she likes. Lady Blue finds this tiresome.

The bar's quiet, but for lampreys murmuring in their wind-whisper way and human drunks muttering in despair.

Lady Blue strains to hear if there are any human words in what the lampreys say. Lady Blue does not believe in God, but it strikes her that the lampreys are like little gods, judging every soul that goes in. Or pretending to. She wonders if the human words in those mouths are even true. She wonders which is worse, calumny or exposure.

While she is thinking, a new man walks in.

You can tell he's from out of town by the uniform, the crisp-cut walk. No one walks so clean and straight in this town. Even spotless Lady Blue tends to slink or to glide, not to march like a fool soldier. The man's clean-shaven, with hair so short it must be military, and a wooden cross round his neck. His eyes are bright green.

"Evenin', sir," he says, nodding to Benny and Lady Blue. "Ma'am."

"Evening," says Lady Blue, nodding back.

"What'll you have?" says Benny.

"Nothing, sir. My name's Abner. I'm from the Department of Emergencies. There's been reports of some disturbance here, sir, so I was sent..." He trails off, his Adam's apple rising. *Reports of some disturbance* hardly covers it.

"You think you can do anything?" says Lady Blue.

"Ma'am," says Abner, "with the good Lord on our side, the Department of Emergencies can always do something. Can't say I've seen a case quite like this, but there's always hope."

Lady Blue takes a sip of her Electric Lemonade. "What if the good Lord is on the lampreys' side?"

Abner laughs. "Wash out your mouth, ma'am."

"And spoil the taste of a good highball?"

"Fair point." He smiles. More intrigued than offended. "Night like tonight, though, shouldn't a dame like you be home, where it's safe?"

"I can take care of myself, thank you."

One of the drunks in the corner grins up at them. "Toughest dame in town, that one. Richest, too."

This seems to perk Abner's interest. Or his worry. "You're not from that big house up on the hill, ma'am?"

"I would be, yes."

His brow furrows. "You… You don't have a spouse or dependents in that house, do you, ma'am?"

Lady Blue looks at him levelly. "What's it to you?"

"Ma'am, I went by that house and there was a front window wide open. You better get back there, round up your people, if they're still there. Beggin' your pardon, of course."

Lady Blue's gaze becomes a stare.

She is sure that she closed every window, sealed every door. Lady Blue pays attention to the details.

"I can walk you there, ma'am," says Abner. He's subtler about it than most, but his eyes have been on her since he came in, more than on the lampreys. Men see Lady Blue and they want to stay with her, protect her. "Not sure what I can do beyond that, but if you need a pair of hands—"

"No," says Lady Blue.

She puts down her Electric Lemonade unfinished and pays, leaving Benny his usual tip. Then she slips out of Old Benny's Pub and runs up the street, in her long blue dress and high heels, as fast as she's ever run to anything.

◂ ▸

Jason is silly, not stupid. He knows what will happen if he opens a window. He cannot have done it carelessly, and Lady Blue knows she did not do it herself. He can only have done it on purpose. To hurt her. To hurt himself.

There is only one thing that makes Lady Blue's husbands betray her.

She hopes she is wrong. Jason is so new. He hasn't started with a single one of the warning signs. He has never toyed idly with the key in her presence; never cast long, brooding looks at it; never asked the wrong questions. Lady Blue will never admit it, but there are tears in her eyes. She does not want the lampreys to have this man. If she is wrong about what he has done tonight, she will protect him with everything she has. She hopes she is wrong.

She knows she is right.

She reaches the house on the hill. The front window is wide open. She unlocks the door, lets herself in, closes it behind her, and shuts and locks the window.

The anteroom is silent and dark. Lady Blue flicks on the lights. She does not see any lampreys, so far.

She walks head held high, no sound but the clicking of her heels, through the five halls and the countless rooms. She thinks something wails faintly, now and again, but is not certain. She does not see lampreys. She does not see Jason. She pauses by the door to the one little room where he can never go. It is shut and locked, but that is no proof of anything.

She checks the closets, even the cupboards. She pauses in the kitchen and draws her best carving knife from its drawer. She saves the master bedroom for last.

On the great canopy bed, Jason is waiting for her, naked, just the way she likes. But he is weeping. His eyes are puffy and red, and the key round his neck drips, fouling the sheets with blood that is not yet his.

Lady Blue goes very still.

"Jason," she says.

He starts toward her, then cringes away.

"Explain this to me, Jason," says Lady Blue without a hint of emotion.

He struggles to speak through his tears. "What did you do to them?"

"To whom, Jason?"

"Your other husbands." The words wrench their way out of him, halfway between a sob and a shout of rage. "All of your other husbands! All h-hanging there, dead, dripping."

"Why did you go in that room, Jason?"

"You were so c-casual. All the time. With the lampreys. And I thought – I thought you must *know* something. I know I promised you I wouldn't look, but the whole town is dying. If I saved the whole town, you'd forgive me, wouldn't you? God would forgive me. Maybe things wouldn't be like they were, but—" He hiccups, chokes briefly on his tears. "But there was nothing about lampreys. There was just them."

"And the window, Jason?"

"I was so scared. And angry. I could hear them wailing outside. I thought, if they want to kill us both, why not? Why should I want to live?" He sniffs loudly. "But they didn't come. And you're going to kill me now, too, aren't you?"

Lady Blue makes no effort to hide the carving knife. Neither does she do anything with it yet. She sits on the edge of the bed next to him. He shies away, but she catches him under the chin with one finger, makes him look in her eyes. "If I didn't kill you now, honey, what would you do? If I held you gently and explained in small words how it started, said I was sorry for scaring you like this, promised not to hurt you so long as you kept my secret? Could you live with me? Could you still be my dearest husband and make me shine from the inside out?"

Jason pulls away, and that's when she knows for sure. He can't meet her eyes, but he sniffs and mumbles, "Yes. Yes, I'd still love you. Please. It could be like before."

"You'd listen to everything I told you? You'd keep it all a secret for me?"

"Please..."

Lady Blue strokes back along his cheek. Tangles her left hand lazily in his hair, like she does every night, when he wants to put his mouth on her. "Then kiss me, honey."

She doesn't draw him closer. She waits for him to move, and he does – away from her, bucking against her grip. They all struggle like this, in the end. "What did you do to them?" he demands again, his voice rising to a shriek.

"This," says Lady Blue. She cuts his throat, spilling his blood over the bedspread.

Then she puts on a little light music.

◂ ▸

Lady Blue is a creature who mourns. Just not the same way as most women. Most of her rage and grief at losing Jason is in the carving knife, the one swift cut that brings closure. The rest must be dealt with in other ways. The essential thing is to keep herself moving and orderly. There are rituals: care of the body, washing of hands and sheets, cleaning of knife, lighting of candles. And there is music. Lady Blue's only real friend at these times is her old vinyl record of Verdi's *Requiem*. Verdi understands about punishment, about actions having consequences, even if Lady Blue's husbands never do in the end. She has everything timed, so that when the last strains of the "Libera me" fade, her house is spotless. Except for that one little room.

She washes her hands as the choir softly murmurs, and then she gets to work. She fetches a coat hanger from that one little room and hangs Jason on it like a suit jacket. The hardest part is carrying the body down the hall and not leaving a trail of blood. She always fails at this, a little, and has to use steel wool and polish to get it off the hardwood, which is factored in to the schedule.

Three feet from the door to that one little room, she hears a wailing like wind.

She pauses. Jason's body lolls in her arms.

"I have no quarrel with you," she says to the walls. "Leave me alone."

The wailing fades, or seems to. It's hard to tell under the music. Lady Blue stands in place and breathes for a moment, considering. She could turn off the record, but that would mess up the ritual. Anyway the "Kyrie" is winding down, with longer and slower pauses between each phrase, and maybe if she waits a moment—

Yes. There is silence. She cannot hear either music or lampreys.

Then the record gets to the good part. She does hear wailing now: the choir wailing in the hands of an angry God, the strings wailing in answer. The wind wails, too. A lamprey materializes in front of her, flexing its mouths with greed.

"I am not one of the men who attacked you," Lady Blue says through her teeth. "I am not your enemy." But she readies her carving knife all the same. She knows that speech is useless, and that it will lunge at her.

Instead, it lunges at Jason.

She is not ready for that. She swipes with the knife and misses. Jason is borne out of her arms, kissed by those hungry toothy mouths. She stands frozen. His body withers before her eyes. The lamprey lets go, dropping him to the floor. There is a bit of a shape to it now, a bit of Jason's cheekbones and his mischievous little beard.

"My name is Jason," says the lamprey, its three mouths shouting to be heard over the despair of the choir. "And I loved you, you bitch. You were my whole life. I'll never forgive you. I'd kill you back if I could. I loved you. I hate you."

Lady Blue grabs it and cuts all three of its throats. Its blood is not red but black and sluggish, like the silt at the bottom of a river. She slices four, five times to make sure, until its mouthy end hangs off the rest of it by a tiny sliver of skin.

She feels confused. This is not how the ritual ought to go. She did not make time for cleaning up two bodies, and she'll never get that black blood out of the hardwood floor.

She tucks what is left of Jason carefully into that one little room, on its hanger with the others. She closes and locks the door, then cleans the key. She decides she will clean up after Jason completely before dealing with the lamprey. He deserves that much.

There is wailing outside the house now, very loud. At some moments it drowns out the *Requiem*. It shakes the windows, batters the eaves. She's killed one of their own, and the lampreys are angry.

She ignores them. She has sealed up the house. There is nothing else she can do.

The best way to get blood out of bedsheets is quickly, with ice water and salt paste, before the stains have time to set. Lady Blue works diligently until her hands change colour with cold. When she has exhausted the first bucket of ice water and is heading to the kitchen for more, she passes the lamprey's body again.

In its pool of sludge-blood, it's twitching. Its throat reforms, and its mouths strain to make words again. "My name is Jason. My name is Jason, my name is Jason, and I loved you..."

This time Lady Blue cuts off its mouthy end completely. Then, to be safe, she cuts the rest of it into pieces and seals each one in a separate Tupperware container from the kitchen. Her carving knife wasn't designed to slice through bone, but it is the best she has. It is long, ugly work. By the end of it, Lady Blue is filthy and twitching herself. The sea-wind has only grown stronger.

The *Requiem* is all the way to the "Sanctus." She should be most of the way through the cleaning now, not making more of a mess. The choir taunts her, singing in mock-joyful chords drowned out by diabolical, chromatic strings. Whatever they are praying to, it is not the nice tame God that the man from the Department of Emergencies wears round his neck.

The lampreys will kill her eventually, Lady Blue knows. As soon as she ventures out of her sealed-up house. Jason and his open window will get to kill her back, after all. Very well. She will face them like a lady. Perhaps she will take a few with her.

Lady Blue stacks the Tupperware containers and puts them in the room with her husbands' bodies. Jason's soul is in there somewhere, after all. Then she trudges back to the anteroom, carving knife in hand, leaving a trail of black blood that someone else will have to clean.

Lady Blue flings open her front door.

The lampreys fly in. Dozens of them surround her. Lady Blue moves without much thought. She stabs with her carving knife, dodging their drooling mouths, and they fall and fall around her. She does not have time to really kill them. Only to keep hurting each one until it can't move closer.

She has no sense of time passing apart from the music – fickle music, pleading and raging by turns. She is surprised to last even a minute or two, but the music goes on and on, and there she is, fighting. Bloody Tom's friends couldn't have lasted this long, and they had three times as many knives.

Lady Blue is not like the others.

It's still a matter of time. For each one that drops, two more sail in on the wind. Finally she doesn't spin fast enough and they blindside her. Six lamprey necks wind around the hand with the knife. Eight more at the other arm – she is suddenly immobilized. She can see nothing but mouths.

The music builds to its final, tragic chorus.

These things are pitiless just like Lady Blue. Like looking in a hideous mirror. Lady Blue has only ever done what she had to, but the lampreys will not see it that way. They will eat the excuses and drink the darkness underneath, the thing even Lady Blue cannot name. Then they will pour it out on the town like it's all she ever was. Maybe it is. For the first time in her life, Lady Blue is terrified.

Mouths latch on to her filthy skin everywhere, not just three but a mass of them. She kicks wildly and accomplishes nothing.

Then there is a scream.

First one lamprey turns back into wind, then another and another, until the horde around her is nothing but a screaming flight, fleeing into the night sky and gone. Lady Blue falls to the floor in a puddle of black sludge.

She puts a hand to her neck, stunned. She is not withered. She does not even feel much pain. She does not seem to be injured apart from one small, round laceration, the kind that only needs a drugstore bandage.

She does not feel triumphant, like a thing that scares gods. She feels hideous and tired.

The music is more or less over. "*Libera me, Dómine, de morte aetérna, in die illa treménda*" the alto spits in a bitter monotone, as if she already knows there is no redemption. There are a few, soft chords, and the recording ends.

Well. The floor is absolutely unsalvageable. She'll have to buy an industrial-grade steam cleaner and refinish the hardwood. Tomorrow.

She washes the carving knife in dismal silence. Then she throws her blood-soaked dress in the kitchen garbage and takes a scalding shower, scrubbing for what feels like hours until she no longer feels lamprey sludge in her pores.

She emerges into the wide, tiled bathroom, haggard but dripping clean. She wipes the fog off the mirror, leans against the sink, and looks sideways at herself. She feels very old, but she is still perfectly smooth, perfectly curved.

She meets her own eyes.

"My name is Lady Blue," she says to the mirror, unsure if it's even true. "I do not know what else I am. And I wish that someone – just one person, just once – could look at my soul and not flee."

◀ ▶

On Thursday night, Lady Blue does not appear at Old Benny's Pub. But on Saturday night, there she is, splendid in something new and midnight blue. She does not feel much like speaking to men, or speaking to anything. But one must keep up appearances.

No one has seen any lampreys since Wednesday night. Red and the other girls say that the monsters must have seen the cross round Abner's neck and fled.

He's still here. The admiring girls seem to make him nervous. Sweat drips down his from his buzz-cut temples. He makes an excuse and disentangles himself from the girls, walking to stare out the window at the night street.

He must know that the girls are mistaken. Lady Blue wonders what else he knows. What else he's hiding.

He isn't a poorly built man. Strong, not with gym-rat muscles like Jason's, but in an understated way that suggests long treks through the woods. Clean, apart from the sweat. White nails. Not even a hint of stubble. Still, Lady Blue is not in the mood to admire men for long. She takes care not to come too close.

"You," she murmurs.

He looks up, startled. "Oh, I recognize you. I hope everything was all right the other night, with the...the window, and all."

Lady Blue takes a sip of Electric Lemonade, cool as you please.

"You don't really know what happened, do you?" she says, low enough so the other girls won't hear.

Abner sighs. "No, ma'am. I'd appreciate if you didn't spread the word around, but I don't. That's why I'm still here. I can't give the Department of Emergencies the all-clear when I don't know why those things are gone, or whether they want to come back."

"Wise choice. But your secret's safe with me."

Abner takes a sip of his rum and Coke, looking back out the window. "I can't say for sure without proof. But I like to think the good Lord did come through. The cross is just a symbol when you get down to it, and those things ain't vampires anyway. But we prayed, we hoped, we stepped in to try to help, and He sent *something* to pull us through. That's how He works, isn't it? Probably sent help in the last place anyone'd think to look. I reckon I can find it."

Lady Blue can't help but smile. It's so cute when they have hope. It ought to be sad, but it draws her in every time, like a moth to a candle. Even – or especially – in the midst of her grief.

Abner looks at her, perplexed. Unconsciously, he fingers his cross. "There's something different about you," he says. "Beggin' your pardon, ma'am. But there's a type of young woman who comes to this sort of place alone, and you're not that type. No, forgive me, ma'am, that's an inexcusable way to say it. Just that it's been two drinks, and I'm trying to figure out why you're here at all."

"I'd like to know that myself," says Lady Blue.

He looks at her ringless hands. "Gettin' away from the husband?"

"Widowed," she says, quite calmly.

He blushes. "Oh. I'm sorry, ma'am, I shouldn't have – I'm sorry."

Lady Blue smiles again. "As penance, why don't you buy me a drink?"

And he does. They're all the same. She sits in her spot, second from the far window with the drapes half down, and Abner brings her a second Electric Lemonade in a frosted highball glass, just the way she likes.

THE FRIENDLY NEWFOUNDLANDER

Joel Thomas Hynes

How can you know, ever really. You cant. Know. Where it's gonna end up. Where you're gonna find yourself. The way time works. The way you work through time. One minute your gear is all stuffed down into garbage bags and slung out onto the street and it seems the next you're all crossing the border together, the modern family, checking out the sunset along the boardwalk, road trip to the desert, taking "sound baths" and crashing in the same motel. Not the same *room* mind, that's a bit far-fetched, but, you know, a couple of doors up the walk and here's Dad's room. And just down by the pool here's Mom and the boy. All's well and everyone gets on. All of a sudden. Dad saying goodnight and hanging out with a cig-arillo and plucking at the guitar when everyone else is off to the bunk. And there's this girl too. Not a girl. But this blonde. She was there at the office chatting with the manager when I walked in. That's me by the way. I'd be Dad. I was being kinda loose just now, conversational, just setting up the scenario in the third person, you know. Being casual. But that can get confusing, I suppose. So, to clarify. I'm not the boy. I'm the Dad. It was *my* clothes and books and shit slung onto the street near on seven or eight years ago when me and the boy's mama called it quits. And it was a bad one, that breakup. But it wasnt, too. It wasnt messy like the way some breakups are messy. There was no going back, that's one thing for sure. There was no falling into bed for old times sakes cause the old times, in terms of the bedroom, werent really the sort of times you'd want to fall back into. Funny how you gets hooked up with a gal, and that very fundamental aspect is not working but yet you hangs around for all them years. Like you're waiting to turn some corner, thinking you'll suddenly find yourself in the midst of this steamy sex life. When it was never there in the first place. Not like rekindling things or finding that old spark or nothing, cause at least there's the *hope* in that situation, the knowledge that things used to be a certain way. But with me and her, they never really were. Maybe there was some sort of psychological thing, sure – I'll give it to you this way just so you dont stray *that* way cause I still needs to be loved even if we're no fun in bed. There's always that game. But the raw sex thing, the caution-to-the-wind, fuck-me-this-way, harder, just-like-that, now, harder, let's-try-this, blah. None of that. None of that. But we are where we are now anyhow. And that seems to be working just fine for all hands. Copasetic, as they says. You dont look back and label it a failure, you know, if you've managed to evolve into this decent and healthy unit that doesnt stress out the boy. Once you irons out all the blame and the emotional blackmailing settles down and everybody moves on to some other bedroom, well that's when things starts to work the way they should, that's when you gets to be the modern family, you know. Modern family. Dad got a house downtown and Mama's over on the South Side. And now we're all out in the desert in California.

Anyhow, this blonde. This blond American gal. In the next room. Sharing a wall with me. I'm out on the patio scratching out a few lines in my notebook, tryna hang onto this dullard melody that keeps floating around in my head, having a smoke and looking out at the desert night, you know. Living. And here's this blonde comes out on her patio and starts chatting me up and within minutes she's commandeered a chair at my table and smoking my cigarettes and spilling her guts about this fella that used to torment her. Says she's gone through that PTSD treatment and everything. They'd be having a racket and he'd be driving, pounding the wheel, saying how he was gonna kill the two of them right this minute, foot to the floor. She bawling, begging him to stop, to pull over and let her out. Me? I just sat there, you know, tuning up the guitar, nodding along, cocking my head this way and that every once in a while. Having an eye down the walkway for the boy. Never know but he might come scrabbling up looking for an extra half hour before bed. His mama's dead to the world, no doubt.

And the wheels, the wheels are spinning in my head, as usual. That's the way these days. Everybody off with their heads up their holes, faces buried in little gadgets, having these exchanges with folks halfways across the world, friends with people they never looked in the eye before. Everybody's at it too. So when finally some stranger starts chatting you up, the wheels gets spinning – is she nuts? One of them girls on the hunt for some fella to save her? Is she some sort of whore? What does she want for Christ sakes? That's how bad it is, see, you walk around feeling half not even there for so long, saying hello to people who barely grunts their way past you, gawking into their little devices, that soon as there's real human contact you dont know fuck all what to do with it. And wouldnt it be nice if it was just some gal recognizing the situation for what it is – decent-lookin fella crashing next door, cold desert night, king-size bed, why not make the most of it, a little adventure, one of them anonymous hookups, no-strings-attached piece of ass. Yeah. No strings attached. But then you gotta think to yourself, you know, what's wrong with me that I cant have a random chat with a good looking woman without it being about fucking? Why you gotta make everything dirty like that, Dad? Why you gotta make everything about cock and balls, tits and pussy? You know you're only looking for sort some of boost, right? Looking for some sort of validation. So desperate for connection you cant even see the human in front of you.

She's nice too, this blonde, her personality, you know, funny and stuff, has a laugh at herself. Working in cosmetics or beauty products, some sort of shit like that. Money in it, no doubt. Comes out to the desert to get out of LA, knows the owner of the motel, stays in the same room all the time, gets a discount. Loves doing these sound baths. Got an idea for a documentary. Always wanted to write a book. Had a fling with an older woman, a teacher. Years ago, this lizzy bit. From the east coast, from over around Maine, says her name is fuckin Mindy, if you can believe that – big-titted blond American girl named Mindy. That's the thing about California though – no one's from here. Never hardly meet a soul born and bred, but they're all from some place else all the time. All migrating to the Promised Land, you know, like that Joad crowd.

Mindy wants to know then, what's the deal anyways, she asks, with that young boy and the lady? How come you're all in separate rooms and shit? Some sort of argument?

Disagreement? So, then it's my turn to spill my guts about where I am and how I got here and I dont hold back one bit neither. Time I'm through I'm pretty much splayed wide open and she's yawning and chattering and shivering under her blanket. Something you dont expect, you know, how cold it gets in the desert at night. I mean, that's what you're told alright, that it's gonna get cold. But you always thinks, yeah cold to *that* crowd, cold to some crowd who are used to drinking fuckin cactus juice and eating fuckin rattlesnake omelettes every morning. But no, this is quite the contrast, once the sun goes down the temperature just keeps on dropping till you swear you never left home. Fuckin Newfoundland in February. Go fuck itself. Dont give me that outdoors shit neither. Dont go preaching to me about sliding and skating and fuckin ski trips. Grey bitter sludgy drizzle and muck for four months straight. Tryna scrounge up the bucks to change your winter tires while you're waiting around for summer to kick in and it never fuckin does. Why in the fuck anyone'd choose to rear up a child there is beyond me. Tell ya what, if that boy wasnt around I wouldnt even go back, or I'd be long gone. Ahhh...that's shit talk though. What kinda world would it be without that little fella in it? How long ago would I have been dead if not for him coming into the world? Dead, jail, on the streets. Somewhere. At least I'm on some sort of path these days, at least there's some sort of drive to have a halfways decent life, if only so's I can offer him the kinda life he deserves. And sure if I fell short on that his mama wouldnt be long fucking off with him either. Nothing's surer. And that's fair as fair too, I dont contest it. Fair enough, I dont want my young feller hanging with no deadbeat, even if it was me. And if it was her that was some sort of waste case, well I wouldnt be long snatching him up out of the way then neither.

This blonde though, Mindy, she just cant fight the cold no more. And here I am and cant hardly move the fingers to play a chord and the guitar gone all out of tune, gone right sharp you know. Next thing Mindy is saying how she's going inside out of it and there's this look across the table, this sly grin, but here I am playing the gentleman I guess, not taking the bait when she's dangling it there like that. Christ, how are you ever gonna get a piece of random ass if you're going around trying to make the ladies think you're not some sleaze looking for a piece of random ass? It's an awful conundrum, as my old grandfather used to say. So there I am anyhow, letting the moment slip through my fingers, watching her hips swaying towards her door, hoping she'll take the leap and turn around and invite me in or some such shit. But she's got the class this one. Mindy. Blond big-titted American girl. PTSD. Fuckin hell, Dad, go for it, you wanker. But then she's gone, the door clicked shut behind her, and I'm standing in my own bathroom hardly able to even look at myself in the mirror. Fuckin dunce.

I calls down to the boy's mama and she answers after a few rings, all groggy and crooked and shit. Wants to know what's wrong, what's up. For the life of me I dialed out of habit, you know, like reaching out in those moments when you just cant face up to the loneliness. It's even on the tip of my tongue to hint around and see if maybe she wants to climb the fence to the pool and hit that hot tub, you know. Call the big time-out on the whole modern family scenario and just have a bit of the other kind of fun for once. But I cant ask her that, I cant. First off she'd only fucking laugh at me, or accuse me of drinking or something, and secondly even if she did say yes, yes I'll meet you at the fence in ten minutes, even if she came at me with that, well I knows full well I wouldnt show up as the same person I envisions myself to be in that situation. I wouldnt bring it, you know, how you always wants this second chance to be the man, be the better lover, the one who cracks it all wide open, go back and remind her of everything she coulda waited for. If you hadda just held your guns, girl, this is what you'd have these days. What's wrong, girl? Swear you never saw a real live sex machine before. Ahhh Christ on it. I hangs up on her, pretty much. Mumbles shit at her. I puts my ear to the wall then and has a listen for what Mindy might be up to, see if I cant catch the rhythm of the bedsprings squeaking, picturing her working the handle of her curling iron up in herself, on her hands and knees in there with her arse stuck up in the air just driving it home, fucking herself senseless with a ketchup bottle, anything she can get her hands on, wishing she could build up the gumption to just come tapping on my window, no talking necessary, just right down to it, fuck each other blind for three straight hours. No strings attached. Yeah, go on over, Dad, knock on her door all friendly like. The Friendly Newfoundlander. Fuckin hell. That's what you gets out here in the world. First off you're right proud when someone somewhere knows where Newfoundland even is. You forgets how fuckin delighted you were to get on that plane and leave it all behind for a while. Then they patters on about seals and fish and maybe high steel and the bumpty Irish accent thing. And you can swallow all that. But then this missus in this little desert gift shop we stopped off at earlier today, she says to me, she says, when I was telling her about back home and stuff, she says Oh yeah, the friendly Newfoundlander, I heard of you guys. She heard all about us. And I caught myself steaming, you know. I stood there and I felt like saying Friendly? Looka here, missus, I knows Newfoundland boys who'd skin you and skull-fuck you and bury you out in the desert for fun. Chalk it all up to a wild night on the beer. Dont tell me about the friendly Newfoundlander. Last going off, the dregs of my drugging days, I watched two mama's boys from out around Gander Bay, two brothers, break every fuckin bone in some young fella's face with two halves of the same hockey stick. Passing a crack pipe back and forth over his bloody moans and talking about some female parole officer they knew, how they'd like to find out where she lived and gangbang her. All a big laugh. Friendly Newfoundlanders. What's his face, sure, there last year, chopped his girlfriend up and stuffed her into a suitcase. Kept her head in the freezer next to the hamburger meat. Friendly enough he was, wasnt he?

There's a thump now, she's still up over there, Mindy. Now she's clearing her throat in that way, you know, that way people does when it's not about clearing their throat but more or less letting someone else know they're up and on the go and looking to communicate something. Fuckin hell boys. Friendly Newfoundlander she wants? I looks down and sees my pants around my ankles and the lad standing to full attention and my right hand is just a blur. Dont know how I made that jump, and it's a bit of a sin you know too, that that's all it takes, to hear a woman clearing her throat through a hotel wall. Sad aint it? How hard up we gets sometimes. Kinda pathetic. She's over there thinking what a fuckin slowpoke I am, not to just have followed right on in behind her when she gave me that look. Rather go on back to his own room and jack himself off. Fuckin ladies' men through and through, them Newfoundland boys. Hell with this I says. What have I got to lose to march over there and put it to her that I'm into having a bit of easy fun? What have I got to lose? All the chit-chat small talk is taken care of, we already knows each other's life fuckin stories. She knows the score. All's left now is to dirty up the sheets. And say she sneers and shakes her head and sends me away, so what? So I'll come on back to my room and finish myself off anyhow. Worth a try aint it? Worth a try, worth a try. Big-titted blond American gal with PTSD. Hell with this.

I bends over to pull up me trousers and tuck myself in when I hears the tap on the door. But is it my door? I listens again. The clock ticking, something squawking out there in the desert night, some creature. The fridge groaning. Then the rap-tap-tapping again, on my door. Fuckin right I says again, fuckin right. You knows she's gonna come to her senses after a while. Sure aint we all red-blooded mammals? Dont we all need a piece every once in a while, for whatever reasons? Random piece of ass out there in the world. No one's shame but your own. I shouts out towards my door, I says Gimme a second! I steps out of the trousers altogether. I slaps the head of my lad a few times and gives the balls a good twist just to get the blood pumping through again. I feels a bit foolish walking across the floor with no pants on and the lad pointing straight up like that. My hand reaching out. A shadow bent across the curtains. I turns the handle and lets the door swing open.

AFTERWORD

CANADA POST ALWAYS RINGS TWICE

I have to admit, I wondered about it – this idea of collecting Canadian noir stories.

After all, that kind of thing isn't really Canadian, is it now? The tradition of noir comes from other places, evokes other things: the lens of Fritz Lang following whistling child-killer Peter Lorre through the shadowed passages of Weimar Germany; the words of Jim Thompson and Cornell Woolrich, telling the downfall of weak men at the hands of bad women, in the dusty corners of America. We Canadians, with our pristine lakes and mountains, and devotion to Peace, Order, Good Government…aren't we a little too good – or at least, goody-goody – for that kind of thing?

But really, I didn't wonder about it for too long. By the evidence in recent years, Canada's a perfect setting for noirish storytelling.

Alberta's booming on the fragile economy of boom-town resource extraction and transient workers. Montreal, not too long ago, revealed itself to be a nest of kickbacks and corruption worthy of a James Ellroy novel. And the late Elmore Leonard is probably the only one who might have kept up with the reversals and plot twists of the Rob Ford cocaine saga in Toronto.

The storytellers in *New Canadian Noir* didn't go for those headline-driven noir stories, though, and I hope you'll agree that their stories – stories that cross genres and settings – are the stronger for it. To single one out would be to single them all, but I don't think there's a genre that hasn't felt the cold touch of a noirist's pen in this volume.

That's the beauty of noir. It's a thing one might call a genre, but one need not. Noir is a state of mind – an exploration of corruptibility, ultimately an expression of humanity in all its terrible frailty. Sometimes that frailty is unbearably sad; other times, blackly funny. But in these stories, it is ever present.

David Nickle

AUTHORS' BIOGRAPHIES

Colleen Anderson is the author of the collection *Embers Amongst the Fallen* and the co-editor of *Tesseracts Seventeen: Speculating Canada from Coast to Coast to Coast*. She was born in Edmonton, grew up in Calgary and now lives in Vancouver.

Keith Cadieux of Winnipeg is the author of the novella *Gaze*, which was short listed for a Manitoba Book Award and long-listed for the 2010 ReLit Award.

Michael S. Chong is a writer living in Toronto. His stories have been published in *Masked Mosaic: Canadian Super Stories*, the Crime Factory specials *Kung Fu Factory* and *Pink Factory*, and K.A. Laity's anthologies *Weird Noir*, *Noir Carnival*, and *Drag Noir*.

Kevin Cockle lives in Calgary, and often incorporates Calgary-inspired economic themes in his work. Author of over twenty stories published in a variety of markets, Kevin has dabbled in screenwriting, sports journalism, and technical writing to fill out what would otherwise be a purely finance-centric résumé.

Patrick Fleming has come to realize, after living in Toronto for just over a decade, that his ratty little heart will always belong to that vital stretch of downtown running from St. James Town to Moss Park.

Chadwick Ginther is the author of the Prix Aurora Award-nominated fantasy novels *Thunder Road* and *Tombstone Blues* with Ravenstone Books. Originally from Morden, Manitoba, he now lives and writes in Winnipeg.
www.chadwickginther.com @chadwickginther

Ada Hoffmann is an autistic computer scientist. Raised in Kingston, Ontario, and now living in the Kitchener-Waterloo area, she uses her spare time to write fiction, some of which has been anthologized in the annual series *Imaginarium: The Best Canadian Speculative Writing*. www.ada-hoffmann.com @xasymptote

Joel Thomas Hynes is a multi-disciplinary artist from Newfoundland, now based in Ontario. He is the author of numerous books and stageplays, including the novels *Down to the Dirt* and *Right Away Monday*. He's written and directed two award-winning short films, released an EP of all-original music, and is currently a writer-in-residence at the Canadian Film Centre.

Claude Lalumière is the author of *Objects of Worship, The Door to Lost Pages*, and *Nocturnes and Other Nocturnes* and the editor of twelve previous anthologies, including, most recently, *Super Stories of Heroes & Villains*. Originally from Montreal, he's now based in Vancouver. www.claudepages.info

Rich Larson was born in West Africa, has studied in Rhode Island, and at twenty-one now lives in Edmonton. He won the 2014 Dell Award and received the 2012 Rannu Prize for Writers of Speculative Fiction. www.richwlarson.tumblr.com

Laird Long pounds out fiction in all genres. Big guy, sense of humour. Born in Duncan, British Columbia, bred in Winnipeg, Manitoba. He's the author of the Clint Magnum mystery *No Accounting for Danger*.

Edward McDermott spends his time writing; when taking time off from his creative pursuit, he enjoys sailing, fencing, and working as a movie extra. Born in Toronto, he is currently sailing off the Florida Coast. Perhaps in the Bahamas. www.edwardmcdermott.net

David Menear has spent most of his life between Toronto and Montreal but has also lived in London, the U.K., and Divonne, France. Currently he is back in Toronto, writing hard and playing tennis with enthusiasm and mediocrity. His short-story chapbook, *One Dead Tree*, was released by DevilHousePress in June of 2014.

Silvia Moreno-Garcia is Mexican by birth, Canadian by inclination, and lives in beautiful British Columbia with her family. Her first collection, *This Strange Way of Dying*, was published in 2013 by Exile

Editions. Her debut novel, *Signal to Noise*, will be released in 2015 by Solaris. www.silviamoreno-garcia.com @silviamg

Michael Mirolla describes his writing as a mix of magic realism, surrealism, speculative fiction, and meta-fiction. A linked short-story collection, *Lessons in Relationship Dyads*, is due in autumn 2015 from Red Hen Press. Born in Italy and brought up in Montreal, Michael now lives in the Greater Toronto Area.
www.michaelmirolla.weebly.com @MichaelMirolla1

David Nickle is a Toronto author and journalist, and the author of numerous short stories and several novels. His most recent books are the story collection *Knife Fight and Other Struggles* and the novel *The 'Geisters*.

Corey Redekop has published the much-admired, award-winning bookworm blockbuster novel *Shelf Monkey* with ECW Press (2007) and the even-more-celebrated, award-nominated zombie satire *Husk* (ECW Press, 2012). Born and raised in Thompson, Manitoba, Corey now nests in Fredericton, New Brunswick, where he works as a librarian (for the money) and writer (for the glory). www.coreyredekop.ca @CoreyRedekop

Alex C. Renwick has a love of Vancouver rain that springs from formative years spent baking in Texas. Her fiction has appeared in *Ellery Queen's* and *Alfred Hitchcock's* mystery magazines and *Imaginarium: The Best Canadian Speculative Writing*. Her collection *Push of the Sky* (as Camille Alexa) was nominated for the Endeavour Award.
www.alexcrenwick.com

Hermine Robinson lives and writes in Calgary, where the winters are long and inspiration is plentiful. Her story "Tipping House" won the 2013 *FreeFall Magazine*'s Short Prose competition.

Kelly Robson moved to Toronto after twenty-two years in Vancouver, and discovered that, no matter where she lives, she'll always be an Alberta girl. She had the great good luck to be *Chatelaine*'s wine and spirits columnist from 2008 to 2012 and absolutely adores Okanagan wine. www.kellyrobson.com

Shane Simmons is a comics creator and screenwriter who also writes stories for anthologies. He was born in Lachine, Québec, and has lived on the Island of Montreal his entire life.
www.shanesimmons.com @Shane_Eyestrain

Dale L. Sproule is the author of the collection *Psychedelia Gothique*. He was born in Alberta, grew up in British Columbia and Alberta, and now lives in Ontario. His stories have appeared in *Ellery Queen's* mystery magazine, *Northern Frights*, *Tesseracts*, and *Pulphouse*. He also sculpts – at least somewhat in the Inuit tradition.
www.psychedeliagothique.com www.dlsproule.blogspot.ca

Simon Strantzas is the author of four acclaimed collections of short fiction, including *Burnt Black Suns* with Hippocampus Press in 2014. His work has appeared in various "best of" annuals and magazines. A native of Toronto, he lives there still with his somewhat understanding and altogether forgiving wife. www.strantzas.com

Steve Vernon grew up in Northern Ontario and visited Nova Scotia at the age of seventeen and never found his way back home again. He has lived in Halifax for the last four decades and has established a reputation as being one of Nova Scotia's liveliest storytellers.
www.stevevernonstoryteller.wordpress.com